Bolan hefted the rifl~~~ ~~~
peered t~~~

As the chopper he~~~
the narrow streets~~~
finding what he wa~~~

D05591689

"There's the Mercedes," the Executioner said,
directing Grimaldi's attention to the white limo. From
their aerial perspective there was no way to tell if
anyone was inside.

Grimaldi took the helicopter lower. A guard lay
sprawled just inside the back gate of the museum,
verifying that the BAO had already infiltrated the
institute. The terrorists now had the perfect spot from
which to launch the missile.

"I can't make out anybody in the tower," Grimaldi said,
circling the spire. "I'm going to have to throw a spot
on it." He leaned over and was about to throw the
toggle switch when the aircraft came suddenly under
fire. Rapid blasts clattered off the fuselage, some of
them shattering glass as they entered the cockpit.

The Stony Man pilot reflexively fought the controls,
doing all he could to keep the Reed from being shot
out of the sky. "I've got to pull back!" Even as the
words were out of his mouth, Grimaldi could hear the
engine misfiring, apparently hit.

"Hold on," he shouted to Bolan. "We're going down!"

DON PENDLETON's
MACK BOLAN®

RAMPAGE

A GOLD EAGLE BOOK FROM
WORLDWIDE®

TORONTO • NEW YORK • LONDON
AMSTERDAM • PARIS • SYDNEY • HAMBURG
STOCKHOLM • ATHENS • TOKYO • MILAN
MADRID • WARSAW • BUDAPEST • AUCKLAND

First edition December 1993

ISBN 0-373-61433-0

Special thanks and acknowledgment to
Ron Renauld for his contribution to this work.

RAMPAGE

Printed in U.S.A.

Yield not to evils, but attack all the more boldly.

—Virgil
70–19 B.C.

The only way to thwart the plans of those who seek to draw attention to their "cause" by spilling innocent blood, is to strike hard and fast.

—Mack Bolan

CHAPTER ONE

With a warrior's stealth, Mack Bolan stalked the ancient cobbled streets of Mougins.

It was late. The tourist crowd had left the small French town hours ago, and although there was activity at some of the more posh restaurants, most of the local residents had retired for the evening. The narrow winding streets were quiet and partially shrouded in a low-hanging fog that drifted up from the surrounding valleys. Cars were forbidden in this particular section of the city, and save for the dull glow of street lamps and a few other traces of modern convenience, it was as if Bolan had been cast through time to the seventeenth century, when Mougins's elevated location and fortified walls had served as a first line of defense against bands of would-be marauders.

Ironically Bolan was there to repel an enemy as well, but his senses weren't on the alert for some medieval foe armed with a club or crossbow. The march of time and progress had bestowed upon the infidels of today more sophisticated means of destruction, and the Executioner knew only too well that he was going up against aggressors whose arsenal included plastic explosives, high-powered assault rifles and, if the warrior's worst fears were borne out, the newest generation of portable missile launchers.

There could be no denying that the stakes were high. The slightest miscalculation, the faintest lapse of vigilance or underestimation of the opposing force could prove fatal, for whenever and wherever Mack Bolan undertook a mission, Death was ever looming close at hand.

The stone pavement was damp from the fog, and Bolan's rubber soles left ghostly imprints as he made his way past the dark edifice of the Chapel of Saint Bernard. By the same token, he was also able to make out tracks left by another, and when he spotted a trail leading into the dark maw of a side alley next to the church, the warrior slowed and released the safety on the 9 mm Beretta 93-R automatic concealed in the pocket of his navy overcoat. Beneath the coat he was further armed with an ammo belt that held three flash-bang stun grenades and two fraggers. He stepped clear of the dim light cast by a sconce lamp mounted above the church doorway, blending into the shadows.

Senses alive, braced for action, Bolan waited.

For several moments it was quiet, then the warrior heard rustling in the alley. He whipped out his Beretta, but eased his finger off the trigger as a pair of small, scrawny cats scampered into view, mewling loudly as one chased the other across the street and up the steps of a two-story apartment building across the way.

False alarm.

Or was it?

The cats, after all, didn't account for the footprints leading into the alley. Bolan kept his gun at the ready and inched forward. He was about to break from cover when he heard a whisper in the darkness.

"I've seen thicker fogs in London."

It was a security code, assuring Bolan that he'd come upon a friend and not a foe. The Executioner stayed put as he identified himself in return, also in code. "It'll burn off by morning."

"That's what I like to hear," the man in the alley whispered. "Come on, but keep the lights out."

Bolan recognized the voice as that of Jack Grimaldi, his longtime friend and the pilot who'd flown him to France from Stony Man Farm in the heart of Virginia's Shenandoah Valley, half a world away. As he entered the alley and his eyes became accustomed to the dark, the Executioner could make out the other man's rugged frame. Grimaldi was armed with a Government Model Colt .45, and slung around his neck was a set of night-vision binoculars.

"Onto something?" Bolan asked as he joined his friend.

"Could be. Here, let me show you...."

Bolan followed Grimaldi down the alley, taking care to sidestep several foul-smelling heaps of refuse piled into rickety trash cans. Equally pungent in the confines of the passageway was the smell of night jasmine growing in planter boxes set on the windowsills of the apartment building opposite the church.

"I came up empty, but Cowboy had some luck downhill," the pilot explained as they walked. "I just got off the box with him."

Cowboy was John Kissinger, who normally confined himself to weaponsmithing back at the Virginia compound but often jumped at a chance to get in some fieldwork with Bolan and the other warriors of Stony Man Farm. This assignment had been no exception and, like Bolan and Grimaldi, Kissinger had spent most of the past two days scouring the countryside north of the French Riviera for clues as to the whereabouts of a team of terrorists calling themselves Blood Against Oppression.

Originally the protest arm of the United Front Against Oppression, a loosely organized confederation of dissident professors and leftist student radicals from various prestigious European universities, BAO had recently splintered off from its founders and adopted a policy of terrorism as a means of drawing attention to its political agenda. Both organizations had been driving forces behind antiwar protests in Europe during the Persian Gulf crisis, and

BAO had capitalized on the ferment, drawing into its ranks not only the more violence-prone protestors, but also a number of Iranians, Palestinians and Iraqi loyalists committed to Hussein's concept of jihad, or holy war against the would-be Great Satan of America and its allies. BAO itself didn't subscribe to jihad per se, but it shared its Middle East members' disdain for the present world order and was committed to any form of upheaval that would disrupt the global influence of the Western World.

BAO had claimed credit for numerous acts of terrorism in Europe and the United States in recent months, and they were rumored to be planning a major assault on Cannes during the coastal city's annual international get-together of film industry luminaries. Denouncing Hollywood as a propaganda mill for the perpetuation of America's subverted values, BAO's apparent intent was to turn the festival into a killing ground in which major film stars would be made to pay for the images of Western decadence they presented to the world. A number of high-profile actors and actresses had purposely stayed away from the festival, while others shrugged off the threat as exaggerated hype.

The authorities weren't about to risk being cavalier, however. Security had been beefed up in Cannes and adjacent coastal cities, and there were several antiterrorist teams roaming the Riviera in hopes of tracking down BAO hit squads. If Grimaldi was right about Kissinger's findings, though, Bolan figured he and the men of Stony Man Farm were going to have the first crack at stopping BAO in its tracks.

Which was fine with Bolan. Over the years, he had seen countless groups like Blood Against Oppression sprout from the ferment of international politics, trying to draw attention to themselves and their dubious causes by spilling the blood of the innocent. He knew that the only sure way to thwart such groups was to beat them at their own game, striking hard and fast before they had a chance to flourish.

There was a second motivation for Bolan's determination as well. According to all available intelligence on the BAO, there was some level of Russian input into their operations. Whether such input involved direct infiltration or merely providing the group with weapons and other supplies, the implications were ominous. If a hard-line arm of the Russian government was attempting to circumvent the cessation of cold war hostilities by creating a puppet terrorist outfit to carry out its private agenda, the Blood Against Oppression had the potential of becoming more than just another small pest on the international scene. With backing, BAO could well join the ranks of such global threats as the PLO and IRA.

And so, in Bolan's mind at least, this was no routine assignment. On the contrary, it had the makings of one of the most important missions he'd ever undertaken.

High stakes indeed.

The alley dead-ended in a small garden planted with herbs and flowers and watched over by a stone likeness of Saint Bernard. The far wall was also part of the city's original fortifications, and as they stood before it, Bolan and Grimaldi could see the surrounding countryside. Much of their view was obscured by pockets of fog, but they could make out a number of scattered villas and smaller homes set in the hills and valleys. Less than five miles away, the lights of Cannes were barely visible as a domelike glow above the southern horizon.

As he unslung the binoculars, Grimaldi directed Bolan's attention to a chalet set back in the hills a few hundred yards away.

"Take a look there, especially the upper balcony."

Bolan took the binoculars and peered through them. The goggles' infrared capabilities compensated for the night's darkness, providing the Executioner with a surprisingly clear view of activity at the estate in question.

"Sentries," he muttered as he focused on two men pacing the upper balcony. One brandished an Uzi, the other a carbine. Both divided their attention equally between surveying the grounds below and keeping an eye on the access road leading to the estate.

"Where's Cowboy?" Bolan asked.

"In a hillside field about fifty yards to the left. He's lying low, so I don't think you're going to be able to spot him."

Bolan scanned the field, which had been partially graded and was cluttered with stacks of lumber and other building supplies. As Grimaldi had suggested, the warrior wasn't able to see Kissinger.

"Well, let's go catch up with him. We don't want him to have to crash the party all by himself...."

JOHN KISSINGER CROUCHED behind a tall stack of bound four-by-eights, maintaining his vigilance on the villa. He was getting impatient and wanted to move in closer, not only to further verify that he had indeed tracked down the terrorists, but also to get a clearer idea of how many there were. But he knew that with sentries posted on the upper floor of the balcony, he'd be spotted through the fog the moment he tried to move away from the building site. Between the stacked lumber and the stone walls surrounding the villa's grounds was nothing but a small valley of tall, green grass.

As he held his position, Kissinger wiped his gun across the sleeve of his shirt, brushing moisture off the barrel and safety. The gun was a QA-18 Stealthshooter, a 15-round automatic of his own design, modeled roughly after the old Browning FN but enhanced with additional features, including a built-in silencer and a flash suppressor. It was an ideal weapon for this line of work, and both Bolan and Grimaldi had QA-18s as their backup weapons.

When Kissinger's legs began to cramp, he shifted slightly and raised his head just high enough to peer over the lumber. He could still make out the sentries on the balcony, but it was activity on the ground that commanded his attention. For the first time since he'd begun his stakeout, Kissinger saw the main gates open. A white Mercedes limousine pulled out and rolled down the driveway to the access road.

Kissinger grabbed his walkie-talkie and tried to reach Grimaldi, but the pilot failed to acknowledge.

"Damn!" He cursed under his breath as he moved away from the pile of lumber and wove his way back through more supplies, all the while keeping an eye on the limo, trying to read its license plates and pick out some other distinctive characteristics he could pass along to the authorities. The car vanished into a bank of fog, however, and Kissinger was barely able to see even the retreating taillights.

He had little time to vent his frustrations, however, because a series of gunshots suddenly plowed into the earth at his feet and began to stitch up the sides of a plastic-shelled portable lavatory directly behind him. He instinctively lunged forward, diving headlong for the nearest cover, a tall mound of decorative river rocks. He groaned with pain as he inadvertently slammed his hip against the larger rocks at the base of the pile. It seemed at first that his contact had been insignificant, but he knew better when he heard a rumble and a clatter and looked up to see the first slew of rocks sliding down on him. He tried to roll clear, but the slide was too fast. In a matter of seconds, he was half-buried and pinned to the ground. He'd somehow managed to maintain his grip on his Stealthshooter, but his arm was weighed down by a few hundred pounds of stone. He wasn't sure if the limb was broken, but already he could feel the circulation being cut off. Struggling only shifted the weight on top of him, rendering him even more immobile. Like it or not, he was trapped and helpless.

And he was no longer alone.

Once he stopped moving, he could hear movement to his right, and as he craned his neck to investigate, he found himself staring at two men armed with Uzis. Both of them had their guns aimed at Kissinger, and from the looks in their eyes, Cowboy felt certain they intended to use them.

CHAPTER TWO

The muffled gunshots sounded like matches doused in water. When he heard them, Kissinger flinched, expecting to feel the hammering thud of bullets slamming into his flesh. Instead, to his amazement, he realized his would-be killers were the ones on the receiving end of the gunfire. Despite fog and nightfall, Kissinger was able to see the flow of blood from exit wounds as the men crumpled before him, dropping their unfired weapons.

Seconds later, two more men materialized out of the fog and stole toward Kissinger, guns in hand.

"Man, am I glad to see you guys," Kissinger told Bolan and Grimaldi as they crouched beside him.

"No kidding," Grimaldi said, hauling boulders off his friend. "I thought you knew better than to get stoned on the job."

"Funny," Cowboy drawled.

As Bolan helped remove the rocks, he asked, "Anything broken?"

"Besides my pride? Hard to say." Kissinger grimaced. "Listen, did you see a limo pull away from the villa a couple minutes ago?"

The Executioner shook his head. "We had to circle past the road and come up the other side of the hill."

"You might want to call into Cannes and warn them," Kissinger advised. "I didn't get a make on the plates, but it was a white stretch Mercedes."

"Hell, given all the big shots hobnobbing around Cannes this week, that'll narrow it down to a few hundred," Grimaldi observed. Still, he keyed his walkie-talkie and patched through to one of the CIA-backed antiterrorist squads working in conjunction with the team from Stony Man Farm. The man Grimaldi spoke to asked him if he wanted to have some agents rushed up to Mougins as backup.

"Negative," the Stony Man pilot replied, eyeing the dead men a few yards away. "I don't think there's going to be time for that. Just make sure you get word to all the teams in Cannes, including Brognola." Hal Brognola was Director of Operations for Stony Man Farm. Though the big Fed usually worked behind the scenes, this time Brognola was on the front line, helping to direct the Cannes security detail.

Grimaldi clipped the walkie-talkie to his belt and resumed helping Bolan with the rocks. Once the fallen heap had been cleared, the two men helped Kissinger to his feet.

"You okay?" Bolan asked.

Cowboy took a few steps, rolling his shoulders and shaking his arms at his sides. He felt bruised all over and wobbly on his feet, but there were no sharp pains indicative of broken bones. "I'm in better shape than those guys," he commented, gesturing at the dead men.

Bolan leaned over the fallen gunmen, quickly frisking them. One carried an expired student ID from Germany's University of the Republic, where the UFAO had been founded almost ten years earlier. The other man had no identification, but around his neck he wore a medallion inscribed in Arabic and stamped with the likeness of Saddam Hussein.

"Republican Guard?" Grimaldi wondered aloud when Bolan showed him the medallion.

"I think so." Bolan rose to his feet. "Probably a deserter who linked up with BAO rather than return home."

"There're supposed to be a lot of them like that," Grimaldi said.

Kissinger glanced over his shoulder. "If there's anyone left at the villa, they're going to start getting suspicious when these guys don't return. I say we make our move."

"I second," Grimaldi said.

Kissinger leaned over and grabbed the fallen German's Marlin 336 CS rifle, which was equipped with a high-powered scope. "I don't want to slow you guys down," he told the others, "but I can at least hang back and give you some cover."

"Good idea," Bolan told him, eyeing the nearby mansion, then turning back to one of the downed gunmen and beginning to unbutton his fatigues. "Let's do it."

ATTIRED IN OLIVE-DRAB camou fatigues and with her hair pulled up in a matching cap, twenty-six-year-old Vera Maris was now the only sentry posted on the second-story balcony of the villa. Several minutes ago her colleague, a fellow university dropout, had gone with one of BAO's Iraqi recruits to investigate signs of suspicious activity at the nearby building site. She'd watched them steal from the villa grounds, disappearing along a dried, fog-shrouded creek bed leading to the distant field. Moments later she'd heard some sort of commotion, but from her vantage point she had only a limited view, and the fog wasn't helping matters. Nerves on edge, she continued to peer across the grounds, her hands gripped tightly around her Uzi submachine gun. The weapon, like many others in the possession of the BAO, had been acquired on the black market during the months of arduous training and preparation that had preceded the group's recent spate of terrorist activities. When supplemented by Kalashnikov rifles and a bevy of other Russian-made ordnance pirated by Iraqi deserters during the chaotic wake of

Desert Storm, BAO's arsenal was imposing. Some of those wielding those weapons were equally formidable; but such was not the case with Maris. Sure, she'd had her share of practice with the Uzi and various other firearms, but she'd yet to draw bead on a human target, and, much as she presented herself to her peers as a ready and willing warrior, the prospect of crossing that line between spouting rhetoric and spewing hot lead had her filled with conflicting emotions.

Maris was a relatively new member of the Blood, enticed into joining less than a month earlier. At the time she had just dropped out of school, both because of poor grades and as a way of revolting against her father, Ed Dauffie. Dauffie, American-born but of Afghan descent, had transferred his entire family from New York to Germany thirteen years earlier when he'd assumed a position with NATO Intelligence. Rarely home, he'd had little opportunity to form, much less maintain, a solid parental relationship with his oldest daughter, and over the years their estrangement had widened in tandem with Vera's growing antiestablishment views. On little more than a whim, Vera had married out of high school, only to divorce a year later and grudgingly comply with her father's insistence that she enroll at the University of Hanover and get a degree. Vera was a poor student, showing little interest in classes, but she found a certain solace in the free-thinking atmosphere of the campus. She was drawn to radical views, particularly those conflicting with the ideals her father stood for. She inevitably developed a reactionary hatred toward her native America as well as the reunified German state. Like many a restless youth before her, she saw these establishments as hulking, monolithic forces whose only purpose was to stifle her free spirit and fit her into some dreary preconceived mold. In time, she came to see the university as yet another unyielding authority figure. She felt destined for greater things and bristled with a growing frustration at her inability to find others who shared her grand vision.

Then, one evening while brooding over a stein of cold ale at a Hanover rathskeller, Maris had fallen in with a group of carousing bohemians, most of them former university students, who'd lifted her out of her sorrows. At first she'd gotten caught up in their festive antics, pitching in to buy rounds of beer and joining them in song, including a number of ribald antigovernment anthems.

By the time the barkeep had ordered the group to leave, Maris was stinking drunk and eager to prove herself to her newfound friends. With surprising strength for a woman weighing less than a hundred and ten pounds, she'd heaved a bar stool through the front window of the rathskeller, then valiantly resisted the bouncers that swarmed around her. The others had come to her aid, trashing the bar in a protracted brawl that only ended when sirens announced the arrival of the local authorities.

Maris had fled with the others, and they'd taken her to their quarters in a dilapidated house down the street from a chemical plant at the outskirts of town.

It was there that she had first met the group's leader, Ali-Jahn Babdi, a charismatic, dark-eyed Turk in his early thirties with an easy smile and a dazzling way with words. When told of Maris's heroics at the rathskeller, Babdi had showered the young woman with praise and toasted her bravado. Thus had begun another bout of revelry, during which time Maris had eagerly taken in not only countless more tankards of ale but also seeming hours of passionate discourse by Babdi, who not only painted a gloriously romantic picture of the noble cause of the Blood Against Oppression, but also seemed to speak as if he had somehow managed to look into Maris's soul and learned all there was to know about her, about her innermost dreams and beliefs, and even about her most secretly kept desires. Within moments after pledging her allegiance to the BAO, Maris had been led by Babdi into a back bedroom. There she'd blissfully placed herself at the mercy of the leader's sexual prowess, and he'd performed acts with her that had previously been only the subject of her unspoken private fantasies. By dawn she'd been sated, and as she'd joy-

ously drifted off to sleep, she remembered hoping
that this dream life would never end.

As fate would have it, her wish had come
true...only the dream had become a nightmare.

Within a week after her induction into the BAO,
she'd witnessed her first killing. It was at the chemical plant down the street from the flat where she'd
been initiated. Under cover of night, she and several
other masked colleagues had stormed the back loading dock, determined to steal a trove of restricted
chemicals used in the making of plastic explosives.
They were armed, and when the workers had resisted and a security guard had stumbled upon the
scene, there had been a flurry of gunfire, during
which the guard and two workers had been killed.
Maris was in charge of grabbing shipping crates
containing the targeted chemicals and had therefore
avoided having to fire her gun. But while fleeing the
scene, the group had encountered another security
guard. Maris had raised her weapon but couldn't
summon the nerve to kill the man. She'd fired wide,
deliberately missing. None of her comrades had noticed, and their own shots had hit the mark with
chilling accuracy. The image of the man's face being
obliterated by the impact of the bullets was still
etched in Maris's mind, and there was rarely a night
that she didn't awaken in a cold sweat, haunted by
the grisly visage.

Of course, the others had readily dismissed the killings as a necessary part of their mission, and the chemicals had been used to create explosive charges that two weeks later had demolished a Hanover restaurant frequented by local politicos. The death toll in that incident had been twenty-six, and when BAO had claimed credit for the killings as part of a rambling declaration sent to the local media, their stock as a terrorist force to be reckoned with had been substantially increased.

By now regularly sharing Babdi's bed as well as learning the ways of terrorism at his side, Maris had followed a group of BAO warriors south to France, leaving a wake of destruction in their path. Although her belief in the ends sought by the Blood rarely wavered, she was increasingly ill at ease about the means the group employed. To some extent she was able to drown her guilt during the interludes of sex and drinking that punctuated BAO missions of brutality, but during more sober moments the deaths continued to haunt her, and she'd begun to regret affiliating herself with Babdi and his band of rogue killers.

Any thoughts of voicing her misgivings or trying to bail out of the organization were stifled, however, when she'd witnessed the fate of Tim Cangelraud, a French recruit who'd joined BAO in Paris the week before, only to decide he wanted out when asked to participate in the bombing of a café on the

Left Bank. Babdi had confronted Cangelraud in front of the entire group and executed him with a bullet through the head before unceremoniously tossing the body into the van that was later left to explode outside the café, adding another six fatalities to the list of the dead claimed by BAO.

And now Maris found herself an unwilling party to BAO's proposed bloodbath in Cannes and elsewhere along the Riviera. A carload of terrorists had just left in a white Mercedes to carry out the first assault, and soon it would be her turn to join in another attack, this one targeting Mougins's world-renowned Le Moulin de Mougins restaurant. The way the mission was laid out, she couldn't avoid being a participant in the killing. Babdi himself had seen to that, specifically designating her to be the one who would place the time bomb in the rest room while dining there the following afternoon.

It struck her as odd that he'd assigned the task to her rather than any of the others. It was so out of character from the way things had been carried out thus far. Maris's darkest fear was that Babdi had caught wind of her doubts and was putting her in a position where she would have to either reestablish her commitment to the cause or betray herself and, in effect, offer herself up as the next grim example of what happened to those who deviated from BAO's bloodthirsty course. The thought that Babdi might use her, his present lover, as just another of his dispensible pawns both appalled and terrified her. How could she have been taken in by such a monster? And why did she remain here, resigned to doing his bidding when she knew the reasoning behind it, when she knew the dire consequences? Better she should throw down her gun, now that Babdi was gone for the night, and flee as fast as her feet could take her. . . .

And yet she remained, feeling trapped, somehow caught in the web of his charismatic influence. With a bitter sadness, she also wrestled with another thought that had been plaguing her in the weeks since committing herself to the cause of the Blood. In joining the terrorists, she had gone a step beyond merely refuting her father and his beliefs; now she had sided with the enemy, an enemy that would just as soon kill the likes of Ed Dauffie as look at him. Maris had broken off all contact with her family when she'd joined BAO, and she doubted that they had the faintest notion that she'd embarked on such a dark course. Were her father to find out, she knew he would be devastated. There had been a time when she would have welcomed such a reaction. But no longer. Now, instead of swaggering bravado, she felt an overpowering sense of shame.

And fear.

In joining the Blood Against Oppression, it seemed as if she'd set out on an irreversible course from which there could be no escape, short of dying.

Maris was shaken from her troubled reverie when she spotted activity down in the creek bed. Two men were striding through the patchy fog, retracing the circuitous course that the sentries had taken to the building site. At first glance they appeared to be the same two men, but as they drew nearer to the side gate and rose up out of the fog, Maris got a better look at them and realized how much tighter their combat fatigues were.

A trick!

She had a decision to make, and she had to make it quickly. From where she was posted, she had a clear view of the intruders and had only to draw bead on them and pull the trigger of her Uzi to gun them down. Or she could call down to the other sentries stationed just inside the walls surrounding the property and leave the killing to them. In doing so, however, she would also alert the intruders, giving them a chance to seek cover or retreat.

Maris raised the submachine gun to firing position, lining the men in her sights as they drew closer to the gate. She balked at firing, though, and finally a third option presented itself as a bullet fired from the opposite direction suddenly bored into her shoulder, carrying enough wallop to send her staggering backward. She struck her head sharply on one of the balcony posts, and in an instant the world around her went black.

CHAPTER THREE

"Nice shot, Cowboy," Bolan whispered under his breath as he eyed the balcony and watched the guard fall from view.

"Yeah," Grimaldi murmured, "but too bad he couldn't have waited until we were through the gate."

"My guess is he didn't have a choice." Bolan reached under the fatigue jacket belonging to the slain Iraqi. He peeled a stun grenade from his belt and lobbed it over the tall stucco wall surrounding the villa. At the same time, Grimaldi leveled his confiscated Uzi at the side gate, riddling the wrought-iron lock and surrounding woodwork with 9 mm parabellum rounds. The lock gave way under the concentrated gunfire, and when the grenade subsequently exploded, its concussive force swung the gate outward, providing Bolan and Grimaldi with an opening to the property.

Just inside the gate, a BAO guard was down on his knees, dazed and half-blinded by the grenade. As Grimaldi charged past him, he lashed out with a well-placed karate chop, striking the guard behind the skull and rendering him unconscious.

The villa grounds were spacious and well lighted. A second gunman stood fifty yards away, peering out from behind a granite fountain sculpture. The terrorist was about to fire an autopistol, and Grimaldi somersaulted to his right as high-velocity rounds pummelled the ground and wall behind him.

Tracking the sound of gunfire, Bolan spotted the terrorist and dropped to a crouch, bringing his Beretta into firing position and squeezing off three rapid shots. Chips of granite splintered off the statue as the bullets sought out their target. One managed to catch the guard in the ribs, doubling him over. Grimaldi followed up with a blast from his Government Model .45, piercing the man's neck and sending him toppling into the fountain.

Signaling to each other, Bolan and Grimaldi split up, with the Executioner charging up a landscaped path that led to the villa's side patio while his counterpart circled around the periphery of the grounds, setting his sights on the back entrance.

Halfway to the patio, Bolan spotted another gunman charging out through the side doorway, cradling a Kalashnikov rifle in his hands. The warrior sidestepped clear of the path, taking cover behind a eucalyptus tree. Enemy bullets thumped against the thick trunk, ripping off shreds of green bark and missing the target by mere inches. Bolan drew a quick breath, then sprang back out into the open, firing his Beretta.

The guard on the patio was about to duck behind a brick barbecue, but Bolan nailed him in the chest before he reached cover. Down he went, misfiring a few final rounds into a planter box overgrown with flowers.

Bolan reached the patio without further opposition. He paused briefly to confirm that the guard was dead, then proceeded to the sliding patio door, which was still open. Without hesitation, he entered the villa.

Like the grounds, the interior of the house spoke of wealth and painstaking upkeep, although it was equally clear that the BAO didn't share the same tastes as the owners. Mud had been tracked across the plush white carpeting of the dining room, and loose food wrappers and unwashed dishes were strewed haphazardly across the antique mahogany table and equally expensive chairs. Cigarettes had been ground out on the finely polished tabletop, and along the walls several expensive paintings and been slashed and stained with thrown bits of food.

Also on the table was a map of France's southern coastline, with scribbled notations around the larger cities. Some of the notes were in Arabic, while others were in Russian. He wasn't familiar enough with any of the script to decipher what was written, but he was certain that the map had been used by BAO to plot strategy. There were Agency people in Cannes who'd hopefully be able to help make sense of the notes.

In the meantime, though, Bolan wanted to finish searching the villa. He wandered cautiously from the dining room into a massive front hallway, complete with a magnificent crystal chandelier and a winding staircase that reached up to the second story. As he started up the steps, Bolan heard a faint sound to his left and whirled around. At the last second he eased his finger off the trigger as he saw Grimaldi step into view from the kitchen area.

"All clear so far," the pilot called up to Bolan.

"Keep checking. I'll take the upstairs."

Grimaldi nodded, crossing the hallway and cautiously heading into the adjacent den. Bolan resumed climbing the steps, then went from room to room, ever ready to engage whatever enemy might be lying in wait. Finally he made his way out to the balcony, where Vera Maris was just regaining consciousness. When she saw the Executioner, her eyes widened with terror and she threw her hands in the air, wincing from the burning pain in her shoulder. She cried out in German that she wanted to surrender, and when she took a closer look at Bolan, she repeated her plea in English.

"Don't shoot, please! I surrender!"

Bolan stepped forward, keeping his Beretta trained on his prisoner. He leaned over, grabbed Maris's Uzi, then gestured for the woman to stand. She obliged, holding one hand against her bleeding shoulder.

"You're lucky to be alive," Bolan told the woman. "You realize that, don't you?"

"Yes," Maris conceded. "I won't try to escape. You have my word."

"I'm going to have to find out how good your word is before I take it. Are you willing to cooperate?"

Maris nodded. She was on the verge of tears. "Yes!" she said, her voice cracking. "Yes, I will help...."

THERE WERE NINE ROOMS on the ground floor of the villa. Grimaldi checked them all but encountered no further resistance. Next to the pantry at the end of the back hallway, he opened a door that led down to a basement. He turned on the stairway light and began to descend the wooden steps. The slats creaked under his weight, despite his efforts to be silent.

He'd taken five steps when a gun barked to life in the far corner, gouging bits of wood out of the stairway railing and whizzing within inches of his face.

Rather than retreat, Grimaldi sprang forward, clearing nearly a dozen steps before landing hard on the tiled floor. He rolled on impact, blunting much of the shock, but a sharp pain raced from his right ankle all the way up his leg. A sprain, he suspected, but he wasn't about to let it hamper him from scrambling across the floor, dodging the next volley from his unseen assailant.

Nearly half the basement had been set aside for a miniature train set, easily the most elaborate one Grimaldi had ever encountered. The detailing on the train was meticulous, and the same fine touch had gone into the surrounding scenery, down to dot-sized ducks floating on a small lake and equally small quail nesting on three-foot-high mountain ranges. Grimaldi was in no position to casually admire the setup, however. He dived headlong behind the mini-Alps, displacing the water from one of the lakes and laying waste to a small-scale freight depot. Downscaled pine trees poked at him as he pressed low against the simulated terrain to avoid another fusillade that pounded away at the mountains. The other gunman had only to lower his aim and Grimaldi would be as good as dead.

The pilot inched forward, seeking out a tunnel that bored through one of the taller mountains. Peering through it, he was just able to make out a lone gunman crouched beside a wet bar jutting from the far wall. He'd apparently emptied his gun, because he was busily ejecting one magazine and getting ready to ram another into place.

Three seconds. That's all Grimaldi figured he had. He made the best of it.

Rolling onto his back, he pointed his .45 at the overhead light.

Two seconds.

He pulled the trigger. The bulb shattered, throwing the basement into darkness.

One second.

Grimaldi pushed off the mountain range and sprang to his feet.

Time was up.

The terrorist blasted away in the darkness, burying more shots into the mountain range, but Grimaldi had already moved out of the line of fire. He retaliated with a lethal stream of .45 slugs, directing his aim at the wet bar.

Upon hearing the clatter of a dropped gun and the scattering of bar stools under the weight of the felled terrorist, Grimaldi moved around the train set and sought out the nearest wall. Reaching it, he moved slowly through the dark silence, groping for another light switch. When his hand fell on it, he readied his Colt, then threw the switch, illuminating the far half of the basement.

For firing in the dark, Grimaldi had fared well. The terrorist lay twisted on the floor, eyes staring vacantly at the ceiling's acoustic tiles. He'd taken one shot through the right cheekbone, another in the chest just above the sternum. Most likely, either one would have been sufficient. The man was clearly dead twice over. He was blond and blue-eyed, with distinctively British features.

Grimaldi felt an odd sensation as he approached the bar. In the past, he'd gone up against enemies of all different colors, creeds and nationalities, but as a rule each assignment usually found him facing only those of one specific makeup at a time. But tonight he'd already encountered an Iraqi, a German, two blacks of unknown nationality and now a Briton. It was eerie, unsettling.

But not unsettling enough that Grimaldi was about to lower his guard.

He stepped over the corpse and circled the wet bar. There was a heavy door behind the bar, and when Grimaldi cautiously opened it, he saw that it led to a small wine cellar. He stepped inside, noting an immediate drop in temperature. The walls on either side of him were lined with wine racks, and nearly every available space was filled with a tilted bottle. In all, Grimaldi guessed there were close to five hundred bottles, and judging from the labels, they were all vintage selections. Definitely not the stuff of bohemians or revolutionaries.

At the far end of the cellar was a small antechamber, most of which was filled by an immense freezer. As he approached the appliance, Grimaldi felt a sudden sensation of dread, and even as he started to raise the hefty lid, he had an idea of what he was going to find.

Or, more to the point, who he was going to find.

An icy fog swirled up out of the freezer, giving Grimaldi a further chill as he glanced inside. Sprawled in a twisted heap at the bottom of the white enclosure were a man and woman, both in their late fifties or early sixties. It seemed a safe bet they were the owners of the mansion. The man, who looked vaguely familiar, wore flannel pajamas and a burgundy velveteen smoking jacket. The woman was dressed in a terry-cloth bathrobe. Both had small-caliber bullet wounds to the side of the head, and their skin was an odd shade of bluish gray. To an untrained eye, it was difficult to gauge how long they'd been dead.

Grimaldi closed the freezer door and left the wine cellar. On his way back to the staircase, his attention was drawn to a bookcase built into the wall. Out of curiosity, he scanned the books stacked on the shelves. Mostly there were philosophy tomes, but he also encountered a few books on radical politics, and one entire shelf was filled with titles touching on both subjects, all written by the same author. Thomas Galton, Ph.D. The name rang a faint bell, and once Grimaldi placed it with the face of the man in the freezer, something clicked. He recalled from the briefing that had preceded this mission that Galton was a university teacher in Paris who'd also been one of the founders of the United Front Against Oppression, the organization BAO had splintered off from.

"Aha," Grimaldi muttered as he trudged up the steps, favoring his tender ankle. "Now we're getting somewhere."

Emerging from the basement, he encountered Kissinger, who'd come over from the building site after witnessing the shoot-out on the villa grounds. Cowboy was limping visibly as well, but seemed far surer on his feet than he had been after first being pulled out from under the toppled heap of river rocks.

"Couldn't content yourself with playing sniper, eh?"

Kissinger shrugged. "I ran out of targets."

"Well, it looks like we have, too," Grimaldi said. Gesturing at the opulent surroundings, he went on to explain the grisly fate that had befallen the villa's owners. He concluded, "So the way I figure it, BAO had Galton's address from back when they were part of UFAO, and they decided to invite themselves over for an impromptu reunion. Galton didn't want to play along and wound up paying the big price."

"That's pretty much it," Bolan called out, stepping into view from the main hallway. He had Maris with him and related the woman's version of events preceding the assault. Grimaldi proved to have been right on the mark about the circumstances leading to Galton's death and that of his wife. But he was less interested in basking in the glory of his deductive powers than focusing on the identity of the BAO's ringleader.

"Ali-Jahn Babdi?" he said. "Is that the same guy they call Ali-Baba?"

"Right again," Bolan confirmed. "And he's got his modern-day forty thieves falling over one another to do his bidding."

Maris stared at the floor, her face flushed with shame. Grimaldi eyed her a moment, then looked back at Bolan. "So, did she give us any idea what Babdi's got up his sleeve as far as Cannes goes?"

"Yeah, she's told me plenty," Bolan said, "and it's pretty grim."

CHAPTER FOUR

Rather than take Route 567, the primary access road from Mougins to Cannes, Ali-Jahn Babdi chose a more roundabout approach, guiding the Mercedes limo along a relatively quiet two-lane road that coursed through winding hills to the small village of Vallauris. Pablo Picasso had put the town on the international map when he settled down in one of its unimposing villas following World War II, and there was a renowned trade shop on the main street as well as a small museum at the Place de la Libération honoring the artist and his work.

But Babdi hadn't come to Vallauris to patronize the arts. Not by a long shot.

Driving past darkened souvenir shops, Babdi sought out Rue de Hesson, an inconspicuous side street that ran back into the hills. There were no street lamps past the first couple blocks, and, combined with the darkness, the last remnants of fog slowed him even further. Finally he came upon his destination, a small, isolated automotive repair shop surrounded by Renaults, Peugots and Citroëns. Veering from the road, Babdi killed the limo's lights as well as the engine, letting the vehicle roll to a stop near one of the rear service bays. Before getting out, the Turk reached under the dashboard and tugged the remote trunk release.

The back hood of the limousine opened slowly as Babdi stepped out into the brisk night air. Three other men got out of the Mercedes as well. Like Babdi, they were well-groomed and wore black tuxedos, looking more like pampered aristocrats than anarchistic desperadoes. A casual sweep of a metal detector, however, would have revealed that each man had an automatic pistol tucked inside his cummerbund.

The night air was rich with the licorice scent of fresh anise and the briny smell of the sea. In the distance, through the quickly dissipating fog, Babdi could see the Mediterranean glittering beneath a waxing moon. Another mountain range blocked his view of Cannes and the isles off Pointe de la Croisette, but the lights of Juan-les-Pins and Cap d'Antibes were visible to his left. He imagined that there were ample deserving targets flaunting their wealth down there as well as in Cannes, but an attack on the peninsula wouldn't have the same impact as wreaking havoc on the film festival. And the Turk was determined that BAO's actions achieve maximum impact. He was through with small gestures. He'd had enough of BAO's offensives being relegated to the back pages of newspapers and shrugged off as just another routine bit of terrorism. He wanted the world's attention, and with the media already swarming over Cannes like jackals crowding a fresh kill, he knew that any blood shed there would be magnified. Yes, he had it all worked out. There would be the mayhem in Cannes, followed immediately by a second incident in Monaco, then yet another in Mougins—three decisive strikes in bold succession, the work of a fearless new force the world would have to deal with. By this time tomorrow night, the Blood Against Oppression would be known throughout the world, and as its leader, Ali-Jahn Babdi would become a household name.

Of course, there were heightened security measures to get around, and such an operation always carried with it the risk of being captured or killed. Babdi was prepared for such contingencies. He'd assigned his best men to handle the job in Cannes, and by the time they were within range of their target, Babdi figured to be miles away, tending to the second phase of his master plan. And while he was doing that, the villa of Thomas Galton would be obliterated by explosives, eliminating those members of the Blood he felt were unworthy of basking in the glory that was to come.

Including his "beloved" Vera.

She had shown such promise at first, with her youthful naïveté and boisterous enthusiasm, with her exquisite olive-skinned body and her willingness to let him have his way with her. He'd even thought for a time that she might help him to forget the woman she'd replaced, Emma Skodynov. But in recent weeks he'd sensed Vera's growing lack of resolve, her timidity in the face of what he'd told her must be done to achieve the aims of the BAO. Was she really so foolish as to think he didn't see her abstain from the killing during their murderous trek from Hanover to the Riviera? Did she really think he couldn't see the cowardice and trepidation in her eyes when he'd suggested she plant a bomb at the Mougins restaurant where her favorite filmmaker was scheduled to have lunch the following afternoon? Of course, he had no intention of having her carry out such a plan. By tomorrow, the survivors of the carnage at Cannes wouldn't be so capricious as to motor up to Mougins for a leisurely lunch. They would be scrambling for ways to leave the country, to get back to the U.S. or their myriad other homelands and spread the fascinating tale of how by sheer luck they'd barely managed to avoid the sad fate of those claimed by the apocalyptic judgment of the Blood Against Oppression.

By tomorrow, Vera would be dead. And along with her, he'd be rid of the weakest links in his organization. He would be particularly glad to be rid of the Iraqis, whose membership numbers were disproportionately large relative to other nationalities in the Blood. That alone was reason enough for concern in Babdi's mind; but he was additionally wary of the group's most outspoken member, Eijai Wahldjun. Wahldjun, formerly a colonel in Saddam Hussein's Republican Guard and a mastermind behind many of the atrocities committed during the occupation of Kuwait, posed an obvious threat to Babdi's leadership, and although the Iraqi was adept at concealing any such intention, Babdi knew the man coveted power—perhaps even as much as he coveted Vera Maris. The Turk had seen the looks exchanged between the two, and it wouldn't surprise him if even now, behind his back, they had slipped off for a shared embrace. In a way he hoped that would be the case, because it would make it all the more fitting when the bomb went off, catching them in the act.

But Babdi had more important things to do this evening than dwell upon vengeance against his underlings. The bomb would take care of that. It was time to focus on striking out against the larger enemy, the Great Satan.

Although no lights were on inside the repair shop, the side door opened and out stepped two men, both dressed in dark, loose-fitting suits, carrying between them a long, narrow wooden crate. Babdi's lips tightened into the faintest hint of a smile at the sight of the crate. He greeted the men with a perfunctory nod and followed them to the back of the limousine.

Once the crate had been set inside the trunk, Babdi motioned for the others to step aside. He reached over and unfastened the latches securing the crate's lid, then gently raised it. Inside, nestled amid a strawlike packing material, was a Lawtin-313 missile system, one of only five such weapons in existence. A prototype for the newest generation of shoulder-launched warheads, the Lawtin, a product of Tucson-based McGaffles-Parez Industries, was as superior to such standbys as the Stinger was to a conventional bazooka. Not only was it nearly half as light as the Stinger system, it also had twice the range without sacrificing accuracy, and it was outfitted to handle a greater variety of warheads. The only downside was the Lawtin's cost, which was more than seven times that of any comparable weapon. Production had been temporarily halted on the weapon while attempts were made to bring down the cost, and the prototypes had been trotted around the globe for demonstration purposes as McGaffles-Parez sought out potential buyers and investors to back a full production run. Blood Against Oppression had caught wind of the company's European tour itinerary, and only this morning a three-man squad had successfully raided McGaffles-Parez's field office in Marseilles and stolen one of the Lawtins slated for a demonstration for NATO's Office of Procurement. One of the three men had been killed in the raid, but the other two had gotten away, and now they were prepared to put the weapon to use on orders of Ali-Jahn Babdi.

"Très bien," Babdi murmured as he ran his fingers over the sleek weapon. He congratulated the men in the dark suits again for the success of their raid, then quickly reviewed with them the plan for the launcher's use later that evening.

Babdi was in the middle of his discourse when he suddenly fell silent, reaching inside his cummerbund for his gun, a Raines 17-shot automatic with a short-cone silencer. Turning around, he and the others spotted a lone bicyclist pedaling downhill past the service station. It was a young man dressed in jeans and a black leather coat. He glanced briefly at the limo, then frowned with confusion at the sight of the gun in Babdi's hand.

Babdi fired twice.

The youth lost control of his bike as both shots drilled into him. He swerved off the road and was thrown over the top of the handlebars when the bike's front tire struck the curb. Dead by the time he landed, the youth sprawled across the cinder driveway and his bike rolled to a stop several yards away, tipping on its side.

Babdi told two of his tuxedoed comrades to dispose of the youth and his bike, then to join the men in the dark suits for the raid on Cannes. He gave the keys to the limousine to one of the men who'd stolen the Lawtin-313. In exchange, Babdi was given another set of keys. As he headed inside the service bay, he signaled to the remaining man in a tuxedo, Roberto Flotman. Flotman was second in command of the Blood Against Oppression, the man who'd helped Babdi launch the organization's first terrorist assaults after its split from the UFAO. Flotman opened the larger garage door as the Turk got in behind the wheel of a four-door BMW. By the time he'd pulled out, the others had finished with the biker and gotten into the Mercedes. Flotman closed the garage door, then joined his leader in the front seat of the BMW.

The Mercedes pulled out and started back down the road. Babdi followed the limousine through the streets of Vallauris and all the way to Golfe-Juan. There, the limousine took a right turn and headed for Cannes. Babdi turned left, heading up the coast until he'd linked up with the Autoroute de Provençale. From there he continued eastward, setting his sights on Monaco.

HAL BROGNOLA FIT RIGHT IN. Dressed in a tux, he freely roamed the Promenade de la Croisette, Canne's main seaside thoroughfare, soda water in one hand, and unlighted cigar in the other. Limousines lined the boulevard, disgorging celebrities and triggering the flash-bulbed cameras of the paparazzi. The air buzzed with excitement as established stars courted the press and up-and-coming wanna-bes feverishly pitched themselves and their projects to anyone who vaguely resembled someone worth sucking up to. Brognola indulged himself in the game a few times, playing along when he was mistaken for a studio executive or independent producer. He found the resulting conversations to be amusing for the most part, laced with an overall inanity that surpassed anything the most savage of satirists might have dreamed up.

But for all his enjoyment of this "walk on the wild side," the big Fed never lost sight of the reason he had come to the gathering. Some of the Stony Man personnel had queried the wisdom of his taking an active role in the mission, but he had waved away their concerns. After seven unrelieved months of running operations out of the confines of Justice and the Farm, he welcomed the challenge of the field.

The big Fed received the relayed message from Mougins regarding the suspicious Mercedes, and whenever a white limo with the telltale hood ornament would roll by, he'd take note. He also kept a trained eye on the crowd as well as the surrounding streets and buildings, looking for any subtle clue that might betray the presence of the Blood Against Oppression—or any other potential disturbers of the peace for that matter. BAO, after all, certainly hadn't cornered the market on hatred for the self-proclaimed Beautiful People who'd flocked to

Cannes for this prolonged orgy of conspicuous consumption. Innumerable organized groups would love to bring this crowd down a notch or two, and there was also that ever-present band of disturbed loners seething around the periphery of success—overzealous fans, psychotic also-rans and paranoid delusionaries who might snap at the slightest provocation and become one-man or -woman whirlwinds of violence.

Brognola was replenishing his soda water at a sidewalk bar when he saw a white Mercedes limousine suddenly veer out of the main flow of traffic and head down one of the narrower side streets. He set his drink down and nonchalantly picked up his stride, reaching the corner just as the limo was pulling up next to the delivery entrance of the Baines Hotel. The side doors opened, and a man with shoulder-length hair hurried out and scrambled in through the side door, followed by two burly bodyguards wearing sunglasses and sharkskin suits.

Brognola was taking note of the bodyguards when he was nearly bowled over by a shrieking hoard of teenage girls charging around the corner. They raced down the sidewalk toward the side doorway, screaming the name of Ronald Gerard, the hottest teen heartthrob on the French pop music scene.

False alarm.

Waiting to cross the street, Brognola glanced at the crowded harbor, where all manner of ships, from small dinghies and inconspicuous fishing trawlers to luxurious yachts and houseboats, were moored to docks littered with party-goers. Far out over the water, a fireworks display further lighted the bay in bursts of vibrant color. Brognola and several other key figures in the security detail had lobbied to have the fireworks canceled, fearing they might provide just the sort of distraction the BAO would desire to increase their chances of staging a successful assault on the festivities. The festival committee had overruled such concerns, however, although they had agreed to limit the number of so-called boom-boom fireworks.

Much as he was impressed by the dazzling shows of lights above the water, Brognola couldn't shake off an intuitive sense of dread. His concerns weren't without merit, either, as moments later a remote pager clipped to his belt beeped to life. He was barely able to hear it above the clamor around him. Reaching down, the big Fed flicked the response button to confirm that he'd gotten the message and would be replying shortly.

Retreating to the lobby of the Baines Hotel, Brognola headed to the nearest stairwell, then yanked the pager out and switched it to its intercom mode, allowing him to establish direct contact with the caller.

It was Bolan.

"We've got something," the Executioner reported. "We're on our way there, but you might want to round up some Company boys and get up to Old Town."

"I'm only a couple blocks from there now," Brognola said.

"Good. Here's what's going down...."

CHAPTER FIVE

The lone airfield servicing the Riviera was more than twenty miles from Mougins and Cannes, but with the force from Stony Man Farm desiring greater aerial mobility, Brognola had called in markers with an old war buddy living in Mougins and secured the use of his private tennis court as a temporary helipad. The man's estate was located less than a quarter mile from the villa of Thomas Galton, and within minutes after the capture of Vera Maris, Grimaldi was at the controls of a Reed-279 helicopter, heading toward Cannes. Bolan was with him. Kissinger had stayed behind with Maris, holding her for questioning and awaiting the arrival of CIA backup forces.

"Hal's on his way," Bolan commented as he replaced the radio mike after conferring with Brognola.

"I just hope that Maris woman hasn't sent us on a wild-goose chase," Grimaldi said.

"There's that chance, but my gut instinct says she was being straight."

"We'll find out soon enough."

Grimaldi was flying just above the fog, but he had to nose up as he approached a mountain ridge line poking through the haze. As soon as he cleared that obstacle, both men found themselves staring down at the glittery opulence of Cannes. Fireworks were still showering the bay with trails of light.

"Looks like one big party, all right," the Stony Man pilot remarked. "And the poor suckers don't even know what's about to hit them if we blow it."

"We aren't going to blow it," Bolan said with quiet determination. "We can't afford to."

In one respect Bolan was referring to the personal risk they were running by aerially approaching terrorists armed with supposedly the most sophisticated portable missile launcher in existence. Both men knew that if BAO spotted the chopper and wanted to shoot it down, the end result would be a foregone conclusion. Once in the sights of the Lawtin-313, there was little Grimaldi would be able to do in the way of maneuvering to shake the missile.

But the men were equally concerned about another grim possibility. Grimaldi finally put their worry to words.

"You think there's any chance they've scrounged up a nonconventional warhead?" he asked. "I know Maris said she didn't know for sure, but if they somehow got their hands on something biological..."

"Yeah. With this group anything's a possibility. All the more reason to make sure we stop them cold."

"On the bright side," Grimaldi said, "we have to remember the Lawtin's just a prototype. None of them has had any amount of experience working it, so there's got to be a margin for error."

"True," Bolan agreed. "That might work in our favor."

"I know it's not much, but, hey, I'll take it."

"I'll take it, too."

The Executioner had already reloaded his Beretta and grenade belt. In addition, he'd helped himself to the Marlin carbine taken from one of the slain terrorists. As the copter swooped down toward Cannes's Old Town, he propped the rifle against his shoulder and peered through the scope, familiarizing himself with the weapon. He knew his capabilities as a marksman, and knew that circumstances might be such that he wouldn't be able to get off more than one shot. If that wound up being the case, he wanted to be as prepared as possible to make that one shot count.

"Well, here we are," Grimaldi announced as he hovered over the outskirts of Old Town. "Should I shed a little light on matters?"

"No, let's try to hold off," Bolan said. Noting that there were two other helicopters in the immediate vicinity, he added, "The longer we can pass ourselves off as being just part of routine security, the better."

"Gotcha."

"Tower's at about two o'clock," Bolan said, indicating a tall spire poking up into the night sky. "Let's close in."

As they floated toward the tower, the warrior scanned the narrow city streets and surrounding buildings of Old Town. Most of the buildings dated back to the previous century, and some, like Sainte Anne Chapel, were more than eight hundred years old. It was an impressive tableau, but Bolan was less concerned with historical landmarks than the presence of something far more contemporary. He finally found what he was looking for.

"There's the Mercedes," he said, directing Grimaldi's attention to a white limousine parked in a cramped alley that ran behind the Museum of Fine Arts. There was no exhaust coming from the vehicle's tailpipe, and from their aerial perspective there was no way to tell if anyone was inside.

Grimaldi took the Reed down lower as they passed over the old brick wall surrounding the museum. Just inside the back gate, a guard lay sprawled on the ground, verifying that the BAO had already infiltrated the institute. When neither Bolan or Grimaldi was able to see any terrorists on the grounds, they were forced to assume that they'd already gained access to their primary destination, the so-called

Duke's Tower, a ninety-foot-high structure dating back to the previous century, when this sprawling estate had originally been built as a summer home for a Russian grand duke. Recently renovated as part of an expansion of the museum, the tower housed temporary exhibits and also offered an unrivaled panoramic view of the bay and the flurry of activity along the main promenade. As such, it was the perfect place from which to launch a missile attack on the unsuspecting festival-goers.

"I can't make out anybody in the tower," Grimaldi said, circling the spire. "I'm going to have to throw a spot on it."

"All right." Bolan slid open the window beside him and pointed the rifle outside.

Grimaldi reached over and was about to throw the toggle switch when the helicopter suddenly came under fire. Rapid blasts of 9 mm parabellum slugs chattered off the sides of the aircraft, some of them shattering glass as they forced their way into the cockpit.

The Stony Man pilot reflexively fought the controls, doing all he could to keep the Reed from being shot out of the air. "I've got to pull back!" he said. Even as the words were coming out of his mouth, though, he could hear the engine misfiring, hit by gunfire.

"Hold on," he told Bolan. "We're going down!"

GRINNING TRIUMPHANTLY, the BAO gunman
watched the disabled helicopter flutter weakly away
from the tower. He was standing on a terrace halfway up the Duke's Tower, holding his Ingram submachine gun. He glanced over his shoulder at his
tuxedoed compatriots, who were still in the cramped
spiral stairwell reaching up to the tower observatory. "Go on up, and hurry! We don't have much
time!"

The others nodded and resumed climbing the stone
steps. Their progress was hindered somewhat by the
unwieldy dimensions of the long box that contained
the missile launcher.

The gunman remained on the terrace, leaning out
over the railing to get a better look at the disabled
helicopter. He could tell from the uneven drone of
the rotors that he'd hit one of the engines, and he
waited expectantly to hear the inevitable explosion
when the chopper crashed on the ground. True, the
noise and fire would draw attention, but if the chopper landed a few blocks away, the crash could serve
as a diversion, giving his cohorts added time to reach
the observatory and ready the missile for launching.

In a matter of seconds, the Reed had fallen from
view behind a three-story building across from the
museum, but there was no explosion. The terrorist's
euphoria gave way to sudden concern. Had the pilot
managed to get the engines running again? Would
they be doubling back, this time aware there was a

gunman in the tower? He fumbled inside his tuxedo jacket, pulling out a fresh ammo clip and reloading the Ingram. As he was doing so, he heard a noise below on the museum grounds. He glanced down, seeing scattered statues in the sculpture garden and the glimmer of moonlight in a reflecting pool. Security lights cast eerie shadows across the grounds, but the gunner could detect no sign of motion.

Then out of the corner of his eye he spied a glint of light bouncing off metal. He whirled, bringing his Ingram into firing position as he spotted someone stepping into view just inside the side gate. Before he could pull the trigger, though, he saw a small flicker of light from the barrel of the other man's weapon.

Shrapnel struck the man's hand as slugs pelted the terrace, but the stinging sensation was nothing compared to the bullets that hit him directly. One bored through his shoulder and another went lower, piercing his chest just above his cummerbund. Slumping forward, the terrorist dropped his submachine gun to the floor of the terrace. He was destined for a much longer fall, however, as he fell over the railing and plummeted to the flagstone pavement below.

BROGNOLA REMAINED in his crouch, gun trained on the terrace, ready to empty the rest of his magazine should any other gunmen appear. When none did, he shifted his glance up to the top of the tower. No sign of activity there as yet, either. He deliberated his next move.

He'd seen the helicopter come under fire and straggle away from the museum grounds, and he was encouraged by the fact that he hadn't heard it crash. That would seem to indicate that at least Grimaldi and Bolan had come through the attack. But, much as he wanted to investigate the matter further, the mission came first. The terrorists had to be stopped, and although he'd nailed one of them, he knew that there were others undoubtedly making their way to the top of the tower.

One option would have been for him to find a position that would provide a clearer view of the tower observatory. With any luck, when the terrorists opened a window to take aim with the Lawtin-313, he'd be in position to intervene. But it would take time to pinpoint the best location, and even when he found it, he'd be forced to play sniper with a handgun rather than a high-powered rifle. No good.

Another option would be to stay put and wait for backup, but Brognola discarded that tactic without consideration. There was no time to play it safe.

The only other viable course of action, in the big Fed's mind, was to proceed to the tower on his own and hope he'd taken out the only sentry covering the BAO's backs as they readied for the missile launch. If he could gain access to the stairs and make his way to the observatory uncontested, there was a chance he could surprise the terrorists and take them all out before they could fire the missile.

All in all, it had the markings of a suicide play. And yet, once his mind was set that it was the last best chance of avoiding the larger catastrophe, Brognola cast aside all worries about his personal safety and headed out. With grim determination, he stole through the shadows until he reached the tower, then slipped through an unlocked door to the stairwell.

Step by cautious step, he headed up into the dark unknown.

CHAPTER SIX

"Here goes . . ."

Bolan and Grimaldi braced themselves as their helicopter descended toward a parking lot two blocks from the museum. There was enough power in the engines to provide a buffering rotor wash and partially cushion their landing, but they still came down hard and at a slight angle, blowing out the right landing wheel. Fortunately the other wheel touched down soon enough afterward to stabilize the craft and keep it from toppling over. Inside the aircraft, both men were jarred by the impact, but shoulder harnesses kept them securely in their seats. Once they had come to a complete stop, Grimaldi quickly killed the engines.

"You all right, Sarge?" he asked his passenger.

"In one piece." Bolan was bleeding from a few superficial cuts and had jammed his knee against the dash transceiver, but the Executioner wasn't one to consider such injuries as anything more than a minor nuisance. He flashed a grin at the pilot. "Nice piece of flying, Jack. You saved our bacon."

Grimaldi shrugged and unclasped his shoulder harness. "Give me a medal later. We still have our work cut out for us."

"Right." Bolan grabbed the Marlin as he climbed out of his seat.

The parking lot had been gated off for the night and no cars were parked around the chopper, but as the men scrambled to the ground, they saw a few curiosity-seekers already making their way to the scene. They were accompanied by a police officer, who shouted at them in French as he waved one arm frantically. His other hand was wrapped around a service revolver.

"Shit," Grimaldi cursed, "We don't have time to deal with them."

"This way," Bolan said, leading his friend away from the crowd to a back wall. The barrier was only four feet high, and despite his bruised knee the warrior had little trouble scaling the top. The police officer fired a warning shot over Grimaldi's head as the pilot followed Bolan over the wall, but he didn't pursue the men.

"What now?" Grimaldi asked, glancing up and down the alley.

The Executioner pointed to a fire escape mounted to the side of the old brownstone apartment building next to them. "I'll head up there and see if I can get the tower in my sights," he said, strapping the Marlin across his back to leave his hands free. "See how close you can get on the ground, then try to draw some fire.''

"Done," the pilot replied, heading out.

Bolan knew he didn't have much time. Unfortunately the ladder reaching from the fire escape's second-story platform to the ground wasn't lowered. To reach the stairs, the warrior first had to run to the side of the building and leap upward, grabbing hold of the bars placed over the ground-floor window. He pulled himself up, then pushed off, shifting his grip to the gridwork on the underside of the fire escape. Hand over hand, he moved out to the railing, then pulled himself up to the platform. Then, unslinging the rifle, he took the steps two and sometimes three at a time.

When he reached the third floor, Bolan quickly abandoned the fire escape and climbed onto the building's flat rooftop. There was a long row of pigeon coops, and the birds cooed loudly and fluttered inside their cages as Bolan stole past, seeking out his best vantage spot, which turned out to be from behind a brick, soot-encrusted chimney. As the warrior had hoped, he was able to secure a clear view of the south face of the Duke's Tower. He quickly raised the Marlin into firing position, then peered through the sights, focusing on the tower's top-floor observatory.

The window was open.

Bolan slowly let his breath out. So far so good. Now he only had to wait.

And he didn't have to wait long.

Less than thirty seconds later, a figure appeared in the window and propped something against his shoulder. Bolan had only seen a drawing of the Lawtin-313, but he knew immediately that the man in the tower was armed with the missile launcher, and that he was preparing to fire down at the festival throng.

As he slowly laid his finger against the trigger, the Executioner lined the other man up in his sights. Once the cross hairs were centered on the terrorist's face, Bolan gave the trigger the slightest additional tug.

The rifle bucked in his hands, recoiling hard against his shoulder as it launched its deadly charge across the clearing.

THE OBSERVATORY WINDOW was made of ordinary plate glass, and as such it exploded into a shower of jagged shards when Bolan's shot blasted through it. The terrorist manning the Lawtin-313 had been spared the bullet, but he was driven back by the flying glass before he could fire his weapon. He let out a scream as several of the shafts stabbed him in the face and hands.

One of the other terrorists rushed over and grabbed the missile launcher as it was about to tumble from the wounded man's grasp. He shoved his comrade aside and brought the Lawtin to his shoulder, taking care to step back from the window so he couldn't be targeted by whoever had fired the first shot. Doing so limited his target area, but as he peered through the launcher's sights, he saw that he still had a number of crowded sections of beachfront to fire at.

Once he had the Lawtin's sights focused on the tile roof of the Municipal Casino, the terrorist smiled and pulled the trigger, bracing himself for the anticipated jolt of the weapon's firing. Nothing happened, however. Cursing, the man drew his eye off the sights and inspected the weapon, realizing that his wounded cohort had apparently tripped the safety catch as he'd fallen back from the window.

The terrorist switched the safety back off and was about to draw aim on the casino again when the door to the observatory suddenly burst open. In charged Hal Brognola. He had the element of surprise on his side, and the split seconds he'd gained were sufficient to give him the upper hand. He quickly took out the man with the launcher, then whirled and fired at a third terrorist, driving three shots into his chest before the guy could so much as raise his own weapon into firing position. That left only the man who'd been wounded by Bolan's sniper fire. Brognola could see the man was clearly incapacitated.

Stepping over one of his victims, the big Fed leaned over and picked up the missile launcher. Unlike Bolan, he had ample opportunity to study the Lawtin-313 and its offensive capabilities. He knew by merely glancing at the missile resting in the launcher that it had been outfitted with a nonconventional warhead. Nerve gas, from the look of it. Brognola didn't even want to calculate the devastation such a weapon would have wreaked had it been successfully fired.

Now, fortunately, he wouldn't have to.

BOLAN REMAINED on the roof, his gaze fixed on the tower observatory, waiting to see if another attempt would be made to fire the Lawtin-313. Minutes passed without anyone appearing in the opening left by the shattered window. Bolan's hopes began to rally, but he maintained his vigil.

Finally he spotted two men stepping out into the sculpture garden. One had his hands placed on his head, and his face was streaked with blood. Behind him strode Hal Brognola, his automatic pistol aimed at his prisoner. His other hand, clutched the infamous Lawtin-313 missile launcher.

"I'll be damned," Bolan murmured, grinning as he lowered his rifle.

The Executioner made his way to the fire escape and quickly scrambled back down to the ground. He was wary of having to deal with the local authorities, but by this time one of the CIA antiterrorist units had arrived on the scene and was running the necessary interference with the Cannes police. The agent in charge was J. T. Dauffie, the thirty-two-year-old brother of NATO Intelligence officer Ed Dauffie.

An eight-year Agency veteran, J.T. had been on the trail of the Blood Against Oppression for the better part of two years, and when the team from the Farm had first been assigned to the Riviera, Dauffie had been the one who had briefed them on what they were up against. He had originally resented the newcomers, but Bolan and the others had quickly proved themselves, and Dauffie's misgivings had quickly changed to grudging respect and a willing sense of full-fledged cooperation.

Dauffie acknowledged Bolan with a nod, then quickly finished his business with the head of the local police. As the Executioner started down the side street leading to the museum, Dauffie broke away from his cohorts and called out, "Hey, hold on a second."

Bolan waited for the other man to catch up with him, then they walked together through the Old Town. The warrior filled Dauffie in on what had happened. By the time he'd finished, they were inside the museum grounds, where Grimaldi had already caught up with Brognola and the surviving terrorist. Brognola quickly described how he'd managed to storm the observatory before a missile could be launched.

"And take a look at what you saved us from," Dauffie said, eyeing the Lawtin's warhead. "If that sucker had gone off, it would have been goodbye Cannes."

"But what about Babdi?" Brognola asked. "He wasn't in the tower, and from what I've heard, he wasn't rounded up in the raid back at the villa."

"Which means he's still out there somewhere." There was a hardened edge to Dauffie's words, filled with anger and frustration.

"So our job's a long way from finished," Bolan concluded.

"Afraid so."

ALI-JAHN BABDI listened intently to the radio as he drove the BMW down the steep road leading to Monte Carlo. It was the top of the hour, and the lead story on the news was the aborted terrorist assault on the Cannes Film Festival. The way the media was handling the story, it was an isolated incident involving a would-be sniper. Details were understandably sketchy, with no mention made of the Lawtin-313 or the fact that the attack had been instigated by Blood Against Oppression.

"Bastards!" Babdi cursed, slamming his fist against the steering wheel. "Incompetent bastards!"

He took out his anger on the accelerator, flooring it and speeding down the same treacherous length of roadway that had claimed the life of Grace Kelly and that of many another ill-fated motorist over the years. A precipitous cliff yawned hungrily just beyond the soft shoulder, and when the BMW briefly overshot a turn and chewed at the gravel, the man riding with Babdi blanched with terror. He didn't dare speak out, however, knowing that any words of caution would only fuel Babdi's rage and bring them even closer to certain doom.

While bringing the vehicle back onto the road, Babdi swerved briefly across the center lane, almost colliding head-on with another car inching its way up the steep incline. He eased off the accelerator and grappled with the steering wheel, bringing the car under control as he continued to spew a torrent of obscenities.

The attack on Cannes had been painstakingly plotted out. He thought he'd assigned his best men to handle the operation. And yet they'd failed him and the cause. Babdi was at his wits' end. How could he expect BAO to become a true force to be reckoned with if he couldn't wage a sustained war against the enemy, a war uncompromised by weak links in his chain of command? It was bad enough he had to contend with weak-willed and treacherous underlings like Vera and that French recruit he'd executed back in Paris. Did he have to suffer incompetents as well? How much longer would he have to endure this hit-and-miss amateurism that had been the undoing of so many other rival groups. He suspected he knew the answer to that one. He'd done the best he could in piecing together his band of marauders, but too often he'd been overeager for devout converts to his word instead of true warriors experienced in the ways of terrorism. Subsequently he'd had to depend on a disproportionate number of novices rather than battle-trained veterans. Maybe it was time to re-think the way he drew in new members, to worry less about bending naive malcontents to his will and more about building a truly deadly strike force. That would mean tapping recruits from somewhere other than universities and the battlefields of the van-quished. He would need to draw in hardened fight-ers, those well versed in the ways of victory. Paradoxically, however, he knew that in order to appeal to such people, he would have to make the BAO a more desirable entity to want to join. And to do that he would have to succeed in carrying out bloodbaths like those planned for that evening.

It wasn't until he'd reached Monaco that Babdi's ill temper finally subsided. He did his best to shrug off the setback in Cannes and focus on the missions that lay ahead. After all, between what he hoped to accomplish in Monaco and the carnage that would be wreaked on Mougins when explosives went off at Thomas Galton's villa, he'd still have his chance to capture the world's attention. This could still be a night of triumph.

Babdi noted the time on the dashboard clock and smiled. In another ten minutes the bombs would go off at Galton's villa, ridding BAO of its weaker members and hopefully killing a few dozen neighboring citizens.

Au revoir, Vera, he thought. He'd miss her favors in bed, but he could always find another woman to fill that role. After this night, all kinds of women would flock to him, drawn by his power like moths to a flame, and he could take his pick. Perhaps one of those moths would be none other than his favorite paramour, Emma Skodynov.

Ah, Emma.

He'd been thinking more and more about her in recent days, wondering if there might be some way he could lure her back to his side without letting her realize the extent to which he longed for her, longed for her special talent in bed, her sharp and gifted mind, longed for another chance to share her company in the countryside near Vitteaux, far away from this other world of bloodshed and strife. He tried to imagine what she might be doing now, miles to the north in Paris. Of course, he hoped she was asleep, alone, dreaming about him. But he realized there was a certain likelihood she might be in bed, but with another lover. The mere thought of it tormented him almost beyond belief, and he chastised himself for risking the mission at hand by allowing himself to be plagued by distractions.

The moment, he reminded himself. Live in the moment, for the here and now. Dwell too much on yesterday and tomorrow, and your todays would be compromised.

Avoiding the casino district, Babdi drove along the periphery of the city, taking note of activity on the streets and looking for any signs of beefed-up security. There didn't seem to be any, but he knew better than to underestimate the enemy. He figured his men in Cannes had probably fallen victim to overconfidence, and he wasn't about to make the same mistake.

Once they'd made their way through the city, Babdi headed into the surrounding hills, where even more lavish estates than those of Mougins stretched out on lush green parcels of land overlooking the sea. One of those estates was home to former U.S. ambassador to France, Floyd Harman. Harman's oldest daughter, Michelle, was currently living at the estate as well, and over the weekend she'd received a visit from her old college roommate, who planned to stay for a few weeks.

Although the Blood Against Oppression might have achieved considerable notoriety by targeting the former ambassador or his family, it was Michelle's old roommate, Audrey, that Ali-Jahn Babdi was more interested in getting his hands on.

Audrey, after all, was the daughter of the President of the United States....

CHAPTER SEVEN

"I'm telling you, I don't know of any other plan."
Vera Maris protested. "I don't know where he is. If
I did know, I'd tell you in an instant. You have to
believe me!"

John Kissinger eyed the woman skeptically. They
were still at the villa. Kissinger had just finished
talking with Brognola in Cannes and was grilling
Maris in hopes of learning the whereabouts of Ali-
Jahn Babdi.

"It's just a little hard for me to understand, that's
all," Kissinger stated, limping as he paced the villa's
spacious den. A doctor was treating Maris's gunshot wound as she sat next to a large oak desk piled
high with Thomas Galton's political writings. The
other surviving BAO recruit was tied to another chair
on the other side of the room. He was still groggy,
having just regained consciousness after being
knocked out by Bolan during the siege of the villa.
Two local policemen were stationed outside the door,
and through the den window Kissinger could see
members of one of the CIA antiterrorist units
prowling the property with flashlights and trained

German shepherd dogs. They were searching for any BAO members who might still be hiding on the grounds, and for any other caches of weapons in addition to those found lying out in the open inside the manor. The dogs were trained in sniffing out explosives, a major concern since Maris had already divulged the plan by which she was to have planted a bomb at Le Moulin de Mougins.

Kissinger turned back to Maris. "Let me see if I have this all straight so far. You knew precisely what was to happen at the restaurant tomorrow, and you also knew detailed information about the planned attack in Cannes—so much so that we were even able to avert a disaster there tonight. Is all that correct?"

"Yes, it is," Maris said. "But you have to understand— Ouch!" The woman grimaced as the doctor applied an antiseptic swab to her wound, cleaning away dried blood and minute traces of infection.

Kissinger forged ahead. "If you knew so many details about these other two operations, how could you be in the dark about a third? And we have to assume there's another operation in the works, don't we? Or do you think that Babdi has just gone into hiding?"

"No." Maris shook her head, blinking away tears of both shame and pain as the doctor began to dress her wound. She glanced up at Kissinger. "Ali-Jahn is many things, but he's not the type to hide. He always wants to be at the head of things. In fact, I was positive he'd be in charge of the operation in Cannes. Are you sure he wasn't among those who were killed or captured?''

"Positive."

"Then I really don't know where he could be. He's very untrusting, very secretive. He never tells anyone everything he plans to do. Even I can never be sure what he's really thinking."

"I think that's pretty obvious," Kissinger said with mounting frustration.

"Don't believe anything she says!" the other terrorist suddenly blurted out from across the room. "She's just his whore, that's all!"

"And what about you?" Maris snapped back. "You're a cowardly murderer who kills women and children just so you can—"

"Whore!" the other terrorist repeated, adding a few choice denunciations in his native Arabic. He tried to move out of his chair and charge Maris, but he was too securely bound.

The French police officers stepped into the room with their service rifles. The two prisoners fell silent but continued to glare at each other. Kissinger sighed and exchanged a few words with one of the officers, then left the den. His pain was subsiding, but he still favored his bruised leg as he made his way down the main hall.

Entering the dining room, Kissinger saw four men huddled over the map on the table. He knew from previous introductions that they were from the French Ministry of Intelligence. One of them had a magnifying glass and was using it to inspect the handwritten notations. Another was typing data into a laptop computer, preparing a code-deciphering program in the event it might become necessary. The senior agent, Denis Scautt, glanced up at Kissinger over the rims of his bifocals.

"Did she talk?" he asked in fluent English.

"Not much. She says she isn't aware of any secondary plot involving Babdi."

"I'm not surprised," Scautt replied. "I understand she's his mistress. Of course she'd cover for him."

"I don't think that's it," Kissinger said. "She seems like she's been scared straight by all this. I believe her."

"Suit yourself. Did you ask her how many members of BAO were staying here?"

Kissinger nodded. "Yeah, she was one of a dozen left behind when Babdi set out for Cannes. We have one in custody and seven in body bags, so there're still four more to be accounted for."

"We've conducted a thorough search," Scautt said, glancing out the window at the officials roaming the grounds. "They must have slipped out in all the commotion."

"We better widen the search then," Kissinger suggested.

"I'll pass along word."

Kissinger glanced over at the men still laboring over the map. "How are you coming with that? Any breakthroughs?"

"Yes and no," Scautt replied. Gesturing at the map, he went on. "This is clearly a scorecard of sorts. There's information here linking BAO to a half-dozen incidents in Germany and France over the past month, and these notations here in Golfe de Napoules coincide with their battle plan for Cannes. But, as far as tipping us as to what Babdi's next move is, well, it's too soon to say. Perhaps there's something to these notes scribbled out in the Ligurian Sea."

"If so, that's a lot of ground to cover," Kissinger said. "From Nice all the way to the Italian border."

"And perhaps beyond that. Let's hope that we can pinpoint things a little better once we translate all the entries."

"I hope so," Kissinger said. "If you do find something, please let me know as soon as—"

"Aha!" the agent with the magnifying glass suddenly exclaimed.

"What is it?" Scautt wanted to know.

The other agent pointed to the Arabic lettering on the map in the area just off the coast of Cap Martin. "This is a time designation," he said emphatically. After a quick glance at his watch, he added, "For almost a half hour from now."

"It's an attack time?" Kissinger guessed.

"Perhaps."

Kissinger started for the door, calling over his shoulder to the others, "Keep working on it. I'll be in the den."

Cowboy hurried back to the den. Vera Maris's wound had been dressed, and she now had her arm in a sling. The other prisoner had been gagged.

"Making trouble," one of the policemen said by way of explanation.

Kissinger leaned over a radio console on the credenza beside the desk. He put a call through to Bolan, who, along with Grimaldi, Brognola and CIA Agent J. T. Dauffie, had boarded a motorboat in Cannes harbor and headed east along the Riviera coast in anticipation that the notes on the confiscated map would reveal Ali-Jahn Babdi's position to be somewhere in the vicinity of Nice. Brognola took the call, reporting that they had already passed the airport in Nice and were in sight of nearby Cap Ferrat.

"Well, make sure you're at your battle stations and ready to move quick," Kissinger said, "because we've got a time frame, and whatever else Babdi has up his sleeve, he's going to be making his move soon."

As Kissinger went into detail about what he'd just learned from French Intelligence, there was a tapping on the den window. One of the policemen opened the window so they could hear the CIA agent who stood outside with one of the leashed dogs.

"You folks owe this dog the biggest bone you can get your hands on," the CIA agent reported.

"Why's that?" Kissinger asked.

"Because he just sniffed out a time bomb linked up to enough explosives to blow this mansion from here to the bay."

"Oh, my God!" Vera Maris exclaimed.

"When was it set for?" Kissinger asked.

"About five minutes from now," the agent responded. "Give or take a few seconds."

Maris's eyes widened as the horrible realization sank in. "He didn't plan on me going into town tomorrow. He was going to blow us all up tonight!" She turned to the other terrorist. "You, too. Your fearless leader, he was going to have you killed. What do you think of that?"

The man's eyes lost their smug gleam suddenly, and an expresssion of fear crossed his face, soon to be replaced again by a flash of rage. When he made it clear that he wanted to talk, Kissinger gestured for one of the policemen to ungag him.

Once his mouth was uncovered, the man coughed a few times, then stared up at Kissinger, spitting his words out in anger. "Very well, if Babdi would betray me, then he deserves the same."

"Then you know where he is?" Kissinger asked.

"Yes." The terrorist nodded several times. "He tried to keep it from me, but I overheard him discussing it with Roberto. The two of them were going to change cars in Vallauris, then head for Monaco. I don't know if they were going to hit the casino or what, but that's where they said they were going."

Kissinger instructed the police to keep an eye on the prisoners while he went to relay word to Bolan and the others. Taking long, forceful strides toward the doorway, he nearly collided with a stranger just about to enter the room. The man had olive skin and a medium build. He was unshaved and had a look of weary exhaustion.

"Ed Dauffie, NATO Intelligence," he said, introducing himself.

At the sound of the man's voice, Vera Maris stiffened and let out an involuntary gasp. Wide-eyed, she stared across the room, meeting her father's equally dumbfounded gaze.

"Vera?"

The young woman turned away, lowering her gaze. "Hello, Dad," she whispered hoarsely.

DAUFFIE'S BROTHER, CIA Agent J. T. Dauffie, was at the control console of the speedboat owned by one of the CIA's shadow companies on the Mediterranean. It was a powerful craft, easily propelling its way through the frothy surf near Cap Ferrat. Standing beside him on the bridge was Hal Brognola.

"Quite a boat, isn't she?" Dauffie commented, raising his voice to be heard above the droning motors and the crashing of waves off the vessel's prow.

"Yeah, it sure is."

"Comes in handy for work," the agent said, "but there are slow days when we'll just take her out with the fishing gear and leave the radio turned off."

"Sounds great."

"Well, if you're up for it, maybe we'll do it once we get this whole sorry mess with the BAO behind us."

Brognola nodded.

They rode silently for a distance, staring at the coastline off to their left and the cape directly ahead of them. Only a few other boats were out at that hour, and none was even remotely close to their position. Dauffie expertly worked the controls, making their progress through the choppy sea as smooth and swift as possible.

Presently Bolan climbed up to the bridge. From the look on his face, Brognola could guess that the man had just gotten some news.

"Just finished talking with Cowboy," the Executioner said. "One of the prisoners says Babdi and his right-hand man have something planned in Monaco for about twenty minutes from now."

"Any idea what?" Dauffie asked.

Bolan shook his head. "The guy didn't know. Some agents from French Intelligence are trying to decipher Babdi's notes, but they haven't turned up any specifics yet."

Brognola turned to the man at the helm. "How fast can we get to Monaco?"

Dauffie slowly opened both the port and starboard throttles. "We'll be cutting it close," he said, "but I can make it. Only we're going to have to figure out where exactly it is we have to be once we get there."

"They'll be in touch as soon as they come up with something," Bolan promised.

"I just hope that won't be too late," Dauffie said grimly.

"Well, they were able to divert another catastrophe back in Mougins," Bolan said. He went on to explain about the explosives rigged to blow up Thomas Galton's villa and a sizable chunk of Mougins countryside.

Bolan stared at the coastline in the distance. "What we need to do," he said, "is put ourselves in Babdi's shoes and try to figure out his next move."

"Good luck," Dauffie said with a sour smile. "If you figure he's got it in for the well-to-do, all he's got to do in Monaco is show up, close his eyes and lob a grenade in any direction."

"Yeah, but we know he's got to have something more concrete in mind," Bolan replied. "Isn't there some kind of log on all the prime targets along the Riviera?"

"Sort of," Dauffie reported. "We've been putting one together over the past few weeks, but it's all on computer and we haven't worked all the cross-referencing yet."

"Cross-referencing?" Brognola asked.

Dauffie veered the speedboat slightly to his right, sending a spray of sea mist flying up onto the bridge. "Right. We're trying to get a breakdown according to private residences, high-visibility targets, visiting dignitaries—you know, the whole laundry list. Then we calculate the existing security arrangements in terms of manpower, response time, which different agencies are involved and which can be called in at the shortest notice."

"Sounds pretty thorough," Brognola said. "And you've got input from everybody?"

"Close to it. The Company's running it, but we swap info with NSA, FBI, NATO Intelligence, Secret Service, French Intelli—"

"Hold it!" Bolan interrupted.

"What?" Dauffie said.

"Secret Service." The Executioner turned to Brognola. "During our first briefing on the way over here, you mentioned something about the President's daughter being in Monaco, right?"

Brognola nodded. "Yes. She's visiting an old classmate of hers. Daughter of the ambassador to— Dear God! You've got it, Striker!"

Bolan rushed back to the ladder leading down to the cabin. "I'll try to get a call through, but we better pour on the power and get there ourselves."

CHAPTER EIGHT

"And by then it just seemed like there was no way out for me."

Vera Maris sniffed and rubbed at her tears with the back of her hand. She was alone with her father in the den of Thomas Galton's villa. For the better part of twenty minutes she'd been describing her involvement in the Blood Against Oppression. There had been a time when she would have relished the telling and taken joy in the pain it caused her father. But Vera Maris was no longer an insolent rebel filled with self-righteousness. Although she'd refrained from divulging all the details, especially those concerning her sexual relationship with Ali-Jahn Babdi, there'd been no attempt to turn her confession into a diatribe against Ed Dauffie's alleged shortcomings as a parent. She'd spoken with pangs of humiliation and remorse, taking no pride in her actions and making little effort to justify them.

Ed Dauffie had listened silently, standing several feet away near a window overlooking the grounds of the estate. Now, as Vera glanced up from her chair, she saw her father staring stone-faced at the night sky, his face pale in the moonlight, his gaze unfocused, looking far beyond the clouds overhead. He finally turned to his daughter.

"I see," he said softly.

"I'm so sorry," she told him, fresh tears welling in her eyes. "For everything."

Dauffie moved away from the window, letting out a long, labored breath as he ran his fingers through his graying hair. Vera watched him uncertainly, trying to read his mood. Like so many times before, however, she found him a cipher, holding his emotions in, presenting the poker-faced countenance of a perfect spy. Dauffie finally grabbed a chair and swung it around so that he could sit facing his daughter. He took her hand and kissed it, then looked her in the eyes.

"When your grandfather emigrated to the United States before I was born," he told her, "it was for one reason and one reason alone. He loved the idea of freedom, of a democracy where he could work hard to make a better life for his family. He ingrained in me that same love for freedom, and I've dedicated my life to seeing that that freedom is not subverted."

"I know," Vera said, "and I—"

"Let me finish."

"Yes, of course. I'm sorry."

"I will admit that I could have been a better father," Dauffie went on. "Perhaps my obsession with my work clouded my judgment in certain matters, and I'm sure that I share a certain blame for this gulf between us. And, to an extent, I suppose it's true that maybe I drove you to do what you've done."

"No," Vera insisted. "It was my own doing."

"I just want to say this much, Vera," Dauffie said, clutching her hand tighter and holding it up to the moonlight. "You and I, we are Americans, but we are also Arabs in the eyes of the world. And do you know how the rest of the world sees Arabs? Go to the movies, read books and magazines and it's very clear. The rest of the world sees us as ignorant camel jockeys, as sinister bedouins of the desert, as hedonistic oil sheikhs, as terrorist subhumans without regard for human life.

"This organization of yours, this Blood Against Oppression—its members think they pursue a noble cause, that they shed blood in the name of a greater good. No doubt Ali-Jahn Babdi even goes so far as to quote Jefferson about freedom being rooted in the blood of revolution. But these people are not about freedom. If anything, they only fuel more hatred against the Arab world and invite more oppression. It's wrong. It's foolish, it's deadly and it's wrong."

"I realize that now," Vera said. Her voice cracked and she began to sob uncontrollably. "Please, Daddy, can you forgive me? Can you ever forgive me?"

"We need to forgive each other, my daughter." Dauffie leaned forward and drew his daughter close to him, embracing her tightly and stroking her hair. "We'll work this out."

Vera continued to sob as Dauffie rocked her slightly back and forth. He knew well that matters were far from settled. Vera had been an accessory to much of the BAO's recent spree of terror, and she would have to be held accountable for her actions. Even if he was to intervene on her behalf, it was unlikely that he could spare her from having to serve a long prison term.

And there were even more immediate circumstances to be considered. Vera's involvement with the Blood Against Oppression put her on a collision course not only with her father, but also with her uncle. In conferring with John Kissinger, Ed Dauffie had learned that his kid brother J.T. was headed for Monaco to track down Babdi, and if what had happened in Cannes was any indication of the BAO's determination to widen its swath of bloodshed, J.T. could very well be putting his life on the line.

Ed Dauffie wasn't a praying man by any means, but as he sat with his daughter and stared out the window, he found himself sending a silent appeal to God, begging that his family might survive this ordeal intact. He had no way of knowing if his plea was heard, but the moon stared back at him like a grim, unblinking eye, and he felt a cold flash of apprehension course through his body. He held his daughter tighter, hoping against hope that it wasn't too late.

BRAHWA BUERRE TOOK a deep breath, then carefully picked up the large silver tray and carried it out of the kitchen. On the tray was a tea service for six, and it took all the servant's concentration to keep the heavy load balanced as he made his way down the main corridor at Floyd Harman's lavish Monaco summer home. The hall was lined with priceless paintings and tapestries, and flanking the entrance to the library were huge matching vases dating back to the Ming dynasty. Most of the artwork had been collected during Harman's recent six-year stint as U.S. ambassador to France, and in Buerre's mind the art was plunder, an insidious testimony to Harman's hand in helping France and the United States maintain political policies that assured the continued oppression of third world countries.

As one of ten servants attending to the mansion, Buerre, of course, had never divulged his antipathy for Harman's politics, or for the man himself. If anything, he took measures to project just the opposite demeanor. Whenever around Harman or any members of his family, and even around other members of the staff, Buerre acted with the utmost deference and unquestioned loyalty. He was sure that in the former ambassador's eyes, he was considered to be a servant who could be trusted to act with discretion and to go about his business without concerning himself with the matters unconnected to his position and duties. Many a time the Harmans had carried on privileged conversations in Buerre's presence, whether at the dining-room table or in the den or sitting room. In every instance, Buerre performed his duties with stone-faced impassivity, as if he were deaf to any spoken words not directed specifically to him.

All in all, Brahwa Buerre was an ideal spy for the Blood Against Oppression, and he'd served in such a capacity for the better part of five months, after having been introduced to the organization and its leader through a mutual friend, Roberto Flotman. It had been Buerre's desire at first to walk away from his job and throw himself wholeheartedly into BAO's cause, but Ali-Jahn Babdi had convinced him that he could serve that cause better by remaining where he was, a man on the inside.

Buerre had been wary at first, fearing discovery and retribution, but he'd done such a thorough and convincing job of fostering Harman's goodwill that he was considered beyond suspicion. While continuing to flawlessly act out the part of devoted manservant, Buerre had already capitalized on several opportunities to play turncoat as well, overhearing or otherwise securing confidential information of use to the BAO and passing it on to either Flotman or Babdi. Most notably, it was through Buerre's eavesdropping of a dinner conversation between Harman and the developers of the Lawtin-313 missile launcher that the BAO had been able to instigate the successful plot to steal the prototype for use in the planned assault on the Cannes Film Festival.

And now, tonight, Buerre would play an even more significant role in advancing the cause of the Blood.

Steady, he told himself as he passed the library and carried the tea service into the sitting room. It was a large room, ornately decorated with primitive art from one of France's few remaining colonies in Africa. Floyd Harman was seated in his favorite chair, holding court with his wife as well as Gregory and Diane Hufka, longtime friends from the States who were in Monaco on vacation. The four of them were carrying on a conversation while watching the television, which was carrying live coverage of the aborted terrorist attack in Cannes.

"Dreadful savages," Diane Hufka pronounced, glancing away from the TV screen. "I don't understand why we should be made to pay for keeping them in prison once they're caught. Better they should be lined up and gunned down by a firing squad. Don't you agree, darling?"

"Absolutely, Di," her husband responded. "Have to speak their language for them to understand you mean business."

"You might have a point," Floyd Harman conceded with a wan smile, "but it's a little more complicated than that."

"Bah!" Gregory Hufka scoffed. "Spoken like a true diplomat. But I'm telling you, scoundrels like this are beyond diplomacy. They're dogs, or worse, and they should be treated as such."

"Ah, here's tea!" Floyd's wife Pauline said brightly, welcoming the interruption. She reached for a remote control and turned off the television, then smiled at Buerre. "It's chamomile, isn't it?"

"Yes, ma'am," Buerre said as he set the tray down and began to fill the cups.

"Excellent." Pauline leaned over and helped herself to one of the small cookies on the tray. She took a dainty bite, then smiled happily at the other couple. "Oh, and you must try these shortbreads, too, both of you. Chef made them up just this morning and they're absolutely heaven!"

"Oh, I'm not supposed to with my diet and all," Diane replied as Buerre held the cookie plate out to her. "But I supposed I can be wicked this once...."

"Very good, madam," Buerre intoned, offering the woman a modest smile. Once both couples had been served tea, he asked Pauline, "Will your daughter and her friend be joining you this evening?"

"No, they're having a slumber party at the guest house," Pauline said. Turning to the Hufkas, she chuckled. "You wouldn't believe those two... carrying on like schoolgirls! It's too much!"

Buerre's face remained emotionless, but inside he was euphoric. He'd been wary that he'd have to pry more insistently to pinpoint the whereabouts of the two younger women, but Pauline had spared him, and fortunately so. Glancing at the antique clock on the wall, he realized he had only a few more minutes before he was supposed to report to Babdi and Flotman.

"Will there be anything else?" he asked the group.

"No, Brahwa, that will be fine for now," Pauline told him. When Buerre started to pick up the two unused tea settings, however, the woman added, "Wait! Before you take those away, see if the boys would like some tea."

The "boys" were two Secret Service agents standing on the terrace just outside the sitting room. They were part of a four-man team assigned to guard the President's daughter while at the Harmans' estate. If the established pattern was still in effect, Buerre knew that the other two agents were probably stationed out on the grounds close to the guest house. He also knew from his experiences of the past few days, none of the four agents were tea drinkers. To a man, they all preferred coffee. But Buerre had his role to play, so he followed the woman's advice and went to the terrace to ask the two men if they wanted any tea.

"No, thanks," one of the men answered.

The other asked, "You wouldn't have any coffee made by any chance, would you?"

Buerre smiled. "There's a fresh pot brewing. I can bring you some shortly."

"As long as you're at it, I'll take a cup, too," the first agent added.

"I'll bring you a carafe," Buerre promised. "If your partners would care for some, I can take them some, too."

"Sounds good."

"Very well." Buerre excused himself and left the terrace, then the sitting room, barely able to restrain a smile of impending triumph.

Very well indeed, he thought as he headed back to the kitchen. Everything was going according to plan....

LESS THAN A MILE AWAY, Ali-Jahn Babdi sat behind the wheel of his BMW. He was parked curbside next to a small, immaculately landscaped public garden that afforded a panoramic downhill view of a private marina lined with moored luxury yachts and sailboats. Roberto Flotman was a few yards away, pacing before a pay phone. When the phone rang, Flotman immediately grabbed for the receiver.

As he watched Flotman take the call, Babdi reached into the pocket of his coat and withdrew a sheet of folded paper. He slowly unfolded it, revealing a detailed map of the Harman estate and all surrounding properties. Babdi had committed the map to memory, but he wanted to refer to it as he went over final strategy with Roberto. Flotman claimed to have memorized the map as well, but Babdi wasn't going to take any chances. Not this time.

The plan was simple enough. They were going to raid the estate, kill as many people as possible, with the exception of the President's daughter, who they would kidnap. With Audrey in their hands, the BAO would be in a position to command global attention and also strike some hard bargains for her release. They would stretch out negotiations as long as possible, not only to allow them more time to publicize their cause, but also to draw the support of other terrorist organizations. If he could get other groups to rally behind him, and in such a way that he was looked upon as a de facto leader of their coalition, Babdi figured he could emerge with infinitely more clout than he could ever hope to amass with his current recruiting measures. He could be like a Mafia don, a godfather lording over a sprawl of specialized groups committed to his bidding. There would be no more shrugging him off as merely a master of forty thieves. Forty thousand, perhaps. Perhaps even more.

As he mulled over his self-envisioned destiny, Babdi gave only passing notice to the lights of a speedboat approaching the nearby marina. If anything, the boat served only to draw his attention to one of the yachts, which he knew belonged to Floyd Harman. Babdi had briefly given thought to stealing the yacht and keeping Audrey captive aboard it, but he ultimately dismissed the plan as too foolhardy. The yacht would be far too conspicuous, and it would limit them to the water, where there were far fewer places to hide than on land.

Less than two minutes later, Flotman hung up the phone and returned to the BMW.

"Good news?" Babdi asked.

Flotman nodded. "She's staying at the guest house," he said, pointing to the map in Babdi's hands.

"Excellent. Easier to attack, harder to defend."

"The only downside is that we would have to wage a separate attack on the main house if we want to inflict more casualties," Flotman speculated. "But Buerre is helping with that, too."

"How so?"

"He's just served some laced tea to the Harmans and their house guests," Flotman reported. "A mild sedative to make them drowsy. He's also making coffee for the Secret Service, and he's going to give them stronger doses. Enough to knock them out."

"How long will this take?"

"Not long. No more than half an hour."

"Fine," Babdi said, starting up the engine. "We'll wait thirty minutes, then we'll strike."

"I GUESS WE'RE JUST NOT as young as we used to be, eh?" Floyd Harman said, stifling a yawn as he rose from his chair and helped his wife to her feet. The Hufkas were already standing, both visibly drowsy from the onset of the sedative Buerre had put in their tea.

"Well, it is late," Gregory Hufka pointed out.

"Brahwa will be here in a moment," Pauline told the other couple. "He can show you to your room."

"Nonsense, Polly," Diane said. "We know the way, don't we, Gregory? Gregory?"

Diane's husband blinked his eyes, almost having fallen asleep on his feet. "Absolutely," he said absently.

"You didn't hear I word I said!"

"Yes, but I agree with you, pet, as always"

"Oh, you're just impossible sometimes, Gregory."

"I try my best."

The two Secret Service agents saw the others preparing to leave and came in from the terrace. Pauline turned to them. "You boys don't need to come in on our account."

"Yes, ma'am," one of the agents replied.

"Of course," Diane said with a vixenish twinkle in her eyes, "if Pauline and I were a couple years younger and didn't have these two old goats to contend with, well, that'd be another story."

"Diane!" Pauline squealed. "How naughty!"

"Don't mind them," Gregory told the two agents, who were both red-faced with embarrassment. "They get this way when they've had a little too much tea."

The two couples were on their way out of the room when the doors to the sitting room opened. Brahwa Buerra entered, carrying servings of coffee on the same silver serving tray he'd used earlier.

"We're all turning in, Brahwa," Floyd said, giving his servant a good-natured pat on the back. "See you in the morning."

"Good enough, sir," Buerre said. He bade the others good-night as he set the tray down.

Suddenly the phone rang.

Floyd Harman frowned to himself. "Who on earth could that be at this hour?"

Buerre felt a wave a panic run through him. As the phone rang again, he moved away from the cart, but one of the Secret Service agents was closer to the receiver and waved him away.

"Don't worry, I've got it." The agent picked up the phone, adopting an officious tone of voice. "Harman residence . . ." His expression hardened as he listened to the person on the other end of the line. "What? Are you sure?" He glanced at his partner and muttered, "We got a problem."

"What on earth . . ." Harman muttered.

As the two couples lingered near the doorway, worry taking the edge off their fatigue, Buerre poured the coffee as calmly as possible. His mind was racing, however, as was his pulse. He wasn't sure what had happened, but it seemed clear that the BAO's mission was somehow in jeopardy. His instincts told him that he wasn't yet under suspicion, and he deliberated keeping his cover awhile longer. But as he picked up snatches of the agent's conversation, he realized that Babdi and Flotman hadn't been apprehended as yet. If he didn't take some kind of action, they would likely be wandering into an ambush when they came to raid the mansion. He couldn't let that happen. Too much thought and planning had gone into this, and after all these months and years of growing rage against the likes of the Harmans, Buerre wasn't about to deny himself his big chance to strike back. No, it was time for him to act, to show both Babdi and Flotman that he was worthy of the Blood.

"We'll get right on it," the agent finally said before hanging up the phone.

"What's going on?" his partner asked.

"The BAO," the first agent said hurriedly as he reached for a walkie-talkie clipped to his belt. "They're coming after Audrey. I've got to warn the other guys."

There were gasps of disbelief from the Harmans and Hufkas. Buerre, however, was committed to what he had to do, and the moment the agent reached for the walkie-talkie, he sprang into action.

Mounted on the wall directly behind Buerre was an artfully crafted African hunting spear. For the Harmans it was nothing more than another decorative part of their art collection, but to Buerre it was a functional weapon, and he put it to quick use the moment he got his hands on it. With a swift, vengeful thrust, he rammed the spear's nine-inch tip into the chest of the agent closer to him. The man reeled backward, dropping the walkie-talkie. His aorta punctured, he toppled to the floor, spewing torrents of blood onto the milk-white carpet.

The older couples were too dumbstruck by what they'd just seen to react, but the other agent hurriedly reached inside his coat, pulling out his automatic service pistol. But Buerre had already yanked the spear from his first victim and cocked his arm so he could hurl it across the room. By the time the other agent could release the safety and prepare to fire his gun, the spear had plunged into his neck, severing his jugular.

"Oh, my God!" Pauline Harman wailed, her face white with terror. She shrank from the grisly tableau before her, and her husband reached out to hold her up as she fainted.

Diane Hufka opened her mouth as well, but she was horrified beyond words and could only let out an inarticulate scream. Gregory, trying to shake off the effects of the sedative, moved sluggishly to his right, groping protectively for a poker dangling from a wrought-iron rack next to the sitting-room fireplace.

Emboldened by his actions thus far, Buerre rushed across the room, snatching up one of the slain agents' automatics. He turned on the two older couples, his eyes alive with bloodlust and unveiled hatred.

"Brahwa!" Floyd cried out. "For the love of God, put that thing down and—"

"No!" Buerre interrupted, firing the gun into his master's face. "No more orders!"

CHAPTER NINE

The guest house was a one-story bungalow set on a bluff at the edge of the Harman property. Tall eucalyptus trees surrounded the house, sheltering it with their wide, drooping branches. A sandy path led down to the family's private beach and the nearby marina, but on those days when the hundred-yard walk to the bay seemed too long, there was also a large black-bottomed pool just off the back patio. Secret Service Agent Mike McHoren was standing vigil near the pool when he heard what sounded like a gunshot coming from the direction of the main house.

He grabbed his walkie-talkie and tried to reach the two agents posted inside the main house but received no answer. Immediately on his guard, he moved quickly out of the circle of illumination cast by the pool lights, crouched next to a small cabana and pulled out his automatic.

In quick succession, he heard four more reports. There could be no mistaking the sounds now. Someone was going gun-crazy inside the main house.

Moments later, a shadowy figure darted around the side of the house, and McHoren held his fire as he recognized his co-worker, Agent Tom Partral, who had his gun out, too.

"Tom! Over here!" McHoren whispered from his hiding place.

Partral broke his stride and cut to his right, heading across the patio toward the cabana. As he passed under the glow of the overhead pool lights, there was a sudden burst of gunfire, this time coming from a much closer position. Partral let out a shout of pain as bullets ran a deadly course up his right leg and through his rib cage. Staggering off-balance, he toppled into the pool, turning it red with his blood.

McHoren stared with disbelief at the floating image of his slain partner, then a second fusillade tore into the pool lights, shattering bulbs and throwing the patio into darkness.

The cabana was less than a dozen yards from the back door of the guest house. When the door opened and McHoren saw the silhouette of the two women in the doorway, he bolted from cover, shouting, "Get down! Now!"

Before Audrey or Michelle had a chance to react, McHoren lunged through the opening, arms outstretched, roughly tackling them both to the floor. Their screams and cries of fear were quickly drowned out by yet another blast of gunfire. Glass shattered as bullets pounded the back door.

"Stay down and get away from the door!" Mc-Horen whispered to the women as he rolled away from them. Eyes wide with terror, they obeyed him, crawling across the floor to the living room.

McHoren could feel a burning sensation in his shoulder. He wasn't sure if it was a dislocation or a bullet wound, but at this point it didn't matter. He tried to block out the pain as he crawled clear of the doorway, then slowly rose to a crouch, ready to defend the women as best he could.

Outside it became suddenly quiet.

McHoren could hear the women sobbing behind him, and the sound of his pulse seemed deafening. A cold sweat enveloped his right hand as he tightened his grip on his automatic. Given the odds he felt he was up against, the weapon seemed woefully inadequate.

Time seemed suspended as the agent remained near the doorway, waiting for the unseen assailants to make their next move. Just as McHoren was beginning to entertain the notion that perhaps the gunmen had fled, there was a loud crashing sound at the front of the bungalow.

Someone was breaking down the front door.

McHoren jumped to his feet and strode past the women, gesturing for them to stay put as he headed for the hallway. He'd only taken a few steps toward the front room when Audrey saw a shadow fall across the back doorway.

"Look out!" she cried out as Ali-Jahn Babdi slipped quietly in through the opened doorway.

McHoren whirled, but Babdi had the drop on him. The Turk's gun blazed, its 9 mm rounds striking the Secret Service agent at point-blank range. Audrey and Michelle screamed in unison as the agent spun backward, slammed into the wall behind him, then slumped to the ground.

Roberto Flotman emerged from the front room, joining Babdi in the living room. Together they stood over the trembling women, who continued to scream. Then Babdi calmly raised his gun and fired three shots into Michelle, silencing her.

Audrey fell silent as well when Babdi turned the gun on her. He refrained from pulling the trigger, however. Glancing over at Flotman, he said, "Go check on Buerre. I'll take care of our little princess here."

ONCE THEY REACHED the private marina, J. T. Dauffie maneuvered the speedboat alongside the nearest dock. They were confronted by a security guard holding a high-powered flashlight in one hand and a double-barreled shotgun in the other. Squinting against the harsh glare, Brognola flashed his identification and quickly explained their business. The loud blare of a power generator made it hard to carry on a conversation, however, and to compound matters the guard spoke only halting English. Obviously confused and suspicious, he kept his gun and light trained on Brognola. It wasn't until Dauffie shouted down in fluent French that the guard finally grasped the gravity of the situation. Setting aside the flashlight and shotgun, he helped Brognola moor the boat. Dauffie killed the engines and clambered down from the bridge, joining Grimaldi. Bolan emerged from the cabin moments later. He looked grim.

"The locals are on their way," he told the others, "but I can't reach anybody at the mansion."

"That's not good," Dauffie said. He turned to the guard and asked if anyone from the Harman estate had been to the marina that evening.

"No," the guard said. When Dauffie asked if he'd witnessed any suspicious activity or seen any other unauthorized boats try to enter the marina, the man shook his head.

Bolan glanced uphill, barely able to make out the mansion's rooftop. "Let's split up and move in. Hal, Jack and I will take the main house."

"I'll take the guest house," Dauffie said, gesturing at the marina guard. "He can come along for backup."

"All right," Bolan said. "Let's do it."

The two teams cleared the dock and started up the sandy path leading to the Harman estate. Once they reached the first terrace, Bolan led Grimaldi and Brognola off to the left while Dauffie and the marina guard veered right, circling up through neatly planted rows of bougainvillea and azalea toward the guest house.

Once they were within sight of the bungalow, Dauffie traded hushed whispers with the guard, then they fanned out in opposite directions. While the guard continued to steal through the floral guards leading to the front door, Dauffie broke from cover, racing across the dewy lawn toward the back patio.

The first indication that something was amiss came when Dauffie spotted shards of glass from the shattered pool lights strewed across the patio. Immediately his attention shifted to the pool. There was enough moonlight for him to see a Secret Service agent floating facedown in the blood-darkened water.

"Shit," Dauffie murmured.

From inside the bungalow came a muffled cry. Dauffie spun around. Ali-Jahn Babdi was standing in the back doorway, holding the President's daughter close to him as a human shield, one hand clamped over her mouth. The Turk's other hand clutched his automatic, and he pumped three quick silenced shots into the CIA agent before Dauffie could so much as bring his own gun into firing position. Dauffie sagged to his right, grasping at the edge of a picnic table to support himself. His legs gave out on him, though, and he collapsed across the table, dropping his gun to the ground.

Audrey shrieked into Babdi's hand as she watched Dauffie fall. The Turk jerked her sharply to one side, slamming her into the doorjamb.

"I told you to keep quiet!" he seethed, pistol-whipping the woman's head until she was unconscious. He crudely flung her over his shoulder and was starting to carry her off when the marina guard suddenly circled around from the front of the house. Babdi raised his automatic and spent his last two shots, dropping the guard before he could use his shotgun.

Babdi hurried to Dauffie's side, shifting Audrey's deadweight on his shoulder as he grabbed the agent's gun. For several seconds he remained crouched beside the picnic table, ready to fend off anyone else.

Once he felt the coast was clear, Babdi hefted his burden and was about to head out when he heard a muffled groan at his feet. He glanced down and saw his enemy stirring on the ground. The agent was lying on his back, and he barely had enough strength to open his eyes and crane his neck for a better look at his assailant.

Without losing his grip on Audrey, Babdi took Dauffie's gun and crouched low enough to place the barrel less than two feet from the agent's head. He waited to see the look of horror that flashed across Dauffie's face, then pulled the trigger, delivering a point-blank kill shot. Dauffie's head snapped back with a dull thud, smearing the concrete with blood and the ravaged tissue of his brain.

Babdi tucked the stolen gun in Audrey's lap and carried her off down a flagstone path leading away from both the main house and the marina. The BMW was parked fifty yards away, in an empty field on the other side of the wall that enclosed the Harmans' property. As part of the master plan, Buerre had earlier seen to it that the gate in the wall was left unlocked, allowing his coconspirators access to the grounds. Once Babdi passed through the gate a second time, he shifted the woman into the back seat of the BMW, then got behind the wheel and drove off.

"Yes!" he shouted triumphantly as he wheeled clear of the field and onto the main road. The mission had been costly, and things hadn't gone entirely as planned, but the bottom line was that he'd done it.

The President's daughter was his....

CHAPTER TEN

Once they reached the main house, Brognola and Grimaldi headed in opposite directions, circling the periphery with slow caution, guns out and ready to fire. Bolan, meanwhile, stole his way up a winding outside staircase that led to the second-story terrace.

The terrace was immense, and much of the area covered with huge potted palms and rows of planter boxes filled with blooming flowers. Strategically placed outdoor lights shone on the plants, filling the terrace with wild splashes of color. Bolan moved alongside the palms flanking the mansion's south wall, peering through huge floor-to-ceiling windows for signs of intrusion. When he reached the door leading into the sitting room, he looked in and saw what he had expected to find. Warily he opened the door and stepped in for a closer look at the carnage.

In addition to the two slain Secret Service agents, the Harmans and Hufkas were also sprawled across the floor, all dead. The Executioner found little consolation in the fact that the President's daughter wasn't among the victims. He stepped over the inert form of Floyd Harman and entered the upstairs hallway.

The assailant had inadvertently stepped in blood while fleeing the sitting room, and the warrior was able to follow a set of tracks halfway down the hall before they stopped, with a wide crimson smear indicating that the killer had spotted the trail he was leaving and wiped his shoes repeatedly on the carpet until the blood was off his soles.

On a hunch, Bolan backtracked and headed the other way down the hall. In what looked to have been acts of wanton vandalism, two vases lay in pieces on the ground outside the library, and several tapestries had been ripped from the wall. The warrior carefully stepped around the broken shards, his Beretta up and tracking.

He was about to head downstairs when he heard a faint sound coming from one of the upstairs rooms. He continued down the hall, pausing outside the doorway to Floyd Harman's private den. Inside, he could hear the rustling of papers and the sound of someone trying to pry something open. Two men were whispering.

"Let's just go!"

"No, not until we get this safe open! He's got a fortune stashed in here. Cash, jewels. I've seen him put it away."

"We don't have time to—"

"Freeze!" Bolan ordered as he strode into the room.

Roberto Flotman was standing by the window behind Harman's desk, watching Buerre gouge at the woodwork framing a wall safe located above an oak bookcase. As he spotted Bolan, he reached for his automatic.

Too late. The Executioner had fired his Beretta. The triburst of 9 mm parabellum rounds drilled into the terrorist, driving him back with so much force that he shattered the window before slumping to the floor.

Buerre had been using a large African hunting knife to try to free the safe. He briefly considered trying to hurl it, but when Bolan turned his gun on him, Buerre knew there was only one way he was going to survive this confrontation. He let the weapon drop and quickly raised his hands above his head.

"Don't shoot!" he pleaded.

"Babdi," Bolan demanded. "Where is he?"

"I don't know who you mean. I'm just a servant here. This, this animal killed everyone and said I'd be next if I didn't show him where my master kept his—"

"Spare me the sob story," Bolan interrupted, taking a step forward and grabbing Buerre by the coat collar. "I want to know where Babdi is, as well as the President's daughter. Now!"

Buerre swallowed hard. "The guest house."

"You're sure of that?"

"Positive!" Buerre wailed.

Bolan pinned one of Buerre's arms behind his back and guided him out of the library. "Why don't we have a look."

Brognola and Grimaldi were on their way up the main staircase. They stopped near the body of a slain maid. Grimaldi called up to Bolan, "It's a bloodbath down here. Looks like they wiped out the entire staff."

"All except one," Bolan said, indicating Buerre.

"What about Audrey?" Brognola asked.

"He says she's at the guest house. Babdi's supposedly there, too."

"Let's get over there," the big Fed growled.

"Why don't you stay here with this guy," Bolan suggested, leading Buerre down the steps to the landing. "I'll head over there with Grimaldi and check things out."

"Yeah, you're the professionals," Brognola said wryly. "Go."

It didn't take them long to backtrack to the bungalow, but by the time they showed up, it was already too late. There was nothing for them to see but more bodies, none of which belonged to Audrey or Ali-Jahn Babdi.

"Damn it!" Grimaldi cursed. "We were so close! If only we'd come here instead—"

"Look, it's done," Bolan said gravely. "Let's check the marina. Maybe we'll catch up with them."

The men charged down the sandy path back to where they'd moored their boat. The marina looked every bit as deserted as it had when they'd arrived. No boats were missing.

Bolan headed for the CIA speedboat, calling over his shoulder to Grimaldi, "I'm going to radio the locals to lay a dragnet. There's still a chance we can nab them."

NOT WISHING to draw attention to himself, Babdi drove cautiously along Rue Ruser, the five-mile long road boasting some of the most exclusive residences of the Riveria. In addition to the Harmans, the stretch was also home to a retired prime minister, several owners of casinos in nearby Monte Carlo and some of the country's wealthiest business barons. As such, it wasn't surprising that even at this late hour a private security guard would happen to be making the rounds in a patrol car. When Babdi saw the car approaching, he tried to remain calm. His suit was torn and slightly disheveled, but he was sure he could pass a cursory inspection. However, the prone figure of the President's daughter in the back seat wasn't likely to go unnoticed if anyone happened to look inside the BMW.

As the other car drew nearer, Babdi steered with one hand, using the other to draw his automatic and release the safety. He continued to drive on, and as the two cars passed, he glanced over and offered a nod of acknowledgment. The uniformed guard in the other car responded in kind and continued on.

Babdi exhaled slowly. That had been close.

Glancing in his rearview mirror, the terrorist saw the retreating taillights of the patrol car. Then, without warning, the other vehicle suddenly turned sharply to its left, making an impromptu U-turn.

Babdi pressed his foot against the accelerator. The BMW shot forward, jostling Audrey in the back seat. The road ran straight for a few hundred yards, giving Babdi a chance to increase the distance between himself and the patrol car. Then, as he rounded a sharp turn, the Turk spotted a side road to his left and wrestled with the steering wheel to change his course. He shut off his lights as he made the turn, then pulled off the road and stopped the car behind a thicket that hid it from view of the road.

Killing the engine, Babdi bolted out of the car, gun in hand, and positioned himself on the far side of the thicket. As he expected, within moments after overshooting the turnoff, the patrol car backed up and changed directions, heading up the side road. Babdi tracked the driver with his gun, then squeezed off three rounds.

The passenger's window of the patrol car exploded and the bullets rammed into the driver, killing him instantly. He slumped over the steering wheel and his foot slipped off the accelerator. The vehicle continued to roll on its own for a few dozen yards, then drifted off the road and tumbled out of view down a steep ditch. The engine died.

Babdi returned to the BMW and dragged Audrey out of the back seat. She was coming to, so he knocked her out again with the butt of his automatic, then hauled her behind the BMW and placed her in the trunk. Then, getting back into the driver's seat, he pulled back onto the side road and drove into the hills. At some point he was sure he'd link up with another main road that would take him to the autoroute, and from there he'd be able to take the girl into hiding and plan his next move.

The road was narrow and winding, forcing Babdi to drive slower than he wanted. Several times he nearly overshot hairpin turns and slammed through the guardrail. Finally, though, he cleared a crest and came upon a four-lane road, complete with a sign telling him a right turn would lead him to the autoroute, a mere four miles away.

Before Babdi had much time to congratulate himself on his unerring instincts, however, he rounded a corner and saw two patrol cars parked diagonally across the pavement, forming a makeshift roadblock. The officers were outside their cars, setting up bright orange cones in the middle of the road.

The terrorist went for his gun again, rolling down his window as he approached the blockade. When the officers moved away from their cones to attend to him, Babdi calmly raised his gun into view and fired. At point-blank range, neither man had a chance to go for their own weapons. Cut down, they fell to the pavement alongside the cones.

Babdi tossed his gun onto the seat beside him and abruptly jerked his steering wheel, flooring the BMW as he tried to speed around the patrol car closer to him. He miscalculated, however, and clipped the car with the rear quarter panel of his vehicle. Accelerating as much as he was, this slight nudge was enough to force Babdi to lose control. He slammed his foot on the brakes, but only succeeded in forcing the car into a more severe tailspin. Crashing sideways through the guardrail, the BMW left the road and became airborne, plunging down a deep ravine strewed with massive boulders. In a matter of seconds, the car was gone from sight, lost in the darkness.

CHAPTER ELEVEN

Given the trail of death and destruction left in his wake, it wasn't difficult to determine the escape route taken by Ali-Jahn Babdi after his abduction of the President's daughter. Within an hour after the BMW had crashed into the ravine, Bolan and Grimaldi were standing by the severed guardrail as a pair of helicopters flew in tight circles overhead, illuminating the area with spotlights. Behind them were the two patrol cars used in the roadblock. The officers gunned down by Babdi had already been taken away in body bags, the latest casualties in the night's growing list of victims claimed by the Blood Against Oppression.

"Down there," Grimaldi said, pointing. "Just to the right of that big boulder."

Bolan looked in the direction Grimaldi was indicating, easily spotting the splintered trunks of several pine trees. Then, another twenty yards downhill, he made out what looked to be the underside of an automobile.

"Yeah, I see it," he said.

The road had been closed off by the authorities, but an official van had pulled up moments before, and a rescue team was already unloading equipment. Bolan went over to the vehicle, seeking out a worker who could speak English. When he found one, he flashed an ID that identified him as an agent of the U.S. Justice Department.

"The man who went down in that car is armed," Bolan told the rescue worker. "I want to go down with my partner and check things out before you send your people in."

"If you insist," the worker said, "but we've answered many calls for wrecks in this ravine, and we haven't found any survivors yet."

"I do insist."

"Very well."

"We'll need to borrow some equipment," the Executioner said.

"Do you know how to use it?" the man asked skeptically.

"I wouldn't ask if we didn't."

With the grudging assistance of the rescue crew, the two Americans were quickly outfitted with climbing harnesses and special smooth-soled klettershoes. After loading their hardware slings with carbiners, chocks and nuts, the two men ventured back to the guardrail. Climbing ropes were anchored to the rail, then flung down into the dark chasm. The choppers continued to hover overhead, but their spotlights were supplemented by twin klieg lights mounted on top of the rescue van. The resulting illumination was harsh and eerie, making the ravine seem like some surreal, almost extraterrestrial, landscape.

By the time Bolan and Grimaldi were ready to make their descent, two police cruisers had arrived, dispatching sharpshooters armed with high-powered rifles. They took up positions along the lip of the ravine, ready to provide cover for the two men as they headed down. Nonetheless, Bolan kept his Beretta within easy access, and Grimaldi's Government Model .45 remained secured in its shoulder holster.

Once they'd added flashlights to their gear and linked themselves to the ropes that would serve as their lifelines, the Stony Man warriors started down the precipitous incline. The irregular surface of the mountain provided adequate hand and footholds in many spots, allowing them to make good time. Less than twenty yards down the slope, Bolan came across a long, fresh gash in the rock, with paint imbedded in the stone from the force with which the car had landed.

"Looks like we're on the right track," he called over to Grimaldi, who was following a parallel course down the rock face.

The pilot eyed the scarred rock and nodded. "I've got to agree with that guy up there, though. No way could Babdi have survived this. Audrey either, for that matter."

"Yeah, but this has to be done."

Bolan paused to anchor a chock, then, after testing it to make sure it would hold his weight, he tightened his grip on the climbing rope and began to lower himself hand over hand down a stretch of smooth rock. When he touched down on a cluster of boulders, he loosened his grip on the rope. His weight displaced some of the rocks, however, and he quickly grabbed the rope to prevent himself from being carried down with the small avalanche he'd started. The falling stones echoed loudly through the ravine, raising small clouds of dust.

"Are you okay?" Grimaldi called out as he eased his way down close to Bolan.

"Yeah. Just misjudged a step."

"Good thing we decided to wait around for the equipment."

"Right."

They reached the severed pines without further incident, and from there it was just a short haul to the larger boulders where they'd seen what they'd assumed to be the getaway car used by Ali-Jahn Babdi. Instead of the BMW, however, they discovered that the chassis was part of a rusting Renault that had obviously tumbled into the ravine months, if not years, before.

"Damn," Bolan muttered.

"I don't believe it," Grimaldi said. "But then I guess there're probably a few more heaps down here, too."

"We've got to be on the right track, though," Bolan said, backtracking to the nearest pine tree. "This trunk was sheared off tonight, no doubt about it."

"Well, then we'll just have to keep looking, that's—"

Bolan raised a hand to silence Grimaldi.

Both men listened intently, trying to tune out the distant drone of the helicopters. Then they heard it again, the sound of something moving through the brush about a dozen yards downhill. Keeping one hand clenched to the lifeline, Bolan reached for his Beretta and took aim in the direction of the sound. Grimaldi got out his .45 as well and glanced up, squinting through the glare of the spotlights and signaling for someone to shine a beam farther downhill. One of the choppers responded, drifting to its right.

Bolan took a cautious step out onto the rusting hulk of the Renault and pinpointed the noise as coming from underneath one of the fallen pine trees. He was about to call out when the spotlight swept across the tree, betraying the iridescent eyes of an animal concealed amid the branches of the tree. Moments later, a wild deer bolted from cover, seeking out a tenuous footing as it scampered away from the men.

"Well, that was good for the pulse rate," Grimaldi stated, lowering his gun. "How many more false alarms do we get?"

"Maybe it wasn't a false alarm," Bolan said, looking back at the fallen tree. "I think I see another car down there."

Grimaldi peered through the tree's limbs and saw it, too—the unmistakable gleam of chrome reflecting the bright glare of the searchlights. "Bingo," he murmured. "Let's check it out."

The two men cautiously lowered themselves the remaining few yards to the tree, then worked their way through the branches to the twisted remains of the missing BMW. The roof was flattened and the front end was crushed in as well, suggesting that the car had somersaulted down the ravine before coming to a stop. Bolan crawled down to the driver's side of the vehicle, noticing immediately that the door had been ripped clear of its hinges and was nowhere to be seen.

Neither was the driver.

"He got away," Bolan murmured.

"What's that?" Grimaldi called out from the other side of the car.

The Executioner shook his head. "Babdi must have jumped out as it was going over," he speculated. "Or he got out before and just sent it flying."

Grimaldi shined his flashlight inside the car, checking the back seats as well as the front. "Yeah, that looks like the size of it, all right. But what about Audrey?''

''Back here.''

Grimaldi withdrew the flashlight and looked up. Bolan had circled behind the BMW and was inspecting the rear end. The trunk was still locked, but the hood was dented inward along the right corner, providing an opening barely wide enough to peer in through. Bolan had his flashlight aimed at the opening.

''Oh, my God! She's in there?''

''Yeah.'' Bolan set the flashlight aside, then rolled up his sleeve and reached into the opening. His arm just managed to clear, and he groped in the darkness until his fingers closed around the woman's wrist. He waited a moment, then turned to Grimaldi with a look of disbelief.

''She's still alive. . . .''

''ARE YOU SURE you don't want me to take you to a hospital?''

Ali Jahn-Babdi shook his head. The question had been asked in French and he responded in the same language. ''No, I'll be fine.''

''Well, if you say so. . .''

''Yes, thank you.''

Babdi was riding in the front seat of a run-down truck driven by a ruddy-faced, middle-aged man whose soiled clothes smelled of fresh-dug soil. The man, who'd introduced himself only as Marc, lived nearby in La Turbie but worked nights as a grave digger at the cemetery next to the Church of Saint Michael the Archangel in La Grave, an hour's drive to the north. He'd been driving home after work when he'd spotted Babdi hobbling in a daze near an intersection a quarter mile from the stretch of mountain road where the BMW had gone over the side. Babdi, who even now had only the vaguest recollection of being thrown clear of the car and miraculously landing in the gravel just shy of the ravine, had been on the verge of collapse after trying to put as much distance between himself and the roadblock that had proved his undoing. Marc had helped him into his truck and offered to give him a ride to the nearest police station to seek assistance. Babdi had talked the man out of that plan, asking instead if he could just have a ride to La Turbie. Marc had agreed, thereby avoiding the need to drive south past the roadblock that would undoubtedly have led him to suspect Babdi's involvement in the deaths of the slain policemen. Instead, Marc had struck a westbound course, linking up with the Upper Corniche, one of the three major thoroughfares servicing the easternmost stretch of the Riviera.

Once on the highway, Marc accelerated. The truck rumbled and shook in protest, but the grave digger kept a firm hand on the wheel, keeping a straight course. The laboring whine of the engine was torture for Babdi, whose skull was throbbing with pain, as was much of his body. He closed his eyes and took a few deep breaths, trying to bring himself under control.

"Hmm," Marc said, glancing to his left. "Take a look back there, would you? I wonder what that's all about?"

Babdi looked back and saw two helicopters with searchlights hovering above a nearby mountaintop. He was still slightly disoriented, but it seemed a safe bet the copters were somehow involved in the attempt to either track him down or deal with the victims he'd cut down during his mad flight from Monaco.

"I don't know," Babdi told the other man. "Maybe someone robbed one of the casinos."

"That would be a first." Marc chuckled. "Usually it's the other way around, eh?"

Babdi forced a smile, sending a jolt of pain through his jaws. "I guess so. . . ."

"Is that what happened to you?"

The Turk frowned. "I don't understand."

"I think I do." Marc nodded knowingly as he looked at Babdi's ruined suit. "It happens quite a bit more than you'd imagine, so you shouldn't feel bad."

"I still don't follow you."

They were heading up a steep grade, and the truck was falling quickly back in the flow of traffic. Marc paused to blast his horn and shake a fist at a motorist passing his truck, then told Babdi, "Let me guess what happened to you. You had a nice dinner in Monte Carlo, then decided to spend a little time at the tables. The next thing you knew, it was past midnight and you'd lost all your money...maybe even more than that. Maybe you borrowed from a loan shark, just enough to win back what you'd lost, or so you thought. When you lost that, too, the enforcers dragged you out into the hills and worked you over. And then I found you. You don't want to see the police because you are embarrassed at having let this terrible thing happen to you. Is that it?"

Babdi couldn't believe what he was hearing, but he played along. "Something like that."

"I thought so!" Marc said triumphantly. He downshifted the truck, struggling to clear the last few hundred feet to the top of the Grand Corniche. "I like to think I am a good student of human nature. I see someone, I take a good look at him and try to guess what his story is. You'd be surprised how often I'm correct! Like with you..."

Babdi humored the man as he rambled on, but his thoughts were elsewhere. Grateful as he was to be alive under the circumstances, the Turk was still hard-pressed to hold back his rage at having come so close to his objective, only to see it all fall from his grasp because of his own carelessness. Now, on the night of what was supposed to have been his greatest triumph, he was faced with the prospect of complete defeat. His organization, what there was of it, had been decimated, either killed or taken prisoner; he himself had nearly died trying to abscond with one last pawn in his quest for glory; and here, in this final indignity, he found himself riding shotgun with a half-crazed grave digger starved for conversation after long hours of dealing with nothing but holes in the ground and bodies in wooden boxes.

As they approached the crest of the Grand Corniche, fifteen hundred feet above sea level, Babdi pointed to a large monolithic structure rising up from the earth. "What is that?"

"Trophée des Alps," Marc told him. "Built by the Emperor Augustus, back before the days of Christ even, if you can believe it. Ah, it's a beautiful sight, especially in the summer, when it's all lighted up and glorious."

"Could you take me to see it?" Babdi asked.

"Well, it's late now. It won't be open."

"I know that. But I'd really like to see it. It's important."

Marc shrugged. "Ah, well, if you say it's important."

"Yes, please."

As Marc sought out the next exit, Babdi looked the other man over. They were roughly the same size, although the grave digger's hands and feet were considerably bigger. That wouldn't matter, how-

ever. It was the fit of the clothes that concerned
Babdi more.

As they left the Upper Corniche and headed down
a dark side road leading to the monument, Babdi
suddenly leaned over and began making coughing
sounds. He also reached discreetly across the floorboards for a tire iron.

"Please, stop the car," he begged, closing his fingers around the makeshift weapon. "Pull over! I'm
going to be sick."

"Yes, yes, all right," the grave digger said, easing
the truck off onto the shoulder.

As soon as the vehicle stopped, Babdi sprang upward and turned sharply, ramming the tire iron into
Marc's chest. The man screamed with pain as the
projectile slid between his ribs. His eyes blazed with
sudden fury at this unexpected betrayal and he
reached for Babdi, grabbing him by the throat.

"Judas!" Marc seethed, trying to strangle his assailant.

Already weakened from his earlier ordeal, Babdi
could feel himself becoming light-headed. In des-
peration, he twisted the tire iron and drove it deeper
into the grave digger's chest until it finally struck the
heart. Within seconds, Marc loosened his grip and
the life went from his eyes. Babdi let go of the tire
iron and shoved the other man away from him. The
corpse slumped against the horn, sounding it. Babdi
pushed him clear of the steering wheel, then laid him

out across the front seat. He hurriedly began to pull off the dead man's coat, trying to keep it as unbloodied as possible.

As he began changing into the grave digger's clothes, Babdi told his most recent victim, "You're not the judge of human nature you thought you were, old man...."

CHAPTER TWELVE

The morning sun burned off the last traces of fog as it rose above the French Alps. The sky was a brilliant shade of blue, reflecting itself off the calm waters of the Mediterranean. All in all, it had the making of a beautiful day on the Riviera—provided one didn't bother to turn on the news or pick up the morning paper.

The headlines screamed with grim tales of bloodshed and mayhem, painting a picture of the entire Côte d'Azur caught in the grips of rampant terrorism. Despite official attempts to conceal the identities of those responsible for the previous night's incidents, there had been leaks to the press and the Blood Against Oppression was receiving all the publicity Ali-Jahn Babdi had been striving for. Even though the BAO's attempted siege of Cannes had been successfully thwarted, in light of the grisly carnage visited upon Monaco, the two events held the same frightening impact in the public mind. There was a sense of growing panic, a fear that no place was safe. The film festival in Cannes was all but shut down, as stars with any stature felt certain that they had been the intended targets of the previous night's incident and weren't about to risk the same fate that had befallen the more prestigious victims of what the media had already christened the Massacre in Monaco. Similarly the casinos in Monte Carlo were virtual ghost towns forsaken by patrons wary that the next terrorist attack would be on a major public venue. And all along the coast from Menton to Montpelier the gossip mills were working overtime to fan the flames of paranoia. Tourists, particularly Americans, were calling their vacations off and fleeing the country in droves. Air traffic in Nice and Marseilles had ground to a virtual standstill, not only due to the influx of passengers trying to book early flights but also because of the need for bomb squads and security forces to thoroughly comb each arriving and departing plane for the presence of explosives.

A state of emergency had been declared, bringing forth the militia into the public eye as both a deterrent to would-be terrorists and a source of reassurance for the worried populace. It was debatable, however, whether the constant sight of uniformed, weapon-wielding officers calmed fears or heightened them.

Locked in this mind-set of unchecked fear and trepidation, few souls, if any, had the faintest idea that the Blood Against Oppression now consisted of little more than a scattered handful of members and one battered man trekking north through the French heartland in a run-down truck, wearing grave digger's clothes and seeking a quiet place where he could lick his wounds.

It was against this backdrop of hysteria that Mack Bolan walked up the front steps of the Sainte Catherine Medical Center in Monte Carlo. It was a small, private facility catering to the well to do, and on this particular morning there was even more security than usual. In addition to the visible contingent of armed soldiers guarding the exits and perimeter of the grounds, Bolan had also spotted a half-dozen roof-top snipers atop the hospital and several buildings across the street. The reinforcements had been stationed since late the previous night, when an ambulance had wailed down from hills near La Turbie, carrying the daughter of the President of the United States. Audrey had been rushed immediately into surgery, and when the Executioner had set out for Sainte Catherine's after a quick nap and shower at his hotel, the woman was still reportedly in the operating room.

Bolan had shown his Belasko ID to get through the gates, but he was required to pass a second security check before being allowed into the medical center. He was on a list of individuals authorized to enter the wing of the hospital where Audrey was being treated. A conference room on the top floor had been set aside for officials dealing with the terrorist incidents of the night before. Bolan entered the chamber as John Kissinger was briefing the group on the results of the interrogations of Vera Maris and Joihof Elaid, the two BAO terrorists apprehended at the villa of Thomas Galton in Mougins. Also in the room were Hal Brognola, Denis Scautt from the French Ministry of Intelligence, Lieutenant Wilhelm Mead of Germany's antiterrorism strike force and Ed Dauffie, who was haggard from a sleepless night and still reeling from the news that his brother had been slain in Monaco, most likely by the same man who'd lured his daughter into the deceitful embrace of the Blood Against Oppression.

"And based on what they've told us, besides the men who slipped away from Galton's villa, there are only two other cells of BAO membership remaining," Kissinger told the group, "and both prisoners agreed that the allegiance of those parties is marginal at best."

Mead raised a hand and said, "I suspect one of those cells is in Hanover. We've had a group of five men under surveillance since the raid on a chemical plant there a month ago. They haven't made any moves yet, but we know they have past affiliations with both the BAO and the UFAO."

"Those men are BAO loyalists, no question about it," Dauffie said tiredly. "My daughter mentioned them."

"You have all our sympathies in this matter, Mr. Dauffie," Scautt said, "but don't you think that under the circumstances, you might be a little too closely involved to be effective? I think perhaps you should step back and let—"

"Step back and let someone else beat me to the bastard who killed my brother?" Dauffie snapped. "Who almost killed my daughter, as well? Do you really expect me to step back from that?"

"I only meant that—"

Dauffie slammed his fist on the table. "I'm here and I'm going to stay here. Now let's get on with this."

There was a momentary silence in the room. Then Brognola turned to Dauffie.

"What about Babdi?" the big Fed asked. "Did your daughter say if he was close with any of these men in Hanover?"

"She said she didn't think so," Dauffie replied.

"I would tend to agree," Mead responded. "Still, I've doubled our surveillance teams in the area in case he shows up."

"Wise idea," Brognola said. "The last thing we can afford is to let Babdi keep up his momentum. John, where's that other cell?"

Kissinger skimmed the transcripts from the interrogations. "Domrémy. Some small hamlet to the north. It's Roberto Flotman's hometown."

"It's the hometown of Joan of Arc as well," Scautt interjected with an ironic smile. "Another martyr who went out in a blaze of glory." He took off his bifocals and brushed back his unruly hair as he regarded the others in the room. "Personally, I think we are being misled to think a cell might be located there."

"Why?" Bolan asked.

"It's quite simple, really. If the BAO has members there, they would have to be keeping a very low profile. In a small town like that, everyone knows everyone else's business. It would be foolish for terrorists to think they could hide in such a place."

"My daughter didn't mention anything about Domrémy," Dauffie said.

"All the same," Brognola replied, "it might bear looking into. We don't have that many leads, and it couldn't take that much time to effectively search that small of a town, right?"

Scautt shrugged. "I'll make the arrangements."

Dauffie asked the Frenchman, "I'm told your people were analyzing a map found at the villa in Mougins. Did anything come of that?"

"Nothing significant," Scautt confessed. "I mean, we translated all the entries, and they all had to do with the attacks planned in Cannes and Monaco. But there is no new information, nothing that would help us track Babdi down."

"I'm afraid we've come up empty-handed with this Brahwa Buerre fellow, too," Brognola said. "His only contact was with Flotman and Babdi. He never so much as met with anyone else in the organization."

"You got him on the polygraph?" Dauffie asked.

Brognola nodded. "He read true as an arrow when he spelled out his role in the attack on the Harman estate, and there was no fluctuation when we got into other matters. He says he was friends with Flotman and that's how he met Babdi. He wanted to join the group, but Babdi figured he was more valuable staying put."

"We have to look beyond just Babdi and his immediate followers, you realize," Scautt said. "With all that's happened, it's safe to assume the BAO is going to become a bandwagon every aspiring terrorist wants to jump on. We've already received contact from five different outfits declaring solidarity with Babdi, and another two that claim they're the ones responsible for last night and not the Blood Against Oppression."

"So let's cut to the chase," Bolan said. "What's our next move?"

"Well, we have to deal with those two cells to the north," Scautt said, "and we also have to be on the lookout for the men that got away in Mougins. They could be still in the area, or maybe they're fleeing to the north to regroup with their cohorts."

For the better part of an hour, the group discussed master plans and contingency plans aimed at defusing the volatile atmosphere in the region. Beyond the obvious decision to bolster local security in hopes of snaring the men who'd fled from Galton's villa in Mougins and to neutralize the BAO cadres in Hanover and Domrémy, there was little consensus. Scautt proved to be the biggest obstacle, largely because he felt that the French should be allowed a larger proportionate say since matters were transpiring on their soil.

As the meeting was adjourning, a hospital surgeon showed up at the conference room with the preliminary results of the operation on Audrey. He looked haggard from the long ordeal, and blood stained his greens.

"It looks as if she's going to survive," the man reported. "Unfortuately we haven't been able to bring her back to consciousness yet."

"She's in a coma?" Bolan asked.

"Yes," the surgeon responded. "I'm afraid so."

CHAPTER THIRTEEN

Not surprisingly other parties in addition to the Western Powers had an interest in the whereabouts of Ali-Jahn Babdi and any surviving remnants of the Blood Against Oppression. In addition to the nickel-dime terrorist outfits Scautt said were clamoring for a piece of the BAO's glory, there were many agencies with far more clout monitoring the events of the past twenty-four hours, including Russian Intelligence.

There were few people within the intelligence community who'd seriously considered that the fall of the Berlin Wall would translate into a permanent softening in the cloak-and-dagger operations of the CIA and its Russian counterpart. Such cynicism wasn't without foundation, as neither agency was about to forsake its distrust for the other regardless of any warming of the political climate between their governing bodies. By and large, the tactics and objectives of espionage for both outfits remained unchanged, even during the turmoil in the Persian Gulf, when Soviet backing of the UN resolutions against Iraq had led some to believe a new age of understanding between the superpowers was about to be forged.

For the record, of course, that morning the Russian head of state had issued statements of deep regret and moral outrage against the savagery of the Blood Against Oppression, and there were the calls for Ali-Jahn Babdi to be brought to justice for having perpetrated such crimes against civilization. Behind the scenes, however, there were those who were secretly pleased with what Babdi had accomplished and wished him the best of luck in eluding capture and living to strike again. And within certain quarters, the BAO's brief reign of terror was, for the most part, openly supported, despite the fact that Babdi had, to date, rebuffed any and all attempts to be drawn under anyone's yoke. Now, the thinking went, perhaps Babdi would be in a different frame of mind.

Or, as Russian Intelligence agent Emma Skodynov put it, "I think Ali might be ready to dance with the Bear this time."

Skodynov was discussing the matter with fellow agent Anatoly Klemberk as they stood before Grand Cascade, an artificial waterfall located near Longchamp racetrack in the Bois de Boulogne.

"Well, I suppose you would know that better than most," Klemberk mused, smiling as the morning breeze dampened his gaunt face with mist from the waterfall. "But, in your case, I think the more fitting analogy would be to say he's ready to sleep with the Bear, yes?''

"Maybe you have a point, Tony," the woman replied, matching Klemberk's smile with one of her own.

Emma Skodynov was a radiantly beautiful woman of thirty-one, with faintly reddish hair, high cheekbones and penetrating hazel eyes. She had charm and wit to go with her beauty, and it came as little wonder that her initial role with the former KGB had been that of a courtesan. Used essentially as a pawn in the strategies of male spymasters, she'd spent the better part of four years bedding diplomats, military officers, foreign agents, and any other figures her mentors hoped to compromise by luring them between the sheets.

Emma had greater ambitions, however, and once she was able to convince her superiors that she had a keen mind as well as a desirable body, her stock within the agency had quickly risen. Able to speak as well as read in half a dozen languages, she secured assignments in all phases of intelligence work, developing an informed overview of agency operations. She was adept at learning the use of weapons, too, and impressed officials with her ability and willingness to kill in the course of duty if the need arose. Of course, she retained her prowess in the sexual arena, but increasingly it was left to her to decide when she wished to bring those skills into play on behalf of any given mission.

A little over a year ago, Emma had been unexpectedly assigned to a small team of European-based specialists charged with laying the groundwork for a productive Russian involvement in the newly formed European Economic Community.

Or at least that was her official duty as far as Moscow was concerned.

Emma might have been drafted out of Russian Intelligence, but her primary allegiance remained with the organization that had nurtured her. She was particularly indebted to the Gray Hand, an inner sanctum of right-wing officials dedicated to hurtling their nation back into a position of emnity with the West. They had several reasons for such a stance, both ideological and financial. Having cornered the black market for most high-priced goods in the former Soviet Union, the Gray Hand was naturally wary of any changes that would bring more goods into the country through channels they had no control over. And so, at the same time Emma was trekking from one European financial capital to another supposedly plugging the cause of Russian participation in the EEC, her clandestine mission on behalf of the secretive intelligence organization was quite different.

One of Emma's first assignments for the Gray Hand had been to infiltrate the then-newly formed

Blood Against Oppression and see to what extent they could be influenced into serving the Hand's private agenda. She had had little problem getting into the organization, learning quickly that Ali-Jahn Babdi's ego was such that he would accept anyone into his ranks who showed him admiration bordering on idolatry. Once within the ranks of BAO, Emma had exploited Babdi's sexual proclivity, pandering to his appetites as a means of getting him off guard enough to gauge his malleability to Russian control. She'd quickly learned that Babdi was as antiauthoritarian as he was egocentric, and her ultimate recommendation to her superiors was that Babdi and the BAO would serve the RI best by being left alone to pursue their own course and destiny. Her advice had been followed to a large degree. No official overture was made to Babdi, but Russian Intelligence had provided indirect assistance to the BAO, both in terms of funneling recruits into their ranks and providing them with Kalashnikovs and other weapons through mutual contacts in the black market.

Emma had left Babdi and the BAO in Hanover less than two weeks before Vera Maris had been recruited to replace her as Babdi's mistress. The parting had been amicable, largely because of Emma's tactful handling of the situation.

Sensing that Babdi had wearied of her novelty and was on the verge of seeking out a new lover, she had confronted the situation head-on. She'd told the leader that it was in his best interests not to confine himself with their ongoing relationship, that a great lover like himself needed the constant challenge of new bedmates to keep him from losing his edge.

Babdi had marveled at her shrewd insight and understanding of his unique nature. Viewing her with newfound respect, he'd had no suspicions when she'd volunteered to bow out gracefully and at the same time to continue to serve the cause of the Blood by seeking out recruits at campuses in Paris.

In a way, she'd kept her word, sending Babdi a few enlistees, including those who'd helped to steal the Lawtin-313 missile launcher and later attempted to fire it on the crowds at Cannes. But in reality, once in Paris she'd resumed her official job as champion of Russian commerce while moonlighting with Klemberk on behalf of the Gray Hand, working to help fuel an ongoing feud between France and other NATO members on certain policy matters regarding the Persian Gulf.

It had been a particularly grueling mission, requiring long hours and steady concentration, but it had paid off, as just two days ago France had successfully managed to get NATO to downscale its presence and involvement in the Gulf on the theory that by definition the organization was obliged to focus itself more on matters directly impacting the North Atlantic.

In global terms it was hardly an earth-shattering development, but for Russian Intelligence, which was eager to eliminate any and all potential threats to its own influence in the Gulf region, the vote was particularly gratifying, and both Emma and Klemberk were in line for high commendations for a job well done.

Now, Emma was ready for a new assigment, and as Fate would have it, it looked as if her path and that of Ali-Jahn Babdi were about to cross again. She'd just gotten the word from her contact from the Gray Hand that morning. In the wake of what had happened the previous night on the Côte d'Azur, Russian Intelligence was of the opinion that, although Babdi's reputation had been enhanced by the bloodshed in Monaco, the losses he'd sustained there as well as in Cannes and Mougins had severely weakened the Blood Against Oppression. More than any time previously, it seemed that Babdi might be ripe for recruitment.

There was, of course, one big catch.

"You'll have to find him first," Klemberk told Emma as they wandered away from the waterfall.

"I think I can manage that."

"You're sure?"

Emma laughed. "When you share the bed of a braggart, he'll open his soul to you if you know how to push the right buttons."

CHAPTER FOURTEEN

Given the ramshackle condition of the grave digger's truck, Ali-Jahn Babdi considered himself lucky
to have been able to drive through the night without
suffering mechanical breakdown. It had been an arduous journey, to be sure, made even more tortur-
ous by Babdi's decision to avoid major thoroughfares in favor of secondary roads that led through
scenic but slow-traveling back country.

The vehicle had plodded along dutifully, and by
the dawn's first light Babdi was driving through Dijon, more than two-thirds of the way to his destination. Only then did a metallic tapping in the
crankcase signal serious problems under the truck's
hood. Babdi had forged on, logging a few more miles
and returning to country before the engine finally
seized. Fortunately the Turk had just cleared a rise
and by letting the truck roll downhill, he was able to
build enough momentum to get off the road and veer
his way down a dirt path leading into a small forest.
Exhaustion took its toll, and when he laid across the
front seat for what he planned to be only a few min-

utes of rest, Babdi quickly slipped into a deep slumber.

Three hours later, the terrorist opened his eyes against the glare of the midmorning sun. For a moment he was filled with that fleeting but resolute sense of disorientation that comes with awakening in unfamiliar surroundings. Even when he quickly recalled the circumstances that had brought him to this remote locale, Babdi's system remained at full alert, adrenaline fueling through his system as he sat upright, chastising himself for having lowered his guard.

Hearing a sound outside the truck, the Turk groped through his grave digger clothes, unearthing his automatic pistol. The sound was repeated, coming close to the passenger's door. Babdi slowly reached over, closing his fingers around the door's handle. On a count of three, he jerked the handle and flung the door open, ready to gun down whoever was sneaking up on him. He held his fire, however, when a sheep scurried clumsily away from the truck, bleating noisily. There were other sheep nearby as well, and when Babdi took a closer look, he saw that an entire small flock was making its way past the truck.

Babdi secreted his gun inside his stolen coat as he spotted a pair of young boys bringing up the rear of the flock, skipping along the dirt trail as they waved their shepherd's staffs in the air. The boys were singing in unison, but they both fell silent at the sight of the truck parked in the middle of the path.

The Turk got out of the truck and smiled at the boys. "Hello," he said in French.

"Hello," the older of the boys replied as he eyed Babdi.

"My truck broke down," Babdi explained. "I was tired, so I pulled off to rest."

"Can we help?"

Babdi shook his head. "No, thank you."

"I could go get my papa," the second boy volunteered. "He could bring his tractor and—"

"That's not necessary," Babdi assured the youths. He glanced over at the sheep, who had continued forging deeper into the woods. "You boys don't want to let your sheep get away, do you?"

"No."

"Then run along. And thank you again for your concern, but I will be all right."

The boys looked at each other, then, with a shrug, they headed off, once again skipping as they hurried to catch up with their sheep. Soon they were singing again as well, filling the woods with their cheerful voices. Babdi watched them awhile, an eerie smile pressed across his face.

"Oh, to be innocent," he murmured. "Young and innocent."

Ali-Jahn Babdi had little recollection of his own childhood, and of the memories he retained, few were happy. He vaguely recalled growing up on a goat farm in his native Turkey. It had been a simple existence, and in that simplicity there had been a certain happiness. There were times even now when he would drive through the country and just the smell of the land would evoke a sense of that distant time, before the night his parents were mysteriously whisked away by the police, never to be heard or seen from again. Babdi had been only five at the time, and he'd had no idea his mother and father had been involved in any kind of conspiracy against the state. Even when his uncle had tried to explain matters to him, it hadn't made any sense, any more than it had made sense to him when he found himself shuttled from his native country to France, where his uncle had a job at one of the Loire Valley wineries.

For the next five years, he'd been bounced from one boarding school to another, never fitting in, always feeling abandoned and alienated from the world around him. At ten, he'd finally run away, living on the streets and falling into the company of young hoodlums who taught him the basics of survival. He'd already learned to distrust and despise authority, and his friends on the street taught him how to channel that hatred to his advantage. They'd taught him how to rob and cheat, to fight and, when necessary, to kill. All in all, it had been the perfect breeding environment for a terrorist, and more often than not Babdi had the fatalistic sense that he'd been put through such a difficult life as a part of his destiny, that all the suffering had been for a reason—to harden him so that he could ably assume the reins of an outfit such as the Blood Against Oppression and carry out its agenda with necessary cold-hearted brutality.

And though Babdi had succeeded in his dreams and lived up to his self-created standards, there still lurked inside him that small kernel of vulnerability, that occasional restless yearning for the untroubled joy of the childhood he'd had before that fateful night when his parents had disappeared and his life had changed forever.

There were parts of France that closely approximated the Turkish farmland of Babdi's memory, and it was to such areas that the Turk fled when he felt the need to step back from his more immediate circumstances and gain some perspective. He'd been in this region recently, in fact. Shortly before he and Emma Skodynov had parted ways, he'd taken her to a modest country inn near the small village of Gresigny. For three days they'd lived the life of honeymooners, staying in bed until noon, then packing a picnic lunch to take out into the hills, where they'd seek out a private spot where they could eat, drink wine and make love under the sun. Babdi had confessed to Emma that he'd come here often, but always on his own, when he wanted to be alone with his thoughts. He'd told her of his childhood, of the lost innocence he came here to reclaim. She'd listened patiently, and though she couldn't offer him innocence, she was more than able to use other means to help take his mind off matters. At the end of their interlude, as they were on their way to rejoin the other members of the Blood, Emma had told him she hoped she hadn't spoiled the area as a retreat for him. At the time he'd assured her she hadn't, and even now he felt that he was right to have come here to think through his next move.

Of course, there was a strategic significance to coming here as well. He had a handful of followers in the area, and at some point he was certain he'd be linking up with them.

As Babdi walked back to the main road, he found himself staring up into the surrounding hills and recalling, not his childhood, but those three days of passion shared with Emma. Perhaps that should be his next move, he found himself thinking. Perhaps he should venture to Paris and track Emma down. With any luck, she'd have assembled more recruits eager to join BAO in the wake of what they'd accomplished the previous night. He could rebuild his forces with her at his side.

But first things first.

Babdi was still more than six miles away from Gresigny, and he was too exhausted to consider walking the distance. By the same token, he didn't want to risk hitchhiking. Fortunately, when he reached the road, he saw several tour buses parked in a lot several hundred yards away. Beyond the buses, two round stone turrets rose into view. Babdi guessed they were part of the Château de Bussy Rabutin, a sweeping residence dating back to the days of Louis XIV. As he drew closer, Babdi saw the rest of the château and realized he was correct. The house held no particular interest to him, however. He was pleased to find the parking lot filled with vehicles other than the buses.

Trying his best to look inconspicuous, the Turk lingered at the periphery of the lot, sitting down on a park bench and perusing a newspaper left behind by one of the tourists. His pulse quickened as he read the official accounts of the previous night's terrorist incidents in Cannes and Monaco. From his perspective, he could tell that the press had been left in the dark about much of what had happened, but there was some information that was news to him. Particularly disturbing was the realization that the President's daughter had miraculously survived the crash of the BMW in the hills near La Turbie. True, she was in a coma, but Babdi would have much preferred that she'd died. It would have been a more decisive blow against the West.

But on the whole he felt encouraged by what he read, and his spirits rose. The climate of fear throughout the country was unfounded, he realized, but an illusory victory was better than none at all.

Now he only had to think of a way to parlay circumstances to his advantage.

Out of the corner of his eye, Babdi saw a small Honda pull into one of the far parking spots. A couple got out and headed off toward the château, not bothering to lock their doors. Setting down the paper, the Turk sauntered casually over to the Honda. Once certain that no one was looking, he slipped inside the vehicle and reached underneath the steering wheel. Babdi had learned to hot-wire cars when he was in his early teens, and although he'd since moved on to greater crimes, he hadn't lost his touch. In a matter of seconds, he had the Honda running and was on his way out of the parking lot.

Less than ten minutes later, Babdi pulled up to the unassuming facade of Wintze Inn. He eyed himself in the rearview mirror, pulling down on the grave digger's hat and fussing with his hair to make himself less distinguishable from the mug shot of himself he'd seen in the newspaper. At one point during the drive he'd been faintly concerned that he might be recognized from previous stays at the hotel, but he'd quickly dismissed such a likelihood. For starters, during those earlier stays, he'd always been far better dressed and groomed, and he'd gone out of his way to be as inconspicuous as possible. Of course, that had been hard to do the time he'd come here with Emma Skodynov, but in that situation he suspected that most people's attention had been on the woman, whose flamboyant and dazzling beauty provided an ideal front behind which an escort could go easily unnoticed.

As hoped, Babdi entered the inn without drawing any undue attention, and fortuitously there was a new clerk at the registration desk. He offered a polite smile and inquired in French as to the availabilty of a room. The clerk answered to the affirmative, and in what Babdi considered an omen, he was able to register for the same second-story room he'd stayed in with Emma during their recent visit to the area.

He registered as Josef Hardolph, the name on his falsified passport, which listed him as a journeyman carpenter from Lahr, a small German border town. The real Hardolf had been slain during the Blood Against Oppression's flight from Hanover several weeks earlier. His bullet-riddled body, weighed down with rocks, had been cast into the Rhine River during the dead of night.

There was a small dining room with a tavern just off to the right of the reception area. Babdi paused to buy a baguette sandwich and a bottle of wine before heading upstairs. His room was nothing fancy, but he liked it because it was at the end of the hall and situated over the boiler room, affording him more privacy than any other suite. There was also a terrace just off the bedroom that offered a breathtaking view of the countryside, with the Château de

Bussy Rabutin rising majestically above the hills in the distance.

Babdi plugged the bathtub and wolfed down his sandwich as he waited for the tub to fill with water. After stripping off his clothes, he opened the wine and climbed into the tub, soaking his aching limbs as he slowly sipped from the bottle.

The room came with a radio, and he listened with interest to a news station filing live reports from the Riviera. He was concerned about the paucity of details regarding what had transpired the previous night in Mougins. There was mention of terrorists being seized in a raid outside the village, but no exact location had been given, and it wasn't clear how many prisoners had been taken. The implication was that the time bomb Babdi had left at the Galton villa hadn't gone off, but he also realized that in an attempt to quell any potential public hysteria in the town, the press might have been deliberately misled into believing that any explosion at the villa had been part of the raid. The uncertainty tore at him. What if Vera Maris was still alive? Or Eijai Wahldjun and the other Iraqis? Had they escaped, or were they in custody? And if they were in custody, would they turn against him?

Babdi finally shut off the radio and tried to close his mind to the turmoil. Rest. Once he had a chance to rest, he could think more clearly and sort things out, decide what to believe, what course to take.

Getting out of the tub, he drained the last of the wine, then washed his soiled clothes in the bathwater and hung them to dry near the register. After cleaning and reloading his gun, he placed it under his pillow, then pulled up the covers and closed his eyes. Within half a minute he was asleep.

"WHO KNOWS where Babdi might be?" Eijai Wahldjun whispered contemptuously. He glared at his three Iraqi comrades, looking for any trace of misplaced loyalty to their absentee leader. "Who cares?"

The others stared back at him silently, their faces masks of impassivity. They were huddled in one of the back pews of an ancient church in the heart of old Nice. The building was massive, with tall, vault-like ceilings blackened by centuries of candle smoke. Tongues of flame flickered now in the front corners of the church, where devout peasants and members of Nice's working class knelt before statues of Saint Michael and the Blessed Virgin Mary, offering up prayers to go with the donations they'd made when lighting candles. There was a handful of tourists mingling along the side aisles, too, drawn by the church's renowned stained-glass windows and hand-carved baptismal font. Besides the Iraqis, there were perhaps two dozen other people sitting or kneeling in the rows of pews. None was close enough to overhear the hushed murmurings of the terrorists, however.

"Babdi may be dead now, for all we know," ventured Ardi Corro, the youngest of the group.

"Exactly!" Wahldjun stated. "But it does not matter! What matters is that we have bred fear in the hearts of the infidels. They have struck a blow against us, too, so it is imperative that we strike back and let them know we are not afraid!"

Corro nodded, but in his eyes was a flicker of fear. The previous night he had seen several of his cohorts gunned down at the villa in Mougins, and he'd been terrified that the intruders were going to find him and kill him as well. It was Wahldjun who had come to his rescue, grabbing him by the collar and jerking him toward the back gate. They'd stolen a car and driven to Falicon, a small hamlet north of Nice, spending the night in a dilapidated barn.

They'd left at dawn, deciding to spend the day in Nice, mingling with the crowds while they tried to learn more of what had happened to the rest of their group and what action they should take next. They'd heard that the assault on Cannes had been repulsed, but that Babdi and others had apparently been behind a successful attack in Monaco. As for their fellow members back in Mougins, the word was that prisoners had been taken. And from the moment he'd heard the latter news, Wahldjun had been proposing that the Iraqis take the incentive to do something to free those prisoners. Corro suspected that Wahldjun was really more interested in exerting his authority than aiding the prisoners, and the young man trembled inwardly at the thought that he would soon be asked to lay down his life as part of a ploy for Wahldjun to wrest power from Ali-Jahn Babdi. He dared not voice his fears, however, because he knew that Wahldjun could be every bit as merciless as Babdi when it came to dealing with those unwilling to bend unquestioningly to his will.

"I have a plan," Wahldjun whispered to the others. "I've given it thought all through the night and all morning. Here is how we must proceed...."

For the next few minutes, Wahldjun laid out his proposed scenario, and although Corro was filled anew with terror at what he was hearing, he held his fear at bay and offered only the most obedient nods of his head whenever he felt the older man's eyes on him.

Once the plan had been laid out in its entirety, the four Iraqis left the church, entering a bustling city square. Diners crowded around tables set outside several restaurants facing the square, and the air was rich with the smell of fresh-baked breads and pasta. The Iraqis split off from one another, taking separate ways through the narrow side streets of the Old Town. They reunited half an hour later at the outskirts of town. Corro broke into a parked utilities van and hot-wired the engine. The other men stole into the back of the vehicle, where the windows were all covered over. Only then did they pull out the automatic pistols they'd kept secreted in the folds of their peasant garb.

"All right," Wahldjun told Corro. "Let's go—and keep your eyes open for what we talked about."

"I will," the young man said, pulling out into traffic and heading for one of the secondary roads that paralleled the main route to the airport. They passed numerous high-priced hotels, and, as Wahldjun had predicted, security measures had been stepped up, not only outside the buildings but also along the street. In some cases private security officers were out in force, but in several instances Corro spotted members of the national militia in their distinctive uniforms. And finally, after nearly an hour of winding through the streets to a run-down industrial section of the city, he came across the situation he'd been looking for.

At the end of a deserted street lined with boarded-up warehouses, four soldiers, either just relieved or about to go on duty, were playing cards together on a bench near their vehicle, a camou-painted pickup truck with a plastic rain shell.

"This is it," Corro called over his shoulder to the other Iraqis.

Wahldjun crept forward and peered over the young man's shoulder, smiling with expectation.

"Well done," he murmured, patting Corro's shoulder. "You know what to do next."

As Wahldjun dropped back with the others and braced himself near the rear doors of the van, Corro drew in a deep breath. He wasn't sure if he had the nerve to carry out his part of the mission, but he had no choice now but to find out.

Jerking the steering wheel sharply to his right, Corro veered the van into the curb, striking it so hard that he was flung against the driver's door. He quickly grabbed the handle, then flung the door open and dived out into the street as if thrown clear of the van. He landed hard on the pavement, but blocked out the pain, knowing that to register any sense of feeling would thwart his charade. He did his best to mimic a seizure, flailing his limbs in all directions.

The ruse was effective, drawing the attention of the soldiers and getting them to approach the stolen van without drawing their weapons. All four were riveted on Corro, and three of them moved in to try to subdue the young man out of fear he was going to hurt himself. Corro yelled and tried to fight them off, doing his best to keep them preoccupied.

In the background, the rear door of the van silently swung open and the other three Iraqis stepped down to the pavement. Before the militia officers had a chance to suspect they'd been duped, the gunmen were on top of them, able to carry out their executions with a single shot to the back of the head of each soldier. Blood was shed, but except for a few stray splotches, the dead men's uniforms were still clean.

"All right!" Wahldjun told the others as he grabbed one of the slain soldiers. "Let's get them in the van! Bring their weapons, too."

As the terrorists dragged their victims across the pavement, Corro spotted Wahldjun watching him. "You did very well, soldier," the older man complimented him.

"I did what was expected of me," the young man replied.

Once back inside the utilities van, the Iraqis quickly shed their peasant garb and donned the uniforms stripped from the slain officers. In terms of weapons, the militia had been armed with M-14 rifles, longtime standbys in the NATO arsenal. With their greater magazine capacity, they would prove worthy supplements to the terrorists' handguns.

"All right," Wahldjun instructed. "Now, into the other truck."

"What about the bodies?" one of the Iraqis asked.

"We'll leave them here and lock the doors," Wahldjun said. "Look around. This isn't a trafficked street. By the time anyone finds them, we will have already made our move. Now let's go!"

As the men filed out of the van and strode toward the other vehicle, they were startled by a sound coming from an alleyway across the street. Wahldjun whirled and spotted a bedraggled transient stumbling out of the shadows. The old man's clothes were in tatters and he walked with a severe limp, supporting himself with a makeshift cane. He blathered incoherently as he stepped into the street, gesturing at the Iraqis, then at the small pools of blood marking where the French officers had been gunned down.

"We don't have time for you, old man." Wahldjun raised the barrel of his stolen M-14 and pulled the trigger. Bullets drilled into the transient's chest. He pitched forward, landing facedown on the littered street. When he made an effort to lift himself up, Wahldjun took aim again and lodged a single shot in the man's skull.

"Get him out of here," he said to the others, "and cover the bloodstains."

While the men sought out scraps of litter to lay across the puddles of blood, Ardi Corro crouched over the beggar and hefted him by the armpits, dragging him back into the alley. It was narrow but long, extending the better part of a city block. Beyond it Corro saw the green hills of the countryside. For a moment, it occurred to him that if he was to drop the body and run, he could distance himself from the others and flee into the hills. From there, he could either continue to hide out on his own, or he could seek out the authorities and plead for mercy. Either course struck him as better than to remain with Wahldjun and face the prospect of certain doom.

"Ardi!" one of the other Iraqis suddenly called out, startling the young man. "What's taking you so long?"

"I...I wanted to make certain he was well concealed."

He proceeded to wedge the slain beggar between the brick wall of the alley and a stack of crumbling cardboard boxes. After toppling the boxes so that they covered the man, Corra glanced a final time at the green fields at the far end of the alley, then sighed with resignation and headed the other way, joining his rifle-wielding comrades.

Eijai Wahldjun was waiting for them near the back end of the military pickup. He was staring inside the cargo bed, grinning with a look of savage triumph.

"Our plans have changed," he told the others, gesturing for them to look inside the truck. Corro peered inside, seeing that the pickup was loaded with clearly labeled crates—C-4 plastique.

During his brief tenure with the BAO, Corro had worked with plastic explosives enough to know their potency. And if the crates were all full, he knew that there was enough destructive power packed into the back of the pickup to demolish any entire warehouse on this block.

"I'll give Babdi credit for this much," Wahldjun said as he pried the lid from one of the crates and confirmed that it was indeed filled with plastique. "He always said it was best to stage two-pronged attacks. That's what we will do now. We'll keep our original plan, but with one exception. We'll put most of these explosives into the other van, then one of you will be going for a ride to provide a little distraction for the rest of us...."

CHAPTER FIFTEEN

"There, try that."

John Kissinger glanced down at the brace that had just been applied to his injured leg. He could barely see any flesh for all the padding and metallic hinges. Yet, to his surprise, when he stood, the brace felt nowhere near as cumbersome as he'd anticipated. Sure, it restricted his movement to some extent, but there could be no denying that it lent sturdy support to the wounded leg. He took a few tentative steps across the hospital room, then glanced back at the physician.

"Works like a charm, Doc."

The doctor directed Kissinger to pivot on the leg, telling him, "There are still going to be plenty of things you can't do, as you can see, but the brace will enable you to stay on your feet—much as I'm still advising against it."

"Well, much as I hate to be a bad patient, this just isn't a good time for me to be laid up." Kissinger glanced over at Bolan, who was standing by the window. "We've got a full dance card, right?"

Bolan nodded. "Yeah, we can use the extra manpower, that's for sure."

They were on the top floor of the orthopedic wing at Sainte Catherine's Medical Center. Through the window, Bolan could see one of the French sharpshooters stationed on the roof, which overlooked the bustling streets of Monaco. The sun was high in the sky, throwing short shadows across the roof. Bolan had accompanied Kissinger to the wing after the meeting with the other security forces earlier that morning. Grimaldi had left to check out the repairs on the Reed helicopter, while Brognola had been assigned the grim task of reporting to the President on the condition of his daughter.

The doctor grabbed her clipboard and started for the door, advising Kissinger, "Well, you'll do what you have to. I'd suggest you at least try to avoid any lateral movement with the knee for at least a week. No sharp turns, no twisting—"

"No basketball," Kissinger interjected with a grin.

"Definitely no basketball." The woman smiled back. "And good luck—to both of you."

Once the doctor had left, Kissinger tried running in place a few seconds. Feeling no pain, he planted one foot and pivoted slightly to one side, stopping almost immediately when a stabbing pain ran along his leg.

"Yeow!"

"Guess you better make sure you follow doctor's orders, Cowboy."

"Yeah, yeah," Kissinger grumbled, sitting on the edge of the bed so he could slip back into his pants.

"How much did that woman tell you about the men who fled the villa?"

"Not a lot. She said she wasn't surprised that they ran off like they did. All four of them are Iraqis, and one's from the Republican Guard. The way she paints them, they're just overgrown schoolyard bullies. They talk and play tough as long as nobody stands up to them, but when push comes to shove, they're cowards."

"Does she think the whole outfit's like that?"

Kissinger shook his head. "No. But she conceded that the ones she feared most have already been killed or captured. Except Babdi, of course."

Brognola strode into the room with the haggard, no-nonsense look of a man laboring under a heavy load and a tight deadline.

"Got through to Washington?" Bolan asked.

"Yeah, I sure did," Brognola reported, "and the Man's fit to be tied."

"Can't really blame him, can you?" Kissinger asked.

"No, I can't. At any rate, I need you guys to get your stuff together, pronto. We're going to the airport."

"What about the follow-up meeting?" Bolan asked.

"It's not our problem. The President wants us to hit the Blood back, as fast and as hard as possible. And since we haven't been able to track the stragglers down here, that leaves the cell in Hanover. They're still under surveillance, and Mead said he'd have his people hold off long enough for us to get there. So let's move it!"

"Right behind you," Kissinger said, buckling his belt and stabbing his feet into a pair of shoes.

The three men left the room and headed for the elevator, Brognola leading the way.

"If the Man wants quick retaliation," Bolan said, "why not just let the Germans move in now?"

"Because he wants it to be a U.S. response," the big Fed replied, reaching the bank of elevators and pressing a button to call a car.

"As far as the media's concerned, you guys are going to be a special task force from one of our NATO bases in Germany."

"Fair enough."

As they started to descend, Brognola added, "I've also spoken with Katz in Italy. Once they wrap up things, he's going to bring Phoenix Force here to help out."

"Sounds good," Kissinger said.

Yakov Katzenelenbogen was the commander of Phoenix Force, another contingent of specialty warriors based out of Stony Man Farm. The five-man team was in Italy, tracking down a cell of the Red Brigades said to be plotting a terrorist attack on members of the G-7, meeting in Rome. Bolan and Kissinger had worked alongside Katz and the other members of the Force on countless occasions, and the prospect of having them join the war against the BAO increased the chances of succeeding with the mission.

When the elevator reached the ground floor, the men emerged and started across the lobby. Before they could reach the main doorway, however, they were accosted from behind.

"Wait a sec, guys."

The men glanced back and spotted Ed Dauffie striding toward them from the other wing of the hospital.

"What is it, Ed?" Brognola said. "We're just on our way to the airport."

Dauffie caught up with the men and followed them outside. "Look, it's nothing urgent. I just wanted to give you guys a little grief for bailing out and leaving me to deal with Scautt."

"You don't care for him?" Brognola asked.

"He's a pompous pain in the ass who's got his priorities backward and should be pushing pencils in some bureaucratic cubbyhole instead of being here on the front. But, hey, other than that, he's a great guy."

"Talk with Mead," the big Fed suggested. "Maybe if the two of you coordinate, you can finesse Scautt into the background when the other French reps show up for that second meeting."

"It's worth a try," Dauffie said, following the others to the parking lot. "If we can link the Hanover incidents and make this more of a NATO matter than just trouble in France, it could work."

"Good luck."

"Thanks. I just want to up the odds that I'll be in on the action when we corner Babdi. After what he did to J.T. in Monaco, I owe him one."

Dauffie backtracked to the hospital as the others piled into Bolan's rental car. The Executioner took the wheel, Brognola rode shotgun and Kissinger took the back so he could stretch his bad leg across the seat. The two security guards stationed near the front entrance waved them through. Bolan pulled into traffic, stopping at a light at the first corner they came to.

"I think Dauffie's right on the money about Scautt," Kissinger observed as they waited for the light to change. "There's something about him that really rubs you the wrong way."

"As long as that's all there is to it, I wouldn't worry," Brognola told him.

"What are you saying?" Bolan asked. "You don't trust him?"

"Let's just say I'm glad he's not in a position to make any unilateral decisions."

As Brognola and Kissinger continued to discuss the French Intelligence officer, Bolan fell silent. His attention was on an approaching utilities van on the other side of the intersection. It was the only vehicle in its lane, and it had slowed to a crawl more than thirty yards from the passenger crosswalk. Behind the wheel was a swarthy-skinned man in a military uniform. The warrior didn't like the way it added up, and when he shifted his gaze to the rearview mirror and saw the hospital in the background behind him, his mind flashed to one of the darkest incidents in the history of U.S. dealings with terrorist factions.

Beirut. A truckful of explosives driven into a barracks filled with U.S. servicemen. More than two hundred fatalities.

"We've got trouble," he announced, rolling to a stop.

"What's up?" Brognola asked, but the Executioner was already scrambling out of the parked car.

On the other side of the intersection, the van suddenly lunged forward, screeching rubber as its tires clawed at the pavement. Bolan planted himself in the middle of the oncoming lane and whipped out his Beretta, the van speeding toward him as he drew a bead on the driver.

Just as Bolan pulled the trigger, the van veered slightly to its right. The front windshield spiderwebbed, but the shots missed the driver, who'd leaned to one side while jerking the steering wheel. Without losing speed, the vehicle continued to bear down on the Executioner.

"Get its tires!" Bolan shouted to Brognola and Kissinger without taking his eyes off the van. Like a matador facing off a charging bull, the warrior held his ground as the van crossed the intersection. He eyed the vehicle, noting the position of the front bumper and the side-view mirror mounted on the driver's door.

At the last possible second, Bolan sprang to his right and crouched slightly. The van rushed past, missing him by mere inches. Bolan quickly leaped upward, grabbing the mirror and swinging his feet up onto the front bumper. The slightest miscalculation would have been fatal, but Bolan succeeded in mounting the vehicle. He held on grimly as it continued to barrel headlong toward the hospital entrance.

The driver was wounded but still able to keep his foot on the accelerator. When he saw Bolan pressed against the front of the van, he took one hand off the wheel, rolled down his window and grabbed at the warrior's fingers, trying to dislodge his grip on the mirror. Bolan turned the tables, however, shifting his hand so that he could grab the driver's wrist and jerk on it.

The van swerved again, sideswiping a sports car parked along the curb. Bolan was almost jarred loose, but he held firm and continued to grapple with the driver. At the same time, he could hear blasts of gunfire, followed by the loud popping of the van's tires as they were shot out by Kissinger and Brognola. The vehicle shuddered and veered even more, losing momentum as it scraped along several parked cars.

Once he was sure he had an almost ironclad grip on the driver's forearm, Bolan leaped from the van. The driver screamed in agony as his arm was bent at an unnatural angle to the point where it snapped against the window frame. In his pain, he took his foot off the accelerator, and the van rolled to a stop less than ten yards from the main entrance to the hospital. The guards stationed there had their guns and were aiming at the runaway van. When it rolled to a stop, they rushed forward to apprehend the driver.

Bolan let go of the man's arm and lowered his Beretta as he paused to catch his breath. Brognola and Kissinger joined him.

"Way to go, Striker," Brognola said.

"You guys did all right, too," Bolan replied, noting that three of the van's four tires had been shot out.

The men circled around the van and looked inside, spotting the crates of C-4 plastique.

"Looks like our friend here was bringing a present to the President's daughter."

"He should have stuck to a get-well card," Kissinger observed.

The street became crowded with civilians drawn by the sounds of gunfire. Ed Dauffie showed up moments later as well, flanked by two Secret Service agents. Brognola quickly related what had happened.

"Nice work, guys," Dauffie said.

A call was put out for reinforcements to help cordon off the area and deal with the van's deadly cargo, then Brognola accompanied the guards as they escorted the wounded driver toward the hospital for treatment and questioning. Dauffie remained behind with Bolan and Kissinger, working to disperse the crowd with warnings about the volatile load.

"Looks likes the Blood's going to keep coming at us with all they've got," Dauffie speculated once he was back within earshot of Bolan.

"Probably," the Executioner acknowledged. "And we're just going to have to be ready to deal with whatever they throw at us."

HALF A BLOCK AWAY, Anatoly Klemberk sipped from a bottle of bourbon as he watched the commotion through the window of his third-story hotel room. He'd checked in only a few minutes earlier, having just arrived by jet from Paris. The agent who had picked him up at the airport had passed along word that the President's daughter had been taken to Sainte Catherine's, and Klemberk had quickly surmised that a nearby hotel would be a likely strategic location for him to stay while he monitored the crisis. Judging from what he was looking at, the Russian felt reassured that he'd made the right decision.

Klemberk had packed a compact pair of binoculars, and he put them to use when he spotted what looked to be a familiar figure helping to control the crowd around the disabled van. Zooming in on the face of the man in question, Klemberk slowly smiled.

"Ed Dauffie," he murmured.

CHAPTER SIXTEEN

The second prong of the Iraqi's offensive was faring far better than the first.

Eijai Wahldjun and his cohorts were able to use the heightened military presence at the international airport in Nice to their favor. Under normal circumstances, there would have been closer scrutiny paid when Eijai Wahldjun drove the stolen militia pickup to the first checkpoint at the main entrance to the airport. But with the constant comings and goings of uniformed personnel since the terrorist incidents of the previous night, Wahldjun, wearing a militia uniform and speaking fluent French, was able to bluff his way past guards without benefit of formal orders. Harried as they were with searching civilian vehicles, the guards also waved Wahldjun through without inspecting the back of the pickup, where Ardi Corro sat with Ehki Kirv, the brother of the Iraqi who'd attempted to blow up Sainte Catherine's Medical Center with the explosives-rigged utilities van. Both men were hunched over crates of plastique that had been left on the truck for this operation. Each cradled an M-14 in his lap and had a

9 mm automatic holstered on his hip. Kirv seemed content with his fate, while the younger man still showed signs of wariness and apprehension. Despite a lifetime of indoctrination about the glory of dying in the field of battle, Corro treasured life too much to throw it away on political gestures. He was glad Wahldjun hadn't tabbed him for the suicide mission with the utilities van.

As Corro continued to brood upon his fate, Wahldjun inched the pickup through the chaotic congestion of the airport, grinning. Everywhere he looked there were likely targets for the Blood Against Oppression. All he would have to do was press his foot to the accelerator and turn the steering wheel, and he could plow into the glut of pedestrians and claim more victims than Ali-Jahn Babdi had in the massacre in Monaco. He could achieve the same results with even less effort by stopping the car and emptying his M-14 into the crowd.

But, much as the prospect of an apocalyptic bloodletting appealed to Wahldjun, he was content, for now, to leave such glory to Ehki Kirv's brother and his assault on Sainte Catherine's Medical Center. Here at the airport, Wahldjun had another objective in mind. He was looking for hostage material, people of prominence he could seize and hold under threat of execution while he negotiated his way past Ali-Jahn Babdi into prominence as the central figure of the Blood Against Oppression.

Up ahead, planes of all sizes could be seen taxiing along the runways or taking on passengers at the main terminal. Conventional wisdom dictated that the terrorists seize one of the larger jets and hold its crew and passengers prisoner, but Wahldjun had no interest in pursuing that option. He knew very well that the track record for such hijackings was poor. There were too many logistical problems in effectively controlling a large aircraft and its hundreds of passengers. And, beyond that, it was unlikely that dignitaries or other prominent individuals would be taking public transport out of the area, particularly under the circumstances.

Surveying the pandemonium, Wahldjun's gaze finally locked on a remote hangar, where two stretch limos were parked alongside a sleek, gleaming Dassault Mystère 20, France's answer to the old Falcon private jet. Seating ten passengers and powered by 4500-pound-thrust General Electric CF-700 turbofans, the Dassault had been a longtime mainstay among French businessmen.

The Iraqi watched as a chauffeur emerged from one of the limos and circled around to open the side doors. That was a good sign. If all the passengers hadn't boarded the plane yet, there would be ample time for the terrorists to close in. Wahldjun was even more encouraged when he raised a pair of binoculars to take a closer look at the first couple emerging from the limo.

"Yes," he whispered, grinning. "They will do nicely...."

WITHOUT WAITING for her bodyguards to catch up with her, blond box-office bombshell Dee Clark vaulted from the limousine, latching on to the arm of her leading man and current paramour, Australian heartthrob Keith Stewker.

"I'll tell you what it is," Clark grated as she flicked her cigarette to the tarmac, just missing her chauffeur's feet. "It's a conspiracy by Paramount. They're trying to sabotage my movie just because I walked out on my contract with them!"

Stewker, looking every bit as virile and rugged as he had in his last action thriller, smirked at his current cinematic costar as they approached the small mobile staircase leading up to the jet. "Don't you think that's a little farfetched, Dee Dee?"

"Absolutely not! Those bastards would stoop to anything to get back at me!"

Stewker sighed. "If you say so..."

Touted in the international press as the Tracy and Hepburn of the nineties, Dee Clark and Keith Stewker had flown to the Riveria to help publicize their third motion picture together. Since each of their past two films had grossed over a hundred million dollars domestically and a quarter of a billion dollars worldwide, the new collaboration was being looked upon as a godsend for Hen/Gee International, the fledgling upstart Hollywood company that had wrested the two stars from Paramount in a drawn-out bidding war that had resulted in suits and countersuits filed by both studios. The movie had been a jinxed production from the onset, suffering from numerous setbacks both before and during filming. But Clark and Stewker had overcome all obstacles to turn in another stellar performance that, fueled with gossip about their growing personal relationship, made it seem certain the new movie would be an even bigger blockbuster than its predecessors. Hen/Gee studio chief T. A. Magrane had accompanied his dynamic duo to France to showcase the film at Cannes, but as fate would have it, the thwarted terrorist attack on the film festival had occurred the day before the movie's scheduled premiere. Now the showing had been canceled along with the rest of the festival, and Magrane was leading the flight back to the States. The chief had arrived in the other limo a few minutes before and had already boarded the plane.

As the two movie stars headed for the staircase, their contingent of four bodyguards joined the chauffeur as he struggled to fend off a small crowd of overzealous fans and members of the press who had somehow managed to learn of the stars' departure plans and wheedled their way past a phalanx of security personnel provided by the airport.

"When's the marriage date, guys?" one of the reporters shouted.

"Is it true you get pregnant at the end of the movie?" another cried out.

Halfway up the steps, Stewker paused to wave to his fans and tell the reporters, "No comment, boys. You're just gonna have to tune in to our interview with Barbara Walters to get the lowdown."

"Yeah, right!" one of the reporters groused. "I'm sure!"

One of the few women in the press corps, gossip hound Jackie Ranuel, waited until she was sure she could get Clark's attention, then called out, "Dee Dee, is it true you just had your breasts augmented for your next picture?"

Clark's face flushed red and she spun around at the top of the staircase, glaring daggers at the reporter. "I'll have my lawyers fry you on hot coals for that one, honey!"

"Is that a yes or a no?" Ranuel responded with a faint trace of a smile.

Some of Clark's fans came to her defense and began shouting at the other woman. Camera crews focused on the altercation as Jackie Ranuel traded barbs with Clark's supporters.

"Come on, Dee Dee," Stewker whispered in Clark's ear as he drew her toward the entrance to the jet. "Don't let them get to you."

But the woman wasn't in the mood to listen to her beau. She turned to her bodyguards at the base of the steps and shouted, "Get that bitch and wrap her microphone around her neck!"

The bodyguards, who had been hired as much by Clark's lawyers as by the woman herself, knew better than to carry out such an outlandish order. They continued to hold their ground at the base of the staircase, content to keep the crowd back rather than take any retaliatory action.

"Cowards!" Clark railed at the men. When she spotted a militia pickup roll to a stop near her limo, she muttered under her breath, "Well, maybe these soldiers will at least have some backbone."

Indeed, when the uniformed driver got out of the pickup, he released the safety on an M-14 and fired a short blast of warning shots into the air, silencing the throng gathered around the private jet. When two more men climbed out of the back of the truck, also armed with rifles, the crowd parted uneasily, giving the gunmen clear access to the staircase.

Stewker stepped farther into the jet and glanced back at the seats, asking T. A. Magrane, "Hey, did you arrange for a military escort for us?"

Magrane, a balding, middle-aged impressario dressed in a white silk suit, glanced up from the calculator he was using to figure out how much this aborted trip to Cannes was going to cost his company. "Hell, no," he called, "I'm trying to cut my losses here. You want to get Bambi inside so we can take off? We're wasting fuel."

Stewker was about to reply when he heard the sudden sputter of automatic rifle fire, followed by shrieks of hysteria. Stunned, he headed back to the doorway, just managing to grab hold of Clark as the woman sagged into his arms. Fearing the worst, he looked for signs of gunshot wounds but saw none. The woman had apparently fainted, and when Stewker glanced down the steps he saw the reason why. Their four bodyguards had crumpled into a bloody heap on the runway, and the two soldiers who'd just gunned them down were on their way up the staircase, rifles in hand.

"Back in the plane!" Ehki Kirv shouted, aiming his M-14 at the actor's face. "Now!"

Stewker had been in similar situations countless times over the years, but in those instances he was always following a script in which it was a foregone conclusion that he was going to emerge not only unscathed but also victorious. He had no such delusions this time, however, and he meekly retreated inside the jet, dragging Dee Clark with him.

On the ground, Eijai Wahldjun fired another volley over the crowd's head, driving them farther back. Then he leveled the weapon at Jackie Ranuel and her cameraman.

"You!" Wahldjun commanded. "Follow me. All of you!"

Ranuel protested. "But—"

The Iraqi lowered the barrel of his M-14 and sprayed a quick burst of gunfire at the asphalt near the woman's feet. Ranuel gasped with terror, then pleaded, "Please, don't kill me! I'll come with you."

As her cameraman followed close behind her, he mumbled in her ear, "If we live through this, we're going to have one hell of a scoop."

TRAFFIC WAS BACKED UP all the way onto the main road by the time Bolan, Brognola, and Kissinger reached the airport. Word of the hostage situation had just reached them. Brognola was in radio contact with Ed Dauffie, who, along with Denis Scautt and Wilhelm Mead, was flying by helicopter from Sainte Catherine's Medical Center to the airport. Bolan and Kissinger could hear both sides of the conversation. Dauffie had received news of the hijacking while in the midst of questioning the suicide bomber, and with a combination of threats and persuasion had gotten the prisoner to divulge details about who was calling the shots at the airport for the BAO.

"Is it Babdi?" the head Fed asked.

"No," Dauffie reported. "The guy's name is Ei-jai Wahldjun. Iraqi. Ex-Republican Guard on the wanted list for atrocities in Kuwait. Helped Hussein try to squelch insurrectionists after the war. This is the first link we have on him with BAO.''

"And I suppose he's the one who sent that guy to try to blow up Sainte Catherine's?''

"Absolutely,'' Dauffie confirmed. "Killing Audrey was their primary objective, but they were also looking for a diversion to help make things easier for them at the airport.''

"Has Wahldjun made any contact with us?'' Bolan asked.

"Yeah, he's using the cockpit radio,'' Dauffie replied. "We've spoken to him twice.''

"What about demands?'' Brognola asked.

"The usual list. Release of political prisoners, press access so they can spout off some rhetoric, free passage out of the country to whoever might be twisted enough to take them in. But look, we can get into details later. We're just coming up on the airport now.''

Bolan glanced out the windshield and saw a Bell helicopter floating into view from the direction of the hospital. "There they are.''

"Are you guys landing near the hangar where Grimaldi's inspecting the Reed?'' Brognola asked Dauffie.

"I think so. We're double-checking to make sure it's far enough away from the Dassault.''

"Or else what?"

"Wahldjun says if any other aircraft or ground vehicle comes within two hundred yards of them, they kill Dee Clark."

"Well, we obviously don't want that."

"We're stalling, obviously," Dauffie said. "We said that with so many different demands we're not authorized to give a blanket response. We're gonna have to go through a lot of channels."

"They didn't go for it, did they?" Brognola asked.

"Not really. We have an hour, then they're going to start tossing bodies out of the plane every fifteen minutes."

"And they've already killed some people, right?"

"Affirmative. Bodyguards to Stewker and Clark."

"Well, keep stalling," Brognola suggested. "We'll catch up with you as soon as we can, then we'll try to come up with a plan."

"All right. But try to make it fast."

"Will do."

Brognola signed off, then turned to Bolan. "Well, you heard the man."

Bolan waited for the vehicle ahead of them to pull ahead a few inches, then abruptly veered the rental car off the road. As they sped along the shoulder past the other stalled cars, they were greeted with a variety of waved fists and multilingual epithets.

"Sticks and stones..." Kissinger said. "I'll take the abuse here over what we're getting ready to go up against."

"Amen to that," Brognola said, as Bolan maneuvered around a sign posted along the side of the road. He didn't like the way things were shaping up. Not at all.

CHAPTER SEVENTEEN

Anatoly Klemberk ordered a bourbon on rocks from the waitress, then turned his attention back to Evan Willan, the Russian Intelligence field agent who'd picked him up at the airport. They were in a dimly lighted back corner booth of the bar in the hotel where Klemberk was staying. There was no one else within earshot, but still the men conversed in whispers.

"This is fantastic news," Klemberk said when told of the hostage situation at the airport. "The BAO couldn't have played into our hands better if we had choreographed this ourselves."

"Perhaps," Willan said. "But at some point we need to make it look as if we *did* help them with their plans."

"It will happen," Klemberk replied. "But we'll pick our time."

The waitress returned with Klemberk's drink, and the two men ordered sandwiches. Klemberk admired the woman's bright features and ample figure. He was reminded of Emma Skodynov. She hadn't divulged where she proposed to go to look for

Ali-Jahn Babdi, and Klemberk had initially thought the Turk might have been behind the seizure of the private jet. How ironic it would be if their paths were to cross again here on the Riviera. If Fate was to be so kind, he was sure he'd find some excuse to get himself alone with Emma again. He had one quick tryst with her before they separated, and there was no way a man could sample her favors just once and not be left with a thirst for more.

"Anatoly."

Klemberk snapped out of his reverie at the sound of his name and saw Willan eyeing him with concern.

"Are you all right?"

"Fine," Klemberk assured the other man. "Where were we?"

"You told me you had found the key to Operation Rekindle," Willan said. "What is it?"

"Not what," Klemberk told Willan. "Who. Edward Dauffie. He is the key. Let me explain. . . ."

AFTER THE MECHANIC stepped back from his handiwork, Jack Grimaldi moved in to inspect the patches welded onto the underbelly of the Reed-279 helicopter. The seams were clean and even, reinforcing the rivets holding several metal plates in place over bullet holes left by sniper fire back in Cannes.

"Nice work," the Stony Man pilot said with a satisfied grin. "A little tampering with the engine and we'll have this beast airborne again."

"You don't figure on heading out to that hangar, do you?" the mechanic asked.

"Hard to say," Grimaldi replied. "You never know how these things are going to play out."

They were outside a mechanic's garage at the periphery of the airfield, more than three hundred yards from the captive plane. Grimaldi had received word about the hostage situation a few minutes earlier. At that time, he'd been specifically ordered not to approach the hangar where the BAO had commandeered the Dassault. But, as he'd just told the mechanic, he knew that the orders might be subject to change at any moment, so he continued to oversee repairs on the Reed, determined to have it airworthy in the event it was needed.

"Engine work'll only take another half hour," the mechanic told Grimaldi. "Forty-five minutes tops."

"Good. Keep at it." Grimaldi reached inside the copter for a pair of high-powered binoculars. "I want to take a look at what's going on over there."

"Careful," the mechanic advised.

"That's my middle name."

The mechanic turned back to the bullet-riddled body of the Reed and shook his head. "Yeah, right...."

Inside the garage was a runged ladder leading up to the flat roof. Grimaldi hauled himself up the rungs and swung open the trapdoor, then crawled out onto the hot tiles, lying low to avoid being spotted from the distant plane. Raising the binoculars, he adjusted the ocular lens and brought the Dassault Mystére into focus.

Isolated as it was, Grimaldi could see that the remote hangar was ideally situated for the terrorists, providing them with an unobstructed view in all directions. It would be virtually impossible to approach without being detected. There was no sign that the terrorists had any intention of fleeing, at least not in the immediate future. The Dassault's turbofans were silent, and the mobile staircase was still in place alongside the plane. The slain bodyguards remained sprawled out on the tarmac at the base of the steps, a grim reminder that the BAO wasn't bluffing. Grimaldi thought he could see movement in the pilot's cabin, but he was too far away to tell if it was the pilot at the controls or one of the terrorists.

"This one's going to be tough," he muttered.

Moments later Grimaldi heard the throaty hum of a Bell helicopter approaching the service area. By the time he scrambled down from the roof, the chopper had set down next to the Reed-279. Ed Dauffie was the first to disembark, followed by Denis Scautt and two uniformed officers representing the French military. Wilhelm Mead remained inside the chopper, wearing a pair of radio headphones and speaking to someone through the headset microphone.

"Anything new?" Grimaldi asked Dauffie.

"Mead's trying to negotiate for more time," Dauffie said. "He's not having much luck, though."

"How much time do we have?"

Scautt checked his watch. "Fifty-two minutes."

The older of the military advisers eyed the distant jet and scowled. "Well, we can't let them get away with this. I say we just round up the best force we have here and move in."

"Absolutely not," Scautt said. "If those two movie stars die without our having made every effort to get them out alive, we'll be crucified."

"Stewker and Clark aren't the only hostages," Dauffie reminded Scautt.

"I'm well aware of that," the Frenchman replied with cool disdain, "but let's be realistic. Those are the two that we need to be the most concerned about."

"Is that so?" Dauffie challenged. "I thought this was a terrorist situation, not some public relations stunt!"

"Don't misunderstand me. I care about the welfare of all the hostages. It's just that in the eyes of the public—"

"I know what you're trying to say," Dauffie said.

"Hey, look, guys," Grimaldi intervened. "We're all on the same side here."

Scautt and Dauffie fell silent. The ranking member of the military reemphasized his position. "We can't give in to these bastards. That has to be our first priority."

"No," Scautt retorted. "The safety of the hostages is the most important—"

"If we can put our heads together," Grimaldi proposed, "maybe we can do both."

"You have something in mind?" Dauffie asked.

"At the moment, no. But that doesn't mean there isn't a solution."

Scautt checked his watch again. "Fifty minutes."

Wilhelm Mead emerged from the Bell chopper and strode over to join the others. There was a trace of hope in his otherwise grave features. "We might be able to get them to push back their deadline for killing any more hostages."

"How?" Scautt asked.

Mead sighed, knowing his proposition would meet with resistance. "They know that we're holding two BAO members from the raid in Mougins. They'll give us an extra half hour to bring them here for a trade."

"No deals!" one of the generals insisted.

Scautt ignored his fellow countryman and asked, "A trade for who?"

"The producer and the reporter," Mead said. "They want to keep Stewker and Clark for collateral, and they want the pilot for their getaway. Apparently they're taping some kind of message with the cameraman, and they'll release him later on, provided their tape gets transmitted worldwide."

"I'm not letting my daughter fall back into the hands of those monsters," Dauffie said.

Scautt eyed Dauffie. "I told you you'd have difficulty being objective about this."

Before yet another argument could ensue, the group was interrupted by the arrival of the rental car carrying Bolan, Brognola and Kissinger. The Executioner parked near the choppers, then got out along with his companions. He carried a large roll of papers.

"Sorry we're late," Brognola told the group, "but we swung by the main offices to pick up some blueprints."

Grimaldi leaned to one side, murmuring to Bolan, "You guys haven't missed much, believe me."

Mead quickly brought the newcomers up to date, then turned to Bolan. "Are the blueprints of any help?"

"Maybe. Let's get out of the breeze and take a look."

The warrior led the group inside, then cleared one of the workbenches so he could lay out the blueprints. There were five different sets, showing all the structures at the airport as well as the configurations for utility layouts, roadways and other peripherals. Bolan was concentrating on one of the sheets.

"Here," he said, drawing the other men's attention to the drawing. "This is a network of flood drains all along the coastal perimeter of the airport."

"A precaution against bad tides?" Grimaldi wondered aloud.

"Exactly," Bolan replied, continuing to gesture as he spoke. "They don't happen that often, but when they do the surf can sweep all the way across this one runway and parts of four others. Without the drains, they'd practically have to shut down."

"And what exactly does this have to do with our situation?" Scautt asked.

"The drains feed into six-foot diameter pipelines that divert the water into this reservoir," he explained. "The openings are underwater, but we can access them and then steal up the pipelines to these two drains on either side of the hangar."

"Very good," Dauffie said, eyeing the diagram. "And what about the grates? Are they welded in place?"

"Bolted," Kissinger replied. "We should have no problem getting them open."

"And once we're that close," Bolan added, "we might have a crack at them."

"I don't know," Dauffie mused. "Odds are they'd spot you before you got the grates off, and by the time you were out of the drains and up the staircase, they'd have killed all the hostages."

"We'd have to have a diversion," Bolan said. He turned to Mead. "We could coordinate it with a prisoner exchange, try to make it as distracting as possible."

"Possibly."

"It'd be a help if we could get one of the prisoners to help us spring the trap, too," Brognola suggested.

"Trojan horse?" Grimaldi asked.

"Why not," Brognola said. "Have them get tear gas and stun grenades inside the plane, and it would save us having to try to lob them in through the cabin door."

"Maybe so," Dauffie said, "but once the prisoners show they've betrayed the BAO, they'll be the first to die."

"Not if it's done right," Brognola argued.

"I vote no," Dauffie said.

"Protecting your daughter again," Scautt taunted.

"Look, I've had just about enough of you!" Dauffie charged Scautt but was quickly grabbed from either side by Kissinger and Grimaldi. The two generals, meantime, restrained Scautt.

"Take them both outside until they can cool off," Bolan suggested. "This is the closest thing we've got to a workable plan, and I suggest we hammer it out as quickly as we can so we don't end up with more bodies on the runway.''

IT WAS A FOUR-HOUR DRIVE from Paris to the Wintze Inn. Emma Skodynov cut the time by more than half by piloting the single-engine Socata Rallye aircraft to a sprawling farmland estate near Les Laume owned by Tristam Donlier, one of her most-valued Parisian clients.

Donlier owned several farms in the French interior, including one near Domrémy, but he'd made his fortune in computers, specifically state-of-the-art components for missile guidance systems, including those of the Lawtin-33. Donlier's company had been helping McGaffles-Parez Industries in its attempt to secure foreign investors for the Lawtin, and it was through him that Emma had learned the whereabouts of the demonstration prototype, enabling her to mastermind the missile's theft by the three BAO recruits she'd lined up for Ali-Jahn Babdi.

Of course, Donlier had no idea he was consorting with a Russian Intelligence agent; throughout his dealings with Emma he had been under the impression that she was a representative from the Russian Ministry of Commerce and therefore someone well worth wining, dining and granting favors to. When Emma had called him earlier, asking if she could land her company plane on his private airfield and have the use of one of his cars to tend to a matter of urgency, Donlier had obliged her without asking for so much as an explanation. He was still in Paris at the time, embroiled with investigators looking into the theft of the Lawtin-313 prototype, but he'd called his estate and notified the staff of her needs.

Within moments of landing on the private airfield, Emma was greeted by one of the chauffeurs whom she recognized from a previous visit. She'd asked to borrow an inconspicuous car, but the least ostentatious vehicle in Donlier's garage turned out to be a gleaming yellow, fully restored 1954 Alfa-Romeo.

"Bonjour, madame." The chauffeur greeted Emma with an engaging smile.

"Bonjour, Louis," she replied, transferring a bag from the plane to the car, then slipping behind the wheel. The chauffeur took the passenger seat.

As they rounded a curve, the high-sloped rooftops of the twenty-five-room mansion came into view. Emma eased her foot down on the accelerator, speeding along the dirt road. Off to their right, day laborers could be seen working the fields under the supervision of several foremen.

"When I was here last," Emma said nonchalantly, "Tristan had just transferred in some workers from his farm in Domrémy. How are they working out?"

The chauffeur shrugged. "I haven't heard of any problems."

Emma's curiosity about the transferred workers was more than casual. The men, after all, were clandestine members of the Blood Against Oppression, longtime friends of Roberto Flotman who used their jobs as a means of infiltrating the working class and ferreting out potential recruits for the organization.

"Then I suppose you wouldn't know if they've had any visitors lately," she asked.

"No, I'm afraid I wouldn't." The chauffeur nonchalantly let his left hand roam to the dashboard, where he pressed in the cigarette lighter. "Cigarette?" he asked, producing a pack from his shirt pocket.

"No, thank you," Emma told him. "But feel free."

"Thank you."

Louis lighted a cigarette, then put the lighter back. As he withdrew his hand from the dashboard, he let his fingers graze against the top of Emma's right hand, which rested on the gearshift knob. Emma smiled faintly but offered no further encouragement.

"You drive very well," Louis noted her as she guided the sports car along the narrow road.

"I try," Emma said absently without taking her eyes off the road.

"Drive well, fly your own plane, and you are very attractive as well," the man said. "No wonder Mr. Donlier is so fond of you."

"He's a good man."

"Yes, he's good." Louis suddenly reached over and placed his hand on Emma's right leg. "But I am better. Surely you haven't forgotten. . . ."

Emma made no effort to remove the man's hand, and she said nothing as she kept her eyes on the road. Up ahead was an intersection where a second road led away from the mansion toward the nearest thoroughfare. By the time they had reached the junction, Louis had begun gently kneading her flesh and letting his hand roam up underneath the hem of Emma's raised skirt.

Without warning, she suddenly slammed on the brakes and jerked hard on the steering wheel, sending the car into a tailspin. The centrifugal force pulled Louis's hand from Emma's leg and pinned him against the passenger's door. He closed his eyes, fearing the worst. Clouds of dust rose in the air around the vehicle as it nearly completed a spin, finally coming to a jarring halt in a field of tall wild grass just a few yards off the road.

Louis's heart was racing and he gasped for breath as he slowly opened his eyes, only to find himself staring down the stainless-steel bore of a Korth Combat Magnum.

"Get out," Emma demanded, flicking the saftey off on the handgun.

"Don't shoot!" the chauffeur pleaded as he fumbled for the door handle.

"Now!"

With some difficulty, the man stumbled out into the grass. Emma leaned over to close the door behind him. "Be grateful I'm not in a bad mood, or you'd have a hole where your forehead is. Now get out of my sight. You can walk back to the mansion on your own."

Louis staggered a few steps away from the car, still in a state of shock.

"And you'd do well to forget this happened," Emma advised. She didn't bother waiting for his reply. Slamming the door, she revved the Alfa-Romeo and sped back onto the road, showering the chauffuer with dislodged gravel and stones.

Backtracking a few hundred yards, she detoured off the road, following a set of parallel ruts into the field toward where she'd seen the laborers earlier. As she drew closer, she recognized Zeita Hu-Perzar, one of the BAO recruiters. He recognized her as well and excused himself from the others, striding over to speak with her. They wasted little time on hellos.

"Has Ali-Jahn been here since yesterday?" Emma asked.

Zeita shook his head. He was in his mid-thirties, a lean-faced man with dark eyes and a thin, meticulously groomed mustache. "No. I assumed he was down on the coast. You heard about everything that happened last night, didn't you?"

"Of course. Listen. If he does show up, have him stay here until I get back."

"And if he doesn't?" Zeita asked.

"Talk with the others," Emma said. "One way or another, I'll need you all tonight. Be ready."

"Are these Ali-Jahn's orders?"

Emma shook her head. "I'm asking you this favor. Of course, you must realize that if anyone has been captured and forced into talking, you won't be safe here for long, so it's best you leave soon anyway. I'm offering you an opportunity to make the most of the situation."

"Fine," Zeita said. "I'll speak to the others. We will be ready."

"I knew I could count on you, Zeita."

The man grinned, then turned and rejoined the other laborers. Emma backed the car onto the road.

She continued on until the road linked up with the autoroute. From there it was only a short drive to the Wintze Inn. As she drove she turned the radio on, listening to a classical radio station playing Mozart's *March in D*. The melodic strains helped to soothe her temper somewhat, but the respite was short-lived, as the selection ended soon after, giving way to the news and a report out of Nice that members of the Blood Against Oppression had seized control of a small private plane containing several U.S. film celebrities. Emma thumped her hand on the steering wheel with frustration, assuming at first that Babdi was in charge of the hijacking. When the reporter went on to describe the participating terrorists as being of probable Iraqi descent, however, her hopes rallied.

Perhaps this trip wouldn't be in vain after all.

"VERY WELL," Eijai Wahldjun bartered, "a half hour, and not a second more."

The Iraqi set down the radio microphone and grinned at the ashen-faced pilot of the hostaged Dassault, who was tied to his seat in the jet's cockpit. A younger copilot was similarly bound in the seat next to him.

"You might live to see tomorrow yet, Yankee pigs," Wahldjun said with a sneer as he cautiously moved away from the plane's controls, making sure to avoid exposing himself to any unseen snipers who might be drawing bead on the plane's windshield.

The sneer remained plastered on the terrorist's face as he headed out of the cockpit. It was too soon for jubilation, but deep in his heart he felt that he was going to succeed. The negotiators had agreed to the trade he had proposed—the release of two hostages in exchange for captured BAO members Joihof Elaid and Vera Maris. He was particularly pleased to learn that Vera was still alive and would soon be at his side.

Ah, the gratitude she would express once she was alone with him! After all the sleepless nights he'd endured hearing her making love to Babdi in adjacent bedrooms, there would be great poetic justice in having won her over as his mistress, just as he most certainly was poised to seize control of the Blood Against Oppression from Babdi.

From the cockpit, Wahldjun swaggered into the passenger's cabin, where Ardi Corro had his M-14 trained on Dee Clark, Keith Stewker, Jackie Ranuel and T. A. Magrane. The third Iraqi, Ehki Kirv, was positioned in the rear of the plane, keeping a lookout for signs of anyone attempting to approach the jet. The four prisoners were bound to their seats with cables, while Ranuel's cameraman, Howie Brett, warily roamed the cabin, focusing his lens on the proceedings.

"What did they say?" Ranuel asked.

"A two-for-two exchange," Wahldjun told her casually as he pried open the jet's small refrigerator and helped himself to a chilled can of vegetable juice.

"Which two?" Dee Clark wanted to know. "The women, right?"

Wahldjun smiled at the movie star. "No."

"No?" Clark gasped. "But...but...you have to!"

"I am so sorry, but two beautiful women such as yourselves . . . It would be foolish for me to lose this chance to get to know you better."

"Let them go!" Stewker roared, straining at his binds. "You'll get your friends back no matter who you release. So be civilized, for God's sake, and let the women go!"

Wahldjun drained the juice in one long swallow, then crumpled the can in his fist and flung it at Stewker's face. The movie star grimaced as a jagged edge caught him just above his billion-dollar blue eyes.

"Maybe for God's sake I will keep them!" the Iraqi taunted.

"Stop it!" Clark screamed. "Stop it, stop it, stop it!"

"Oh, please," Jackie Ranuel told the other woman. "It's going to take more than your bad acting to get us out of this!"

"Shut up!" Clark turned to the reporter, livid with rage. "Just shut up!"

"Enough!" Wahldjun shouted. For emphasis, he aimed his gun at them, slowly shifting his aim from one to the other. "Both of you!"

"This is crazy." Magrane spoke up. "Look, you've made your point with the rest of the world and you've gotten your interview with Ms. Ranuel that'll be broadcast around the world. Why not just let us go and take the plane to Algiers or someplace like that? Or if you want a ransom, I'm sure I can talk to my backers and—"

"No!" Wahldjun turned to Kirv. "Gag them! All of them!"

Kirv began ripping pillowcases into long strips to use as gags.

Wahldjun turned to Howie Brett. "Are you filming all this?"

"No," Brett said apologetically. "I didn't know you wanted me to."

"Yes, absolutely!" Wahldjun said, aiming his weapon at the cameraman to reinforce his point.

Brett reluctantly turned his camera on the prisoners, who struggled futilely as Corro applied the makeshift gags. Wahldjun watched with amusement, revelling in the humiliation of his long-avowed enemy.

"This is wrong!" Clark wailed as Kirv prepared to gag her. "This is all so wrong! This can't be happening!"

"Oh, it most certainly is happening," Wahldjun assured the woman. "And we have a few more surprises in store for you as well."

Once all four prisoners were gagged, Wahldjun motioned for Corro to move away from them. Brett stopped the camera.

"No," the terrorist told him. "Keep filming!"

Wahldjun motioned for Kirv to train his M-14 on Brett, forcing the cameraman to keep his film rolling as the Iraqi leader sauntered over to the seats where the two women were bound. He smiled at Dee

Clark and reached forward, clutching the collar of her silk blouse.

"You are a big sex star in America, yes?" he asked. "You have millions of men and boys wanting to have sex with you. But they can't, can they? No, because you are, how do you say it...inaccessible."

Clark stared up at the terrorist with fear and loathing. She tried to say something, but her words were garbled by the fabric wedged inside her mouth. When the Iraqi gave her blouse a sharp, sudden tug, ripping off buttons, she let out a muffled scream.

"Very nice," Wahldjun told the woman, gazing at her black lace bra and the swell of her breasts. He glanced back at Brett. "They are very nice, yes?"

The cameraman took a deep breath and slowly lowered the camera, turning it off as he glanced away from Clark. "Please," he mumbled hoarsely. "I can't do this...."

"You can, and you will," Wahldjun commanded. He raised his gun and pointed it at Brett. "Raise the camera and turn it back on."

Brett took a deep breath, then reluctantly propped the camera on his shoulder. When he turned the camera on, Wahldjun lowered his gun and turned his attention back to Clark, who was now sobbing hysterically. Wahldjun reached down, roughly unfastening the clasps of the woman's bra. The lace fell away, baring her breasts to the camera.

"Here you are, America!" Wahldjun gloated as he dragged his fingers across Clark's chest. "Here is your sweetheart, just the way you've always wanted to see her!"

Clark was almost choking in her hysteria. Keith Stewker raged futilely in the chair next to her, trying to get at Wahldjun. Jackie Ranuel and T. A. Magrane, meanwhile, sat still, watching with frozen horror.

Howie Brett suddenly jerked to one side, flinging his camera off his shoulder. He struck Ardi Corro in the head, knocking the young man unconscious. Brett grabbed the fallen M-14 and dived for cover behind a service cart. Before he could position himself to fire, however, Wahldjun was on him. The leader fired twice, with both shots slamming into the side of the cameraman's head. He died instantly and slumped to the floor. The terrorist whirled and glared at the other prisoners.

"Does anyone else want to die?" he roared. "Maybe I should kill you all right now!"

CHAPTER EIGHTEEN

It had been more than four months since unruly tides had fed the inland reservoir next to the international airport in Nice. The water level was down and white bands of salt ringed the exposed embankments. Some wildlife had taken hold over the years, and as Mack Bolan led John Kissinger toward the water's edge, a flock of small, bright-feathered herons suddenly rose up out of the marsh grass, taking to the air in a mad fluttering of wings. Bolan had reflexively reached for his Beretta, but he released his grip on the weapon as the birds fell into a loose formation as they flew out over the Mediterranean. Beside him, Kissinger and Grimaldi likewise relaxed their guard.

"Always nice to get that little extra boost of adrenaline before show time," Kissinger wise-cracked.

"Yeah, isn't it though," Grimaldi said.

Although airport authorities had shut down the two runways closest to the hangar where the BAO was holding its hostages, flights were still arriving and departing. The men fell silent as a hulking

Boeing 757 thundered overhead, sunlight gleaming off its silverish fuselage.

A vent pipe rising from the foliage twenty yards away marked the spot where the airport sewers fed into the reservoir. The men quickly approached the landmark, plodding through thick grass and tall weeds, then cautiously made their way down the pitched slope of the embankment to the water's edge. They had already stripped down to slacks and lightweight shirts, and once they'd taken off their shoes, they each placed them and their handguns into individual waterproof backpacks already bulging with gas masks, walkie-talkies, flashlights, canisters of tear gas, stun grenades and Kevlar bulletproof vests. Once the packs were resealed and strapped on, the men waded into the briny water.

"Okay, let's do it," Bolan said.

Drawing in a deep breath, the Executioner took another long stride, then dived headlong. The salt water was cold, raising hackles of gooseflesh and stinging the warrior's eyes as he swam downward, following the contoured slope of the embankment. Visibility was poor, but he was able to make out schools of small fish fleeing before him, and, moments later, he reached the barred grillwork covering the dark mouths of two large sewer pipes.

Bolan had secured a key from airport maintenance, and as soon as he reached the closest opening, he quickly sought out the rusting, algae-covered lock. His lungs were starting to burn for want of oxygen. Through the grillwork, he could see the pipe angle sharply upward, leading to much-needed fresh air. So close, yet so far.

The key slid in with difficulty, and when the Executioner tried to turn it, the tumblers resisted. He torqued the key back and forth, trying to pull it free so he could try the other lock. It was no use, though. The key was jammed.

Kissinger caught up with Bolan and quickly realized the problem. He too was running out of air, but rather than lose precious time retreating to the surface, he, like Bolan, was determined to gut it out. Spying an old pipe lying just inside the grating, Kissinger quickly eased it out between the bars, then used it to tap at the lock while Bolan continued to wrestle with the key. The Executioner was beginning to feel light-headed, and the ache in his lungs was almost unbearable, but he tuned it all out, keeping his focus on the key and the lock.

Finally the key turned.

Kissinger had already secured a grip on the bars, and the moment the lock gave way, he tugged with all his might. Bolan quickly joined in, and the grille swung open just wide enough on its encrusted hinges to let them squeeze through.

Expelling spent air through their mouths, the men broke to the surface and gasped refilling their lungs. The air inside the darkened sewers was foul and stagnant, but they breathed it in as if they were atop a mountain on a crisp, clear day.

"Next time, I say we bring along some scuba gear," Kissinger suggested between breaths as he pulled himself up out of the water.

"Let's hope there isn't a next time."

The men had to scale nearly another twenty feet of pitched pipeline before the sewer leveled off. There they paused to catch their breath and don the accessories in their backpacks.

"Ready?" Bolan asked, standing up after tying his shoes.

"As I'll ever be." Kissinger clicked on his flashlight, cutting a bright swath of light through the darkened tunnel.

The men advanced quietly, with the curved walls echoing the faintest scuffing of their soles against the concrete. They covered almost a hundred yards before coming across the first perpendicular shaft leading up to one of the airfield drains. Sunlight filtered down through the grate, creating patterns on the tunnel floor. The men noted that there were ladder rungs anchored into the shaft, allowing access to the surface.

Bolan unfolded a diagram mapping the paths of the various sewer lines. Kissinger shone the flashlight on the paper as they both looked on.

"Okay, we're right here," Bolan said. "Another thirty yards or so, then we'll split up. I'll take this south drain and you take the north."

"Got it."

The men resumed their trek, rounding a curve in the sewer and coming upon the next shaft. Bolan stayed put while Kissinger moved on. As he watched Cowboy head out of view, the Executioner pulled out his walkie-talkie and patched through to Hal Brognola, who was still stationed at the mechanic's garage at the far end of the airfield.

"We're almost in position," Bolan reported. "How are things going up there?"

"Cutting it close. Something's holding up the prisoners, and we're running out of time."

Bolan checked his watch. Brognola was right. Only seventeen minutes remained until the revised deadline set by the terrorists in the Dassault.

"Have you tried to stall them?" Bolan asked.

"Negative. We don't want to risk arousing suspicions.

"Good point," Bolan conceded.

"Grimaldi's got the chopper fixed. I'm going up with him once he's refueled."

"They're going to spot you from the jet."

"Not if we do it right," the big Fed replied. "We've figured out as long as they stay in the plane, there's enough of a blind spot that we might be able to circle around and close in from behind."

"Sounds pretty tricky."

"If anybody can do it, though, it'll be Jack."

"Right," Bolan said. "Listen, I hate to change the subject, but what's happening on the Hanover front? It doesn't look like we're going to be heading up there in the immediate future."

"It's being taken care of," Brognola informed the Executioner. "I got through to Phoenix Force and had them change their itinerary. They'll rendezvous with some of Mead's men in Hanover, then move in on the BAO cell."

"Okay. You and Jack keep us posted. We'll be ready on our end."

"I never had any doubts, Striker."

Bolan signed off, then reached up and grabbed the lowest rung inside the drain shaft. He pulled himself up, hand over hand, until his feet were in position on the ladder. He was now less than two feet from the tarmac, and through the grillwork of the drain he could make out the tail assembly of the Dassault. He withdrew a wrench from his backpack and adjusted it to fit one of the hexagonal nuts securing the drain in position. Thankfully the nut wasn't rusted in place, and he was able to unscrew it with some effort. He moved on to the next one, pausing to take another glance at his watch.

The numbers were running down.

"FIFTEEN MINUTES!" Wahldjun advised his prisoners. "Fifteen minutes and another one of you dies!"

The four captives eyed the terrorist with uncertain fear. They were still restrained to their chairs, still gagged so they couldn't respond verbally. Dee Clark sat hunched over in her chair, trying in vain to cover her bared chest from the Iraqi's lascivious gaze. He'd made no further advances toward her, but the woman feared that any moment he might resume where he'd left off before Howie Brett's attempted intervention. The cameraman lay dead where Wahldjun had gunned him down, a reminder of the price to be paid for resisting the terrorists. After regaining consciousness, Ardi Corro had been dispatched to the cockpit to stand watch over the runway, and his other counterpart was doing the same from a position at the rear of the plane.

The Iraqi picked up the fallen video camera and tested it. The recording light flashed on, and he could hear tape advancing across the heads. His stern gaze gave way to a look of bemusement as he propped the camera on the serving tray, aiming it at the hostages. He moved in front of the camera, crowding the aisle between his prisoners.

"This is another message for the Great Satan," he began, expanding on the remarks he'd made earlier while speaking with Jackie Ranuel. "Let it be known that when blood is shed for our cause, that blood should be on the conscience of our oppressors, who have forced us to use violence as the only means of being truly heard.

"For centuries the Western nations have treated us as chattel, exploiting us for their own material gains, breaking our spirit, turning a deaf ear to our pleas for justice. This cannot be tolerated, and it will not be tolerated.

"These past few days you have seen the power and the resolve of the Blood Against Oppression. And yet this is, as you might call it, only the tip of the iceberg. We call on all our brothers, not only those sworn to Islam but those of all continents, to rise up and join us in spilling a cleansing blood across the land, a blood that—"

T. A. Magrane tried to speak around his gag in an effort to drown out Wahldjun's commentary.

The Iraqi fell silent a moment, turning to glare at the producer. Then, smiling back at the camera, he resumed. "Behold how futile protest will be against the righteousness of our cause."

Taking a step back, Wahldjun secured his grip on an M-14, then suddenly swung the weapon, striking Magrane's face with the thick stock. The producer's head snapped to one side from the force of the blow, then sagged at an unnatural angle as the man lost consciousness. A crimson trail of blood seeped out of the corner of his mouth, spilling down onto the white silk of his coat.

Wahldjun turned back to the camera and shut it off, then told the prisoners calmly, "Twelve minutes..."

CHAPTER NINETEEN

Emma Skodynov parked the Alfa-Romeo in front of the Wintze Inn and started up the main walk. Her revealing dress and the voluptuousness of her stride drew stares from a couple heading down the front steps. The young man behind the registration desk did a double take as she walked into the reception area. Emma knew from experience that her brazen sexuality put her in command of most situations, and it was second nature for her to parade herself in such a manner.

The clerk, in his twenties, smiled sheepishly as Emma approached him. He stammered slightly as he asked her if she wanted to rent a room.

"No, I'm afraid not," she told him in French. "I was supposed to meet a friend here. Perhaps you could tell me if he's been here yet." She proceeded to give a description of Ali-Jahn Babdi.

"I don't believe so," the clerk told her. "But if you could give me his name, I can check the register to see if he's taken a room."

That wouldn't be necessary. Emma had already glanced at the open book on the counter, and the name of Josef Hardolph all but leaped out at her. She noted the room he was staying in and smiled with barely suppressed satisfaction.

"Oh, I'm sorry," she told the clerk, "but he's not staying here. We were just going to meet for lunch."

"Oh, I see."

"Could you possibly do me a favor?" Emma asked.

"I'd be happy to."

"I have a brief errand to run down the road a ways. If my friend should happen to stop by, could you tell him to wait here for me? His name is Wade."

"Wade." The clerk frowned, never having heard such a name before. "Very well."

"Thank you so much," Emma told him, widening her smile and winking at the young man. "I do appreciate it."

"My pleasure," he assured her. She knew he meant it.

Emma left the inn and returned to the parking lot. Rather than getting into her car, however, she wandered idly to the far end of the lot, which led to a large flower garden. Fresh blossoms filled the air with their fragrance and bright colors, but Emma paid little attention to either. Following a circuitous flagstone path, she hurried through the garden, then circled behind the inn to the boiler room. Even through the stone walls she could hear the laboring of the inn's ancient heater, and she was grateful for the noise. It would make her next move that much easier to execute.

There was an old rain barrel propped against the wall to collect runoff from a downspout trailing from the eaves. Emma judged it to be less than a quarter filled. Once she was sure no one was looking, she rocked the barrel loose, turning it over and jockeying it several yards to her right until it was situated directly beneath a second-story balcony. When she subsequently climbed on top of the barrel, she had only to reach up to secure a grip on the lower railings.

Emma's athletic prowess extended beyond the bedroom, and with agility she hoisted herself off the barrel, pushing off the outer wall of the boiler room to give herself enough momentum to swing up to the balcony. She straddled the railing briefly, then stepped down onto the wooden slats of the balcony itself, taking care all the while to remain clear of the doorway leading out from the bedroom.

Emma had left her bulky Magnum under the front seat of the Alfa-Romeo, but as she paused to catch her breath, she unzipped her jacket and pulled out her backup firearm, a palm-sized Bogsley four-shot, one of the world's smallest automatic handguns. It was a toyish-looking weapon, but at close range its .22 slugs could be lethal. Releasing the safety, she inched toward the doorway and hazarded a glance through the lace curtains. Inside, Ali-Jahn Babdi lay in a still heap on the double bed, half-covered by a linen sheet and a down comforter.

"I knew I could count on you," Emma whispered to herself as she closed her fingers on the doorknob. Not surprisingly, she found it locked. From her previous trip she knew the kind of lock, and she'd come prepared. Taking a customized locksmith's shiv from her jacket, she quietly tampered with the lock until it yielded with a dull knock.

Emma slowly opened the door inward, spilling her shadow across the oak-panel floor. She had her Bogsley held out before her, and at the first sign of motion from Babdi, she leaped forward onto the bed, pressing the gun's barrel against the Turk's left temple.

"Put both your hands out at your sides," she whispered harshly in Arabic as she straddled Babdi's back. "And do it slowly."

Babdi hesitated a moment, then carefully brought his hands out into the open, leaving his own gun under his pillow.

"What do you want from me?" he asked, starting to turn his head for a better look at his attacker. Almost immediately, he felt the tip of Emma's gun dig farther into his flesh.

"Keep your head still and close your eyes!" the woman demanded. Leaning forward, she reached under the man's pillow with her other hand and grabbed Babdi's larger automatic. She pulled it out so the Turk could see it, then flung it across the room onto an overstuffed chair.

"You didn't answer me," Babdi told the woman. His voice was calm, guarded. "What do you want from me?"

"You'll find out soon enough."

Keeping her Bogsley pressed to Babdi's skull, Emma reached for her blouse, tearing it open at the collar so that several buttons popped free. She wasn't wearing a bra, and as she slowly leaned forward again, her nipples brushed against the hairy flesh of Babdi's shoulders. As he stirred at the touch, she drew her lips to his ear and flicked her tongue out, making playful stabs at the inner canal.

"I want you, Josef Hardolph," Emma purred, "you big Teutonic stud."

Babdi began to laugh as he let his hands drift behind him, clasping the underside of Emma's thighs. "Then take me, you heathen slut. . . ."

"MY GRATE'S FREE," Bolan whispered into his walkie-talkie.

"Same here," Kissinger reported back from his position on the other side of the plane. "And I've caught a few glimpses of someone peering out the rear window."

"I've seen him on my side, too." Glancing up through the grating, Bolan eyed the last of the five portals on the fuselage of the Dassault. It was the only one whose shade wasn't pulled, and moments later he could see a face framed in the opening, peering out at the surrounding runways. "There he is again."

"Think we could take him out?" Kissinger wondered.

"I'm not sure."

"We might not have a choice."

"I know," Bolan said grimly.

Bolan wasn't concerned about his aim. He was less than twenty-five yards from the rear of the jet, and once he had the grate off, he didn't figure he'd have any trouble fixing the terrorist in his sights. But even though the windows of the jet weren't bulletproof, the warrior knew their density was such that any shot coming from his Beretta was apt to be deflected enough to leave the gunman alive and in a position to kill the hostages.

"Seven minutes," Bolan said. "Have you heard anything from Hal?"

"Negative."

"Well, if worse comes to worst and we have to go it alone, open fire and try to draw them to your side. I'll head for the staircase and hope I can get to the door before I'm noticed."

"That'd be suicide," Kissinger protested.

"I've taken longer shots."

There was a beat of silence, then Kissinger said, "Well, it looks like it might not come to that. Check out over the water."

Bolan shifted inside the cramped shaft, turning his attention away from the jet. Off in the distance, high above the Mediterranean, a small speck loomed closer, taking on the familiar outline of the Reed-279 helicopter. Grimaldi and Brognola were approaching on a course parallel with the fuselage of the Dassault. As long as the chopper remained high enough in the air and stayed on course, it was conceivable that Grimaldi could eventually position his aircraft directly above the jet without having been spotted. There was one obvious hitch, however.

"If the Iraqis step out onto the stairs, that chopper's going to stick out like a sore thumb," Bolan speculated. "Not to mention the fact that they're going to be seen by the prisoners we're exchanging."

"Well, I don't think Vera's going to tip them off," Kissinger said, "and from what Dauffie says, the other guy's going to play along, too."

"Let's hope so," Bolan said. "If either of them double-cross us, we're going to have a massacre on our hands."

Again there was a moment's silence, followed by an ominous update from Kissinger.

"Five minutes."

THERE WERE additional variables Jack Grimaldi had to keep in mind as he jockeyed the Reed-279 through ragged pockets of clouds in the air above the runways. The sound of the engines was the lesser concern, since he was confident that he was flying high enough that the chopper's whine would be lost in the drone of larger aircraft using the other runways. What posed the bigger headache was constantly monitoring his position relative to the sun to make sure he didn't betray his position by casting the Reed's shadow somewhere in range of the terrorists' vision. The high altitude helped somewhat, obscuring the shadow and at times losing it in the clouds. And, of course, while engaging in this aerial hide-and-seek, Grimaldi also had to make sure he didn't wander into the flight paths of arriving or departing jets.

It was just the sort of challenge a veteran fly-boy thrived on.

From the pilot's seat, Grimaldi deftly worked the controls, all the while monitoring ground reports over his radio. Brognola sat quietly beside him, cradling an M-16 in his lap. A Stealthshooter pistol was nestled in his shoulder holster.

"Think it's going to be hard to sit back behind a desk after all this excitement, Hal?" Grimaldi asked, smiling.

"We'll see," Brognola said noncommitally. Physically he hadn't felt this pumped up in ages, but he knew that his days of putting it on the line in the field on a day-to-day basis were long gone. His skills at this point in his life were better suited to pulling strings in the international arena and managing the affairs of the Stony Man operation. However, on occasion he'd have to go to the front line, and this was one of those times.

From their airborne perspective, the men had the best overview of the unfolding drama taking place below. As the clock continued to wind down, Brognola and Grimaldi saw the various pieces being maneuvered into position for what nearly everyone involved assumed was going to be an inevitable confrontation with the terrorists in the grounded airplane.

With binoculars, Brognola could see the drainage grates on either side of the jet, but he couldn't make out Grimaldi or Bolan crouched beneath the grillwork. As well, he had no way of seeing what was going on inside the plane. Conversely there was plenty of visible action taking place beyond the two-hundred-yard area of clearance that had been demanded by the BAO. Military troops were scrambling in all directions across the tarmac, both on foot and in jeeps, establishing a wide perimeter around the remote hangar. In all, Brognola guessed there were close to fifty men involved, all of them well armed and ready to move in at a moment's notice. If not for the hostages, there were any number of ways the jet could be stormed. For that matter, the howitzers mounted on the backs of several of the jeeps could have easily destroyed the Dassault from a distance. But, again, such action wouldn't be ordered except in a situation where it became clear that the terrorists had already executed their prisoners.

Still more troops were being used to maintain order around the main terminal, where word of the hostage situation had leaked, aggravating the already-chaotic state of panic. There was particular concern with maintaining an open roadway all the way from the access road to the garage serving as the makeshift command post for the members of the task force trying to contend with the crisis.

As he continued to stare down at the pandemonium, Brognola's attention was suddenly drawn to a set of flashing lights just inside the main entrance to the airport. A closer look revealed a caravan of two police cars flanked by eight uniformed officers on motorcycles. The big Fed was sure that one of the cars had to contain the BAO members that were supposed to be exchanged for hostages aboard the jet. He grabbed for the radio microphone. As he was patching through to Mead and Dauffie on the ground below, Grimaldi glanced at him.

"The bait's on the way?"

"I want to find out for sure, but yes, I think so. And not a moment too soon."

As Brognola confirmed his findings with the ground crew, Grimaldi checked the console clock.

One minute to deadline.

As WILHELM MEAD hurriedly contacted the grounded Dassault to announce the arrival of the BAO prisoners and negotiate the terms for an exchange, Ed Dauffie sought out his daughter. Vera was in the second of the police cruisers, where she'd been briefed en route to the airport by a French army colonel specializing in hostage situations. The second prisoner, Joihof Elaid, had come in the other car and received his briefing from another officer.

Dauffie spotted Vera the moment she stepped out of the cruiser. He weaved his way through the motorcycle escort to her side, his face revealing his conflicting emotions. In the short time since he'd first stumbled upon her back at Thomas Galton's villa, Dauffie's mind had been in a whirlwind as he'd tried to come to terms with their failed relationship and find the right words that might invoke a true reconciliation. It would have been a difficult, if not impossible, task under normal circumstances. To attempt such an undertaking in the midst of this emotional maelstrom seemed even more futile. Gazing down at her, recognizing his own features in her face, he yearned to call this emergency off and to whisk Vera away to some private, quiet place where they could build upon those few moments of kinship they'd shared at the villa. He wanted to yell to the others that this was the child he'd seen brought into this world, the innocent babe he'd bounced on his knee and amused with googly sounds a seeming lifetime ago, the pigtailed schoolgirl he'd promised on countless occasions to protect from harm and suffering. How could it be that he was now about to send her back into the clutches of a man who had no more concern for her well-being than he would for that of a mosquito nagging him on a hot summer's day?

There was so much Dauffie wanted to do, wanted to say, but standing there before her at the moment of truth, all eloquence escaped him and it was all he could do to mutter a single choked syllable.

"Hi," he told her.

"Hi," she replied, her voice equally strained.

Vera tried to show her father a look of calm determination, but Dauffie could see the fear in her eyes, and an instinctual parental concern roused him from his speechlessness.

"Are you sure you want to go through with this?" he told her. "You don't have to, you know. I can—"

"No," she interrupted. "I want to do this. I need to."

The others were watching, waiting. Dauffie drew a deep breath, reining in his emotions. He took a final step forward and embraced his daughter. She clung to him, closing her eyes as she kissed his stubbly chin and whispered softly in his ear.

"I love you, Dad. I'm sorry about all this."

"Hush," he told her. A cold chill ran through him as he felt the outline of the stun grenades and tear gas canisters secreted inside the bulky folds of the oversize combat fatigues she'd been dressed in. As they pulled away, he swallowed hard, forcing a smile. "It kills me to see you do this, but I'm proud of you. I love you, too, Vera."

She returned the smile. "Let's try to keep it that way, okay?"

"Absolutely."

Wilhelm Mead appeared in the background. The colonel who had briefed Vera in the car led her away, along with the other prisoner. Dauffie battled a fleeting but overwhelming sense of emptiness, then strode uneasily away from the motorcycle contingent until he reached Hal Brognola's side.

"Tough day for you," the big Fed said.

Dauffie nodded, then asked, "Mead cleared the exchange?"

"Yeah. They've decided to release the two women instead of the producer and cameraman. Humanitarian gesture, they called it."

"And you believe them?"

"I think they're playing up to the media," Brognola speculated. "I wouldn't bank on them having much in the way of a conscience."

"No, I guess not," Dauffie murmured, glancing over at his daughter, who was getting her final instructions from the colonel. He wondered if he'd ever see her alive again.

CHAPTER TWENTY

The cabin door of the Dassault Mystère slowly opened. Their gags still in place, Jackie Ranuel and Dee Clark stepped timidly out onto the mobile staircase. To cover her torn blouse, Clark was wearing the *faux* silk warm-up jacket taken off the body of Howie Brett. Both women's ankles bore welts from where they'd been tied to their chairs. Their years of petty feuding were behind them, bonded as they were by the traumatic ordeal they were still very much a part of. As they began to head down the steps, trembling with each step, both were wary that at any moment the door behind them would swing open and they would hear Eijai Wahldjun or one of his men step out with an M-14 and shoot them in the back. As they neared the bottom steps and had to negotiate their way around the twisted bodies of the slain bodyguards, tears rolled unchecked down Clark's mascara-streaked face and she began to sob uncontrollably.

Ranuel retained more composure. When she happened to spot the glimmer of a gun stock just inside the pocket of one of the bodyguards, she fleetingly considered snatching it up and backtracking to the plane to single-handedly subdue the BAO and free the other hostages. She quickly discounted the thought as a foolish whimsy and turned her focus to more practical ways of dealing with the situation. Ever the professional, the woman hadn't lost sight of her cameraman's first words after their apprehension, and in her mind she began rehearsing how she would conduct herself once she was in the media spotlight and in a position to impart her heralded first-person account of being held prisoner by the Blood Against Oppression. It had all the makings of a bestselling novel, and she would be certain to retain theatrical rights, too, so that she could reap an even bigger fortune having the book turned into a movie or TV miniseries.

Once on the runway, the women had been told to walk slowly in the direction of the distant mechanic's garage, and as they set out, both of them felt foolish and awkward covering the distance in their high heels, which pounded loudly on the runway. Ranuel was the first to kick her shoes off, and Clark quickly followed suit. The asphalt was warm to their feet, but the midday sun wasn't hot enough to make the walk unbearable.

After walking a dozen yards, the women saw two other figures making a similar trek toward them. As they drew closer, the foursome exchanged wary glances and Ranuel determined that one of the prisoners being exchanged was a young woman wearing oversize fatigues. The four people remained silent, although Clark ceased her weeping long enough to fix Vera Maris and Joihof Elaid with a look of unbridled hatred.

Then they passed one another, and the hostages turned their attention to the mechanic's garage, looming ahead. During their years in the celebrity limelight, both Clark and Ranuel had toured the globe, visiting the architectural wonders of the world, but at this particular moment neither of them could recall seeing such a wondrous sight as that ramshackle brick building and the swarm of men milling around it. It was all they could do to remember their orders and continue to walk slowly rather than break into a full run to hasten their arrival to that coveted safe haven.

DEE CLARK and Jackie Ranuel had walked within nine yards of Mack Bolan at one point during their march to freedom, but he'd ducked inside the drain shaft, hiding himself in the shadows so as to not draw their attention. For a few moments he was able to detect them by the sound of their shoes on the runway, but once the women went barefoot, he lost track of them, even when he eased his way back up to the grating. Glancing up at the rear portal of the Dassault, Bolan saw the same terrorist he'd seen earlier, peering out, not toward the grate but in the direction the women had headed. From the man's expression, Bolan had no way of judging the progress of the prisoner exchange. With the door to the jet open, he couldn't risk using the walkie-talkie and being overheard, either.

All he could do was wait.

And hope.

The seconds dragged by inexorably. Bolan began to sweat in the confined quarters of the shaft. He pushed gently upward against the grate to reassure himself that it was fully loose and ready to be flung aside at a moment's notice. He ran his hands over his gear, double-checking to make sure everything was within easy access.

Staring up through the cloud cover, he was barely able to spot the silhouetted outline of the Reed-279. It seemed to Bolan that Grimaldi was too far up to be able to bring the chopper into play once the doomsday numbers fell to zero.

Suddenly the air above Bolan came alive with a thunderous roar. Even as he was glancing back up through the grillwork, Bolan knew what had happened. The Mystère's turbofans had been activated.

The terrorists were going to try to make a run for it.

The Executioner dropped down two rungs on the shaft ladder and keyed his walkie-talkie. There was no way anyone was going to overhear him above the rumbling of the jet.

"What's it look like on your side?" Bolan asked Kissinger.

There was a moment's hesitation, then Bolan was barely able to pick up Kissinger's reply through the noise being generated overhead. "The prisoners are almost to the staircase. My guess is they're going to hightail it out of here and negotiate for the men's release later."

"Or they're going to kill them."

"Yeah, that might be the case."

"How long before they can take off?"

"I don't know," Kissinger confessed. "But I'm sure the engines have to be warmed up. And they have to back away from the staircase, too."

"Listen," Bolan said. "Keep your transmission going and I'll do the same. Once the prisoners are inside the plane, give the girl thirty seconds to make her move, then start firing. As soon as I hear you, I'm out of here."

"Got it."

Bolan raided his pack for a gas mask and slipped it on. He regretted the awkwardness of the apparatus and the way it cramped his senses, but if he was to make it inside the jet alive and encounter a discharged cloud of tear gas, he knew he'd be grateful for the protection.

Once he was sure the mask was on tightly, the Executioner set the walkie-talkie on a small ledge just beneath the grating. He wasn't going to be needing it once he climbed up out of the shaft.

What he was going to need was luck, and plenty of it.

"WHAT DID THEY TELL YOU back in the car?" Joihof Elaid asked Vera Maris in a hushed whisper as they walked toward the jet at the far end of the runway.

"Nothing," Vera said. She didn't trust the Iraqi and wasn't about to divulge what the colonel had told her during the ride to the airport.

"You can tell me," Joihof assured her. "We are still on the same side, only now we want to stop Eijai, not aid him, yes?"

"I told you they said nothing!" Vera snapped. "Now leave me alone!"

"They asked you to stop Eijai and the others somehow, yes?" Joihof persisted. "Did they give you any weapons?"

Vera refused to be baited into answering. She walked with her gaze fixed on the jet ahead of them, struggling to put her troubled mind at ease. Her final exchange with her father had been an unsettling one, and her subsequent encounter with the released hostages had tormented her even further. She had felt the hatred and the look of accusation in the other two women's gazes, and she was filled anew with a sense of shame for the wrong turn she'd taken with her life and the dire consequences it had exacted. She knew deep in her heart that there would be no way to reverse the wrongs she'd done. Too many had died, and the fact that none of those deaths had come at her hands did little to salve her guilt. If she was successful in the mission laid out for her, she might achieve retribution on behalf of the dead and save a few lives that might have otherwise been lost down the line, but there was nothing she could do to bring back those who had been cut down by the Blood Against Oppression since she'd aligned herself with them.

They were within fifty yards of the jet, and Joihof was still attempting to insinuate himself into Vera's confidence when they suddenly heard the Dassault turbofans engage. Vera was taken aback. Her understanding had been that the initial prisoner exchange was going to be followed by further negotiations for the release of the other hostages. The colonel had told her that all indications were that Eijai Wahldjun would be asking for monetary ransom as well as guaranteed passage from Nice. But apparently Wahldjun had other plans, which made it even more urgent that Vera succeed in her mission.

She had been told by the colonel that she would have immediate backup once she entered the jet, and it was all she could do to keep herself from glancing up at the helicopter she could barely hear above the drone of the Dassault. As they drew closer to the staircase, she turned her head to one side, feigning a cough as she shot an urgent glance toward the nearest storm drain. Just as the colonel had promised, there was someone lurking beneath the grillwork, and for a moment she thought she'd seen a pair of eyes peering up at her through the bars. It was a reassuring sight, helping her to bolster her courage as she moved ahead of Joihof and stepped around the slain bodyguards littering the base of the mobile staircase.

Vera's heart raced as she ascended the steps, and she clutched the railing to steady herself. Joihof was directly behind her. Up ahead, the open cabin door yawned like the jaws of a great white beast, waiting to swallow her into its cavernous bosom. Then, as she neared the top steps, she saw someone standing just out of view, clutching an assault rifle. It was Ardi Corro, the youngest of the terrorists. Vera would have to negotiate her way past him, then quickly size up the situation inside the main cabin before carrying out the plan. It sounded so simple, but Vera was nearly incapacitated in her fear. Her pulse hammered madly and her throat constricted, making it difficult for her to breathe. For a moment it felt as if she were going to faint dead away and topple backward into Joihof Elaid.

Somehow she managed to scale those last few steps. She looked past the weapon in Corro's hands and offered him what she hoped would pass for a grin of triumph and relief.

"It's good to be free again."

Corro smiled shyly and took a step back, motioning for Vera to pass. Suddenly, however, Joihof bounded up the last few steps and grabbed for Vera as he shouted a warning.

"Search her!"

Vera panicked as she felt Joihof's fingers close around her arms, pinning them behind her.

"Search her!" Joihof beseeched Corro again. "She's a traitor!"

CHAPTER TWENTY-ONE

Grimaldi had brought the Reed-279 down a little lower after getting word from the ground that the engines had been started up on the hostaged jet. It was still important to keep their visibility to a minimum, however, so he had to hold back as soon as he saw the chopper's shadow threatening to slide down off the roof of the private hangar. Brognola, meanwhile, had his binoculars trained on Vera Maris and Joihof Elaid as they mounted the staircase leading up to the jet. He was the first to realize that something was going wrong.

"Bring us down!" he exhorted Grimaldi without taking his eyes off the binoculars. "Now."

"Done," Grimaldi responded, even as he was toggling his joystick to lower the copter.

Brognola watched helplessly as Joihof pinned Vera's arms behind her back and held her at the top of the steps while Corro stepped forward to frisk her. It was going to take a miracle to save the rescue operation from going haywire, and Brognola could only hope the copter could swing down into view in time to distract Joihof and Corro before they discovered the weaponry Vera had brought with her to the jet.

VERA MARIS'S MOTHER had died several years earlier, slain in the course of a purse-snatching by a street punk who'd panicked when the woman had resisted the theft. Vera had been there at the time and had watched with mute horror as the thug had lashed out with a switchblade, stabbing her mother through the heart. As a way of dealing with the emotional scars of so traumatic an experience, Vera had been taking self-defense courses and training regularly in the martial arts for most of the past five years. To date she'd never had cause to use the skills drilled into her during those countless sessions, but now was the moment of payoff.

The moment Joihof Elaid had placed his hands on her, Vera's mind cleared itself of all the clutter that had been assailing her, and she let her instincts take over. With forced calm, she waited for an opportune moment to launch her defense.

She didn't have long to wait.

Confused by Joihof's command to search her, Corro had approached Vera uncertainly, holding his M-14 angled downward. The young man reached out for her clumsily with his free hand, fumbling at the folds of her oversize fatigues.

It was then that all three of them heard a growing whine above the din of the turbofans. Corro was the first to glance up, his gaze drawn by the glint of sunlight off the Reed-279 helicopter banking downward at a precipitous angle. As the Iraqi's eyes widened with disbelief, Vera saw her chance.

Bringing her right knee swinging upward with all her might, Vera targeted Corro's groin and hit him squarely, doubling him over in tortured agony. He dropped his M-14 and Vera quickly kicked it through the railing of the staircase before focusing on the man behind her.

Elaid had been taken aback by the sudden fury of Vera's initial attack, and although he reacted by tightening his grip on her arms, he was outmatched by her frenetic release of pent-up rage. When she suddenly snapped her head backward, Elaid was caught off guard and stunned by the impact of the back of her skull against the bridge of his nose. He took a step back, loosening his grip on her.

Vera next feinted with her left arm, then jerked her right, again backward, breaking Elaid's hold and ramming her elbow sharply into the terrorist's rib cage. The wind knocked from his lungs, Elaid let go of Vera entirely and gasped frantically for air. The woman turned on him, grabbed his right arm, then leaned into him, using her shoulder as a fulcrum as she jerked him off-balance. Going with the momentum she had created, she flung the man not only over her shoulder, but also over the railing of the mobile staircase.

The terrorist screamed as he plummeted to the ground. The drop wasn't far enough to be fatal, but the man broke both arms and dislocated his shoulder, and his head glanced off the tarmac, rendering him briefly unconscious.

In all, it had taken less than ten seconds for Vera to turn her situation around.

But she knew that her work was far from finished. Springing away from the railing, she clawed inside her fatigues, pulling out both a stun grenade and a tear-gas canister. She activated both weapons as she charged the doorway of the jet, just as Ehki Kirv was charging out with his M-14 in firing position.

Vera might have had a chance to protect herself, but she chose to concentrate on lobbing the two projectiles past the gunman. In a way, the mere act of throwing worked to her advantage, as the movement distracted Kirv just as he was squeezing the trigger. What had been intended to be certain kill shots to Vera's chest instead struck low, ripping into her midsection. She staggered back at the impact, losing her footing on the steps. She struck her head against the railing and was ushered into the black void to the reverberating accompaniment of the stun grenade detonating inside the jet.

Eijai Wahldjun had posted himself inside the cockpit after giving orders for the Dassault's turbofans to be started. Hunched next to the pilot, he had peered out at Vera Maris and Joihof Elaid as they'd approached the mobile staircase after the prisoner exchange. He'd advised Dee Clark and Jackie Ranuel that there would be more killing if they told the authorities that the cameraman had already been killed, but he didn't trust them to keep silent, and rather than risk a siege on the plane, he'd changed his agenda, deciding that once Maris and Elaid were safely aboard, they would flee the airfield prematurely and seek the refuge of safer ground before negotiating for whatever concessions the BAO might secure for the release of the remaining prisoners.

But within moments after Maris and Elaid had climbed up and out of Wahldjun's view, the ringleader had been startled to hear sounds of a skirmish atop the mobile staircase. He was about to charge out of the cockpit when he heard the pattering of Kirv's assault rifle and saw both the stun grenade and tear-gas canister roll into the passenger cabin.

Quickly he flung himself back into the cockpit, just as the projectiles went off. The walls flanking the narrow doorway absorbed most of the concussive force directed toward the cockpit, but a shock wave still managed to send the Iraqi sprawling to the floor between the two pilots. He rammed his knee into a control lever and felt a sharp jab of pain race up his leg.

The copilot was still bound to his chair, but the senior pilot's limbs had been freed to allow him to work the controls. Wahldjun was shaken but still conscious, and he quickly kicked the door shut before the disseminating tear gas could waft into the pilots' compartment. Then, grimacing, he struggled to his feet.

"Get us out of here!" he shouted at the pilot.

The pilot stared at Wahldjun with disbelief. "But, that explosion . . . I need to know what kind of damage we sustained so—"

"Didn't you hear me?" The Iraqi yanked out his automatic and pressed it against the side of the copilot's head, then abruptly pulled the trigger. As the pilot watched with horror, the other man's head jerked sharply to one side and bloody gore splattered his side of the cockpit. Wahldjun swiveled, pointing the gun at the pilot's face. "I can kill you just as easily. Now do as I say!"

His hands shaking with fear, the pilot reached for the controls, trying not to turn and look at his murdered companion. Wahldjun, meanwhile, quickly rummaged through a storage cabinet behind the pilot's seat, finally tracking down a gas mask. He jerked it out and slipped it over his head. Once he'd adjusted the straps to ensure a snug fit, Wahldjun paused to track down a fresh ammo clip for his 9 mm automatic.

"All deals are off," he seethed. He meant it, too. Once he'd dealt with his betrayers, he was going to execute the rest of the prisoners.

THE FLOOD DRAIN'S grillwork creaked open on a pair of rusted hinges, and Bolan charged to the surface. On the other side of the jet, Kissinger was already in action, directing his fire at its tires. It was a less surefire tactic than when he'd similarly disabled the utilities van near Sainte Catherine's an hour earlier, but under the circumstances it seemed like the only viable option to keep the jet from getting out onto the runway. The gambit paid off, too, as the cumulative rounds of 9 mm parabellum eventually punctured all the tires. The jet had only managed to pull a few yards away from the mobile staircase, and as the wheels' rims bit into the asphalt, it was clear that the aircraft wasn't going to be going any farther.

"Nice work, Cowboy," Bolan murmured inside his gas mask as he rushed toward the staircase.

Joihof Elaid, dazed and in agony from his broken limbs, nonetheless managed to reach out and snatch the .44 Magnum pistol of one of the slain bodyguards. He grimaced as he propped the gun on the dead man's chest to steady his aim as he drew a bead on the Executioner. Before he could pull the trigger, however, Bolan spotted him and let loose with a quick 3-round burst from his Beretta. Elaid took two shots in the face and slumped lifelessly across the bodyguard as the Magnum clattered to the ground.

Bolan reached the steps and took them two at a time. Vera was lying still and bleeding, halfway up, but much as the warrior wanted to check on her condition, he knew there was no time for it. He charged past her and was about to fire at the man at the top of the staircase when he saw that the man was on his knees, hands clasped on top of his head in a gesture of surrender.

Overhead, the Reed-279 was closing in on the jet. As he reached the top platform of the staircase, Bolan glanced up and saw that Brognola was poised near the opened window of the chopper with an M-16. He quickly gestured for the big Fed to keep an eye on the terrorist, then turned his sights on the doorway to the jet, which was now a good three yards away and blanketed in tear gas.

There was only room enough for Bolan to take four steps before springing forward and flinging himself across the chasm. He arched his back, and the moment his feet made contact with the floor of the plane, he somersaulted forward, cushioning his landing. By the time he was back on his feet, Bolan was inside the passenger cabin.

Through the swirling haze, he quickly accessed the situation. The first thing he saw was the inert form of Howie Brett, and to his right T. A. Magrane and Keith Stewker were slouched over in the front seats, knocked out by the stun grenades. There didn't seem to be anyone else inside the passenger cabin.

Then, out of the corner of his eye, Bolan detected motion off to his left. He turned and saw a goggle-faced man standing in the cockpit doorway. The other man had the drop on Bolan, and before the Executioner could duck for cover, four rapid shots thumped into his chest, slamming him back against the serving cart. Silverware and a sterling water pitcher tumbled down on Bolan as he slumped limply to the floor.

Satisfied that he'd eliminated his most immediate threat, Wahldjun turned from Bolan and glanced out the doorway. Through the fog, he could see Corro kneeling atop the mobile staircase, hands cupped over his head, eyes turned heavenward as if pleading to God for mercy. Wahldjun calmly raised his automatic and pointed it out the doorway.

"This is the fate of cowards!" Wahldjun shouted as he pulled the trigger.

Corro twisted to one side as the gunfire tore into him. As the life fled from his eyes, he managed to glance across the clearing to see Wahldjun standing inside the doorway, enveloped in a swirling mist and wearing a gas mask that made him look like some inhuman avenger.

Wahldjun watched Ardi pitch forward, toppling over the edge of the staircase and out of view. In the distance, the Turk could see a handful of jeeps speeding across the runway. He smiled mirthlessly inside his mask.

"You'll never get to me in time." He returned inside the cabin and calmly aimed his automatic at Keith Stewker.

THE REED-279 WAS within fifteen yards of the jet's roof when Brognola saw Ardi Corro gunned down.

The implications were almost too grim to contemplate. For someone to have been in a position to execute the terrorist, he would have had to get past Bolan, and Brognola knew that the only way the Executioner would have allowed such treachery was over his dead body.

"Put it down on the roof, Jack," he told Grimaldi.

"What are you going to do?"

"I'm going in there," the big Fed replied, jerking the Reed's door open and slinging his M-16 over his shoulder so he could have both hands free. He unslung a gas mask from a hook above the doorway beside him and pulled it on.

With a finesse that could only be the mark of an ace pilot, Grimaldi gently hovered downward, guiding the chopper so that its landing gear straddled the roof of the Dassault Mystère. He held back from setting down completely, however, not wanting to tip off his presence by weighing down the jet any more than necessary. He knew that Brognola was endangering both their lives, but under the circumstances, he couldn't blame him. If he wasn't at the controls, he was sure he'd be out of the chopper the first chance he got, too.

The howl of the Reed's turbines was deafening in Brognola's ears as he eased out onto the steps leading down from the chopper door. The rotor wash beat down on him forcefully, too, as he carefully shifted position so that his back was facing outward. As he glanced over his shoulder and looked down, he saw Kissinger, also wearing a gas mask, storming up the mobile staircase.

Kissinger halted a few steps from the top of the staircase and carefully peered over the cover as he clutched his 15-round Stealthshooter. He couldn't see anything through the gaseous cloud billowing out of the jet's doorway, so he warily signaled an all-clear to Brognola.

The big Fed stepped down to the rooftop of the jet just above the doorway, then drew in a deep breath and secured a firm handhold before swinging down and in through the opening. He landed hard and slightly off-balance but let his momentum carry him into the plane, where he heard a single gunshot suddenly explode from inside the cabin. He reflexively braced himself, sure the shot had been directed at him.

As he waited for that surge of pain, he suddenly saw Kissinger flinging himself across the gap between the staircase and the jet, landing within inches of him and grabbing at his coat for support.

By now Brognola realized that he hadn't been shot after all, and together with Kissinger he ventured into the passenger cabin, gun at the ready.

T. A. Magrane and Keith Stewker were still out cold in the front seats, but neither showed signs of bullet wounds. The same couldn't be said for two men lying in contorted heaps at their feet. Howie Brett lay face down where he'd been shot nearly half an hour ago. Nearby, a second figure stretched out on his back, chest bleeding, goggled eyes staring up at the ceiling. He was clearly dead.

Or was he?

Spookily the man suddenly moved, and not in a natural way. His limbs remained flaccid, offering no support. He moved torso-first, as if being levitated in a magic show. It was only then that Brognola and Kissinger realized what was really happening. There was a second man underneath the corpse, trying to push the body away.

Bolan.

Kissinger leaned over and tugged Eijai Wahldjun's body clear of the Executioner. Brognola lent the warrior a hand, helping him to his feet. There were gaping holes in the fabric of Bolan's coat, but no blood. Through the tear gas it was difficult to make out the tight weave of the Kevlar vest that had blunted the impact of the shots that would have otherwise dispatched Bolan to his final rendezvous with the Grim Reaper.

"You're a sight for sore eyes, Striker," Brognola shouted through his mask with unabashed relief.

"I lucked out this time," Bolan replied, patting his bulletproof vest. He noticed Kissinger cautiously checking out the rest of the jet and assured him, "It's okay, Cowboy. We got them all. It's over."

CHAPTER TWENTY-TWO

As they lolled beneath the sweat-stained sheets, Ali-Jahn Babdi idly curled a strand of Emma Skodynov's hair around his index finger. She, in turn, rested her head on his shoulder and stared at her own fingers as they gently grazed the thin mat of hair on the Turk's chest.

"Was it as good as you remembered?" she asked.

"Hmm...a difficult question," Babdi responded, making little effort to suppress an amused grin.

"Wrong answer." Emma suddenly pinched a few locks of his chest hair and tugged them.

"Ow!" the Turk yelped, swatting her hand away.

"Let's try it again," Emma murmured, letting her hand drift below the covers to Babdi's groin. "Was it as good as you remembered?"

"Better," Babdi said with a smirk. "Most definitely better."

Emma smiled back up at him. "Now that's more like it."

With deft, measured strokes of her hand, Emma coaxed the Turk back into a state of arousal, then shifted her weight on top of him, guiding him inside her. He groaned his approval, cupping her breasts in his hands as she knelt upright and began gently rocking her pelvis back and forth.

"Why have you come back?" Babdi asked her. "And how did you know you could find me here?"

Emma smiled down at him. "How do salmon find their way back to their spawning grounds?"

Babdi shrugged, letting his hands roam freely down the woman's chest. "Instinct, I suppose."

"There you have it."

"That still leaves the question of 'why,'" Babdi reminded her. "Why did you seek me out again?"

"This isn't enough of a reason?" Emma said, huffing slightly as Babdi's thrusts became more forceful and frequent.

"For most, perhaps," the Turk confessed. "But you are not like most."

"Is that a compliment?"

"What do you think, you wily wench!" Babdi laughed. He reached behind her, clasping her buttocks tightly. She laughed back at him, briefly, then they gave themselves in to their shared passion, racing toward climax. Then, with a sated exhalation, Emma slumped forward, lying again across the Turk's bare chest.

"I missed you," she told him, not yet ready to forsake pleasure for business. "Did you miss me?"

Babdi stared up at the ceiling. His passion spent, his mind once again directed itself toward matters taking place beyond this bedroom. "I've been a busy man."

"And no doubt you replaced me with some young virgin."

"I doubt she was a virgin," Babdi confessed, earning himself another tweak in the chest.

"Bastard!"

"You have no reason to be jealous. She was only a reminder of how much better you are."

Emma kissed Babdi's chest, then raised her head and again stared him in the eyes. "Let's be together again."

"It's not that simple," Babdi told her. "Much has happened . . . is happening right now. I won't be having time for this soon."

"If you can deny yourself," she told him, "so can I. Just let me be with you. I can help you."

Babdi frowned. "Help?"

Emma nodded. "I know you were behind those attacks on the Riviera—in Cannes, in Monaco. It had your stamp."

"And . . ."

"And you have made a great mark," she told him. "You are poised for greatness. With the right support, there is no limit to what you might achieve. No limit!"

Babdi eyed the woman suspiciously. "You're not speaking of only yourself, are you?"

Emma shook her head. "I have made some powerful connections in Paris. People you can use."

"People who can use *me,*" Babdi contradicted her. "That's what you mean, isn't it?"

"Not at all," Emma insisted. "Oh, of course, it might be to your advantage to have them think it is you who are doing them the favors, but in reality, you could have your own agenda."

Babdi raised a callused finger and stroked the outline of Emma's chin. "And you . . . Where would you fit in?"

"I would work at your side," she said, "and I would be your liaison with them, your buffer."

"This 'them,'" Babdi said. "Who are they?"

Emma was evasive. "As I said, they are important people."

"NATO?"

"No."

Babdi guessed again. "RI?"

"They make for a better ally than an enemy," Emma told him. "They are impressed by what you've accomplished. You would have a great deal of autonomy."

"And the Blood?"

"You would still be their leader," Emma said, "although from what I understand, there may be those within your own ranks who are challenging you."

Babdi suddenly pushed Emma off him and sat upright in the bed, his face turning red. "What do you mean?"

"You haven't heard?" Emma said. "About the hijacking in Nice?"

"No," Babdi said. "Tell me."

Emma quickly related what little she knew of the incident, including the thumbnail description of the perpetrators.

"Eijai Wahldjun!"

Babdi slammed his fist against the mattress and expounded a string of epithets in his native language. Emma listened without comment, edging away from the Turk lest he suddenly lash out at her in his rage.

There had been a pack of cigarettes in the grave digger's coat, and Babdi lighted one of them and continued to curse under his breath as he stormed out of bed and clicked on the radio. Emma wrapped herself in a sheet and calmly helped herself to one of the cigarettes as well. Propping up a pillow, she sat back in the bed, watching Babdi crouched naked before the radio, furiously twitching the dial, seeking out a station that would bring him the latest news.

Once Babdi managed to find such a station, he haphazardly wrapped a towel around his waist and went to the door to the balcony, turning his back on

Emma and staring at the countryside view as he listened to a sonorous anchorman launch into the news.

Neither Babdi nor Emma were prepared for the latest update. Details were sketchy, the reporter said, but by all accounts the hijack situation at the airport in Nice had been resolved, with all but one member of the rebel faction slain during the liberation of the hostages. In a related story, it was reported that another band of BAO terrorists had been routed at their hideout in Hanover, Germany.

Aside from flicking ashes off his cigarette, Babdi took the news without visible emotion, but when he finally turned away from the doorway, Emma could see that a toll had been taken, and a severe one at that. By her own accounting, she estimated that Babdi's meager force had been decimated to the point where he might have, at best, half a dozen loyalists available to command, and those would be raw recruits in Domrémy, a short drive to the north.

All in all, it was devastating news for Babdi. Conversely, however, things couldn't be shaping up better for Emma. With his minions gone, Babdi was in little position to refuse the collaborative aid of the Russians. Handled right, he could be a vital pawn in the agency's master plan. The trick lay in bringing the Turk along tactfully, in leading him to believe that he was still master of his destiny. Or, as Klemberk had so aptly put it to Emma once, the happiest puppet is the one unaware that he's linked to a set of strings.

"You have them all where you want them," Emma assured Babdi as she rose from the bed.

The Turk didn't answer her, choosing instead to busy himself with stubbing out one cigarette and lighting another. Emma sidled up next to him. Sensing his tension, she refrained from touching him.

"They will be reveling in their victories," Emma told him. "And in doing so, they will drop their guard. If you bide your time and choose your next move wisely, you will be able to strike back hard and let them know just how far you are from being vanquished."

Babdi blew smoke from his second cigarette, mustering the faintest hint of a smile as he glanced at Emma. "Another reason I'm drawn to you," he said. "We think alike."

"Then I'm sure you're thinking that we had best make love again, and even harder, because it may be some time before we allow ourselves such distraction again."

Babdi's smile slowly grew and he held his arms out, drawing the woman into his embrace. As he led her back to the bed, Emma smiled to herself in triumph. She had him right where she wanted him.

"KATZ SAID THEY WERE picked up at the airport and hustled to the hideout so fast they nearly got a citation," Hal Brognola said, relating Phoenix Force's part in the siege on the Blood Against Oppression enclave in Hanover. "They got there just in time to intercept the whole group as it was trying to sneak out in a minivan. The fools tried to shoot their way out and got nailed with everything we could throw at them."

"No survivors?" Bolan asked.

Brognola shook his head. "Not even close, from the sounds of it."

"They were able to identify the bodies at least, weren't they?" Grimaldi asked.

"Yes and no. They know that Ali-Jahn Babdi wasn't among them."

"Damn," Kissinger muttered.

They were standing near the disabled Dassault Mystère, surrounded by various crews dealing with the aftermath of the thwarted hijack attempt. Ambulances had already whisked Vera Maris, Keith Stewker, T. A. Magrane and the jet's pilot to a nearby hospital for treatment. Coroners and other investigators had waited for the tear gas to dissipate before going to inspect those slain inside the jet. A handful of militia officers had been retained to cordon off the area from zealous members of the media and other curiosity seekers.

"What's our next move?" Grimaldi wondered.

"The area around Domrémy," Brognola said. "Scautt's already sent men to start combing the countryside up there for that last pocket of Babdi's followers, but we might as well lend a hand. I haven't talked to the President yet, but you can be sure he's going to want us taking every measure to track Babdi down."

"Any update on Audrey?" Grimaldi asked.

"I called the hospital a few minutes ago. She's still comatose, but they think they might be close to pinpointing what's causing it."

"And if they do?"

"They say it'd be a long shot," Brognola said, "but it might be treatable."

"There has to be something we can do besides playing hide-and-seek with Babdi," Kissinger grumbled. "Haven't there been any more terrorist incidents since the hijacking?"

"Not that we've heard of. Well, there've been some bombings near our embassies in Greece and Italy, but in both cases other factions took credit, saying they were showing solidarity with BAO."

"Which is just the thing we wanted to avoid," Kissinger said.

"And that's why it's so important we get Babdi. Even if we take out everyone under him, he's going to be a threat because he'll have every terrorist wanna-be looking up to him as some kind of hero, or at least a martyr."

"So he could wind up gaining more power by default?" Grimaldi concluded. "Man, that sucks!"

"We'll get him," Bolan promised. "Somehow."

CHAPTER TWENTY-THREE

Ed Dauffie stared intently at the craggy-faced surgeon who'd just emerged from the doorway leading to the operating rooms at Sainte Catherine's. The doctor's face was a mask of weariness and fatigue, offering no hint as to the outcome of his efforts over the past two hours.

"How is she?"

"We're doing the best we can," the surgeon replied. He was wearing a sanitized gown spattered with Vera Maris's blood. "But you have to realize there's been a lot of tissue damage, and she's lost an incredible amount of blood."

"I know, I know," Dauffie said. "But she's going to live, right?"

After a moment's silence, the other man responded gravely. "I can't promise you that. Another team's going to be working on her for at least another two hours. Stopping the bleeding's going to be the biggest challenge. If they can do that and her vitals don't go down any more, well, maybe she'll have a chance."

"Can I donate blood?" Dauffie pleaded. "I'm not sure, but I think we're the same type."

"We can draw a sample and test it," the doctor said, "but even if you're compatible, we're going against the gun here. There's no guarantee we'd have yours ready when she needs it. Odds are we're going to have to go with more units from the bank."

"I understand," Dauffie said. He smacked a fist into his open palm in frustration. "I have to do something for her!"

The doctor rubbed his sweating brow with the back of his hand, then regarded Dauffie thoughtfully. "Are you a praying man?"

"No," Dauffie confessed. "I haven't prayed in years."

"This might not be a bad time to start again." The doctor gestured down the hallway. "There's a chapel down on the ground floor, just down from the gift shop. As I said, it'll be a couple hours before we have any more news...."

Dauffie nodded absently. "Thanks. And thanks for taking the time to talk."

"Just trying to help. Now, if you'll excuse me..."

The surgeon disappeared through the swing doors that led back into the operating room.

Dauffie let out a deep breath. Rather than return to the waiting room, he ventured down the hallway, feeding some coins into a vending machine to get a cup of coffee. He was at Sainte Catherine's, and as he carried his steaming cup to a window overlooking the hospital courtyard, he could see the room where the President's daughter was being monitored. Keith Stewker, T. A. Magrane and the pilot of the hijacked Dassault were in rooms elsewhere at the center, all of them, like Vera, victims of the Blood Against Oppression.

There was a part of Dauffie that wished at least one of the terrorists had survived and been brought here. Then he could have had an outlet for his pent-up rage. He could haved stormed the scum's room and strangled him with his bare hands, glaring into his eyes as he watched him die, shouting that he was avenging his brother's death, the suffering of his daughter.

Dauffie's hand shook from the swelling fury, and when he glanced down he saw coffee spilling over the edge of his cup and onto his fingers. He could feel the burning pain but refused to acknowledge it. He drained what was left in the cup, then crushed it in his hand and dropped it in the trash.

At the end of the hallway, he pressed the elevator button.

Sure, he'd go to the chapel and pray, but only on the condition that his prayers would be heard by the God of the Old Testament, the God who believed in an eye for an eye, the God who would listen to his pleas for revenge upon those who had torn his family asunder.

ONE BY ONE, Zeita Hu-Perzar had contacted the other BAO recruiters working the fields at Tristam Donlier's farm near Les Laume, telling each of them the urgent message passed along by Emma Skodynov earlier in the day. A rendezvous had been arranged for later in the afternoon when their work shift was ended.

Now, as the sun dipped low on the western horizon and most of the other workers were straggling back to their lodgings for food and rest, Zeita meandered through neatly planted rows of grain toward a nearby forest situated at the edge of the farmland. Part of Donlier's private holdings, the twelve acre wooded parcel was fenced off and stocked with wild game for those occasions when Donlier wanted to indulge in his passion for hunting.

One of Zeita's colleagues, a Domrémy native named David Laix, had secured a job guarding the grounds against poachers, and as such the BAO was provided with an ideal place to meet and conduct their business with a reasonable assurance of privacy.

When Zeita reached the compound he found Laix waiting near the main gate, whittling a thick stick with a jackknife. They exchanged greetings as Laix opened the gate to let Zeita through.

"The others are here?"

"They're waiting at the lodge."

Laix closed the gate and quickly fell in step beside Zeita as they headed down a well-worn footpath leading into the heart of the woods, which consisted primarily of birch trees, poplars and an abundance of brilliant green ferns. Birds and squirrels chattered noisily in the trees, and in a clearing off to the men's right, three deer lapped water at the edge of a small pond. Dappled sunlight fell through the treetops, lighting their way as Zeita grimly passed along the latest news he'd heard about the wave of terror instigated by their fellow members of the Blood Against Oppression.

"And so except for Monaco, we've fared poorly," he summed up, snapping a twig off a nearby tree and absently plucking its leaves.

"Poorly isn't the word for it," Laix groused. "From the sounds of it, it seems as if Babdi's heaving us into the furnace like so much firewood, just so he can take credit for the flames."

"Yes," Zeita concurred, "and if that harlot Emma's back pulling his string, you can bet he won't cut his losses and stop."

"As long as it isn't his neck that he's risking, you're probably right."

"I've been wondering," Zeita said. "Perhaps we should see if—"

"Wait!" Laix held up a hand, stopping in the middle of the path. He was staring at one of the nearby trees, and when Zeita followed the other man's gaze, he saw a squirrel clinging to the bark halfway up a thick poplar.

"A squirrel," Zeita observed. "What of it?"

"Watch."

Laix pried open his jackknife again, then took quick aim and gave his wrist an almost imperceptible flick. The knife fled his hand in a blur, hurtling end over end before striking its mark with chilling accuracy. With a triumphant grin, Laix led Zeita to the poplar, where the squirrel was twitching in its death throes, impaled through the back by the knife.

"I collect their tails," Laix boasted, killing the squirrel with a quick blow to the head, then pulling the blade free of the tree and hacking off the creature's tail. "This makes thirty-one."

"A fox guards the henhouse," Zeita stated with a tight smile.

"Donlier doesn't come here to hunt these puny things," Laix defended himself as he discarded the squirrel's body and tucked its tail in his pocket before cleaning the knife on the leg of his pants. As the two men ventured back to the path and resumed their trek through the woods, Laix asked Zeita, "What were you about to say before I interrupted you?"

"I was thinking perhaps there is a reward being offered," Zeita speculated cautiously. He knew that he was on thin ice here. If he'd misread Laix and betrayed his disloyalty to the BAO's cause, there could be trouble, and Zeita knew from experience that Laix could kill a man with the same moral indifference by which he killed squirrels.

"You're probably right," Laix responded non-committally. "If so, the price on Babdi's head would be quite high."

"Exactly."

Laix eyed the other man. "Why do you ask?"

Zeita shrugged, thinking fast. "I'm concerned about our own safety, that's all. After all, if there's a bounty on him and we find ourselves drawn to his side as reinforcements, we'll be fair game as well."

"Very true," Laix mused without breaking his stride.

"And I expect they would just as soon take him dead as alive," Zeita said, fishing for a commitment from his companion.

He finally got one.

"Dead would be better," Laix said. "Dead, he wouldn't be able to pin us as collaborators."

Their conspiracy hatched, the men walked in silence a ways. The trail wound deeper into the woods, where the canopy of the trees was thicker, blocking out more of the sun's dying light. Up ahead, however, was a clearing where the lodge overlooked a large man-made lake stocked with a variety of panfish.

Laix finally spoke. "Of course, we would have to kill the woman, too."

"I have no problem with that," Zeita said. "None at all. I'll even take care of her myself."

Laix chuckled sardonically. "So she's rejected your advances, too, eh?"

Zeita shot Laix a harsh look, then laughed. "Maybe we won't kill her right away, huh?"

"I like the way you think, Zeita."

The men continued to joke with each other as they approached the lodge, a fair-sized structure made of logs, mortar and river rocks. As they started up the steps, the front door opened and another member of their cell, Raffi Minslow, peered out and told them, "We have company."

"Who?" Zeita furrowed his brow as he stepped past Minslow into the lodge.

Tied to a chair in the middle of the lodge's main room was Louis, Donlier's chief chauffeur. He looked groggy, and his face was bruised and swollen from an obvious beating. Standing on either side of him were two other members of the BAO, Bari Sihn and Colaz Douke. Sihn had a leather strap wrapped around his knuckles.

"What the hell's he doing here?" Laix demanded.

"That's what we've been trying to find out," Sihn responded. "We found him lurking outside the cabin a few minutes ago. He's drunk . . . or at least he was before we sobered him up."

Zeita walked over to the chauffeur and stared down at him. "Well?"

Louis slowly tilted his head back to view his interrogator. His right eye was nearly swollen shut, and a thin trickle of blood flowed from his nostrils. He swallowed with great difficulty, then spoke in a hoarse voice. "I just wanted to do some fishing. That's all! I swear!"

"With what?" Douke called out from behind Zeita. "You had no pole, no bait."

"That's why I was here," Louis said. "I thought there might be a pole inside."

"I see," Zeita stated. He turned to the others. "It seems a likely enough explanation."

"Yes!" Louis said hopefully. "I meant no—"

"Liar!" Zeita suddenly turned back to the chauffeur, stiff-arming him in the chest with so much force that the man was knocked backward. The chair toppled to the floor, and with his hands tied to his sides, there was no way for him to break his fall. The back of his head struck the wooden floorboards, almost knocking him out. Before he could have a chance to recover, Zeita leaned over, grabbed him by the hair and jerked him back to an upright position. Louis screamed in agony, feeling as if his scalp were being torn from his head.

"The truth!" Zeita demanded. "I want the truth, now!"

Tears of pain welled in the chauffeur's eyes. "It was that woman."

"Emma?" Zeita asked.

Louis nodded. "She...she humiliated me. I wanted to get back at her."

"What does that have to do with us?" Zeita wanted to know.

"After I saw her talking to you, I kept an eye on you. I saw you talking with these other men. I thought it might have something to do with her, so when I saw some of you heading this way after work, I followed you."

"What did you hope to find out?" Zeita wondered.

"I don't know," Louis confessed. "I was angry. I'd had a few drinks and I wanted to find a way to hurt her. I guess I thought maybe I'd find she was doing something behind Mr. Donlier's back. That's all. I have nothing against any of you. I swear!"

"You swear a lot," David Laix said skeptically as he nonchalantly pulled out his jackknife.

"Who else knows you came here?" Zeita asked.

"No one. And no one has to know. As far as I'm concerned, I never came out here. I never saw any of you come here or—"

"Not good enough," Laix interrupted, taking a sudden step forward. With a swift motion, he rammed his knife into the chauffeur's chest, just below the sternum, then twisted the blade. Louis screamed, a confused look on his face. By the time Laix pulled the blade free, Louis was dead, sagging against his binds.

"We don't have time to waste on him," he told the others as he cut the corpse loose and grabbed his arms. "Somebody give me a hand."

"BESIDES, IF I DON'T leave for at least a few minutes, you'll never get dressed," Emma Skodynov teased as she opened the door to Ali-Jahn Babdi's room.

"Just don't be too long," the Turk warned, eyeing her in the mirror as he lathered his face with shaving cream.

"Leave the mustache," Emma told him, flashing a vixenish smile. "I like the way it tickles."

Babdi frowned with mock anger and pointed his straight razor at the woman. "Go! And don't forget the coffee!"

Emma bowed at the waist like a geisha. "Yes, honorable master. Your wish is my command."

"I'll keep that in mind."

The woman stepped out into the hallway and closed the door behind her. "Pig," she whispered as she traipsed down the corridor. She'd told Babdi she was starved and wanted to buy something to eat in the bar. There was another errand that needed tending to as well, and after stopping off at the bar to order a sandwich, she backtracked to the reception area and slipped into the phone booth.

She had memorized the phone numbers of the six other members of the Gray Hand participating in Operation Rekindle. She quickly dialed the senior agent in Paris who had first approached her about trying to track down Babdi in the wake of the BAO's terrorist attacks in Cannes and Monaco.

"I've found him," she reported.

"You work very fast, Emma," the agent responded with calm admiration.

"Not only that," she went on, "but I've contacted his subordinates in Les Laume. We've arranged a rendezvous for later tonight."

"How much later?"

Emma glanced through the glass door of the phone booth, spotting a clock on the wall. "Six and a half hours from now."

"Excellent."

"Then you've found a plant?"

"One, possibly two," the agent told her. "Gott called an hour ago from Geneva. He's got a Company man for sure, but he's just a paper shag."

"That could be a problem." A paper shag was an espionage agent who dealt mostly with stolen documents and government secrets and had little record using a gun. It would be a stretch to dump such an agent into Operation Rekindle and not expect people to suspect a setup.

"We might be in luck, though," the agent said. "Through Klemberk, of all people."

"Toni?" Emma couldn't believe it.

"Yes. He and another of our people are tailing a member of NATO Intelligence in Monaco. It looks as if they could—"

"Wait," Emma interjected. "NATO? I thought for the plan to work we needed someone from CIA."

"We thought so, too," the agent confessed, "but this man will work even better. His name is Dauffie. As good fortune would have it, his daughter belongs to the BAO."

"No. Are you serious?"

"Yes. She was wounded during the airport siege in Nice. She's being treated at the same hospital as the President's daughter. From what we've been able to learn, she might not survive. Even if she does, Dauffie has a perfect motive for wanting to execute Babdi."

"Perhaps too perfect. Isn't it likely to look like he was acting alone?"

"Not if it's done right," the agent said. "I haven't told you the real reason he fits the plan so well."

"You mean there's something besides his daughter?"

"Yes. He's on record as having done wet work."

Wet work was a euphemism for assassination.

This was too good, Emma thought. "It's documented?"

"Irrefutably. The press will have to be blind not to pick it up, and if they are, we'll leak it to them."

Emma smiled. She felt that special flush of excitement one got when finally piecing together a difficult puzzle. The senior agent was right. If Klemberk could nab Dauffie, he'd be the perfect fall guy.

"What about tonight?" Emma asked. "Should I try to postpone the rendezvous?"

"No. One way or another, we should carry out your end of the plan. I know we can get the shag man to you, and if we're lucky, Klemberk will come through for us in time to bring Dauffie up to you as well. Give us the location where you'll be, and we'll put the wheels in motion."

Emma passed along all the necessary information, then hung up and headed back to the bar for the sandwiches. She paid for the food, then carried it upstairs. When Babdi answered her knock, he was still in the process of getting dressed.

"What took you so long?" he asked.

"Your coffee." Emma leaned over and kissed Babdi's cheek. "I insisted that they brew a fresh pot."

Appeased, Babdi took a bite from one of the sandwiches, washed it down with a sip of coffee, then resumed getting dressed. "I've made up my mind," he told Emma decisively. "Our first objective should be to finish off the President's daughter. *That* would be the strongest response...."

"Perhaps, but it would also be the most anticipated, not to mention the most foolhardy. Eijai Wahldjun already proved that."

"But he failed," Babdi said. "If we were to attempt the same mission and succeed, then there would be no question that I am in control of the Blood."

Emma was tempted to remind Babdi that he'd already failed once to kill the girl, but thought better of it. Babdi was tense, clearly agitated, and Emma knew how easily he could turn on people when he was in such a frame of mind. "With Wahldjun defeated, I don't think anyone is questioning your position. And if they are, they'll know better soon enough."

Babdi weighed her words as he stood before the mirror, buttoning his shirt. Reflexively he straightened his posture and eyed himself with confident resolve. "You're right," he finally said.

The radio was playing in the background, and they both fell silent as the news came on. There was no new information on the terrorism front other than unconfirmed reports that government forces had been sent to the northern provinces of France in hopes of tracking down Babdi and any remaining members of the Blood Against Oppression.

"That's not a surprise," Babdi said.

"Let them look all they want. Donlier's above suspicion, so they aren't going to be searching any of his farms all that closely."

"We still have to get there, though," Babdi reminded her.

"It's not that far, and, besides, I'll bet they're going to be looking around Domrémy first, on account of Roberto."

Babdi nodded, slipping into his shoes. "It's a good thing we moved our men to Les Laume."

"You had foresight, my darling," Emma said, certain he wouldn't remember that it had been her idea to have the men transferred. "That is why we will succeed."

The Turk laced his shoes, doubling the knots, then took a long step across the room, drawing Emma into his arms. He kissed her briefly but passionately, then looked into her eyes. "You make me feel invincible! Do you realize that?"

Emma smiled shyly, willing herself to blush with feigned embarrassment. "Everything feels right when I'm with you, too."

"That settles it, then," Babdi said with an air of finality. "We'll have to stay together."

"Yes," she replied, thinking to herself that they'd be together until she didn't need him anymore.

CHAPTER TWENTY-FOUR

Fully fueled, the Reed-279 had a range of a little over three hundred miles, and it had been necessary for Grimaldi to lay over briefly near Lyon before continuing northward to aid in the search for Ali-Jahn Babdi and the last tatters of his Blood Against Oppression. Bolan was riding shotgun, while Kissinger took up most of the back bench serving as a makeshift third seat. Brognola had remained behind in Nice, forced to beg off due to a strained right thigh sustained when he'd leaped from the chopper during the raid on the Dassault Mystère.

As they flew above the rolling farmland of Côte d'Or and Haute-Marne provinces, Kissinger watched the scenery with a dubious eye.

"We're looking for needles in a haystack, if you ask me," Cowboy said. "Even if the BAO's down there somewhere, all they have to do is lie low and we'll never find them. And it's going to be dark soon, too."

"You won't get an argument out of me," Bolan said, "but like Hal said, we have to hope they aren't going to pull back and hide at this point."

"The odds are they won't," Grimaldi said. "I mean, they've got the world's attention, and from everything I've heard or read about Babdi, he's not going to pass up a chance to milk the media."

"He's passed it up so far," Bolan reminded Kissinger. "Maybe everybody else in the BAO's making a lot of racket, but Babdi hasn't been heard from since Monaco."

"Maybe he's dead," Grimaldi suggested. "That was one hell of a wreck he walked away from in Monaco. Maybe he just managed to crawl clear of the dragnet, then keeled over somewhere."

"It's possible," Bolan admitted, "but we can't count on it."

They continued to discuss the situation as Grimaldi guided the Reed over the countryside. Several minutes later they got the break they were looking for when the radio sputtered to life with an incoming message from Phoenix Force's Yakov Katzenelenbogen, who was calling from an air force base less than three miles away.

"Brognola tells me you guys are wandering into the neighborhood."

"Sure are, Katz," Grimaldi replied. "Hey, congratulations on that mission in Hanover. Sounds like you guys kicked some ass."

"From what I hear you guys didn't do too bad for yourselves, either. But this isn't a social call. You're just in time to give us a hand here."

"What's up?" Bolan asked.

"We just got a distress call from a search team two miles from here," Katz reported. "Seems they wandered into some sniper fire."

"BAO?"

"Can't say for sure, but they're taking a hell of a pounding. We're prepping an Apache for lift-off, but it's going to be a few minutes. If you could swing by and run some interference..."

"Done," Bolan said. "What's their position?"

Katz supplied the coordinates.

"Got it," Grimaldi said, already changing the helicopter's course.

"Good luck."

"Right." Bolan switched off the speaker and glanced at the others. "Well, it looks like the needles have jumped out of the haystack."

THERE HAD BEEN A TIME, earlier in Anatoly Klemberk's career, when he'd been known almost exclusively by his nickname, Chameleon. Back then, the agent's specialty had been fieldwork, particularly tailing and surveillance. There had been few operatives within the organization that had been able to match his combination of infinite patience, street smarts and the ability to effortlessly blend into his surroundings so that he could go about his business with minimal risk of blowing his cover. Although he'd gladly jumped at the first opportunity to es-

cape from the grueling, painstaking demands of such
work, his instincts for the job remained intact, as he
found out during the three hours he and fellow agent
Evan Willan spent staking out the heavily fortified
perimeter of Sainte Catherine's Medical Center.
There were no fewer than eight separate entrances to
the facility, and with posted security guards monitoring activity in the area, Klemberk and Willan had
to pull out all their tricks to keep moving and maintaining an unrelenting vigil without drawing attention to themselves.

Their efforts paid off when Klemberk finally
spotted Ed Dauffie leaving the hospital in the company of Hal Brognola. It was late afternoon by now,
and the NATO Intelligence officer had just been informed that his daughter had come through surgery
in better shape than anticipated. Buoyed by the op-
timistic change in Vera's prognosis, Dauffie had ac-
cepted Brognola's invitation to an early dinner.

Klemberk wasn't put off by Brognola's presence.
If anything, it was more likely to prove a welcome
development than a stumbling block. After all, although Klemberk didn't know the man, he remembered seeing him during the earlier incident with the
aborted bombing attempt by the BAO-driven utilities van and assumed that he had to be somehow involved in U.S. or NATO Intelligence work, and
probably in an advisory capacity. There was even a

chance he'd make a better pawn in Operation Rekindle than Dauffie.

But first, of course, there was much work to be done.

As Brognola and Dauffie pulled out of the parking lot at Sainte Catherine's in the latter's car, Klemberk and Willan were poised to follow them in separate vehicles. Klemberk had given Willan much of his training back in Moscow, and the younger man had learned well. Working in tandem according to well-practiced strategies, the two agents were able to switch off every few blocks to ensure that they wouldn't tip themselves off.

After driving through the city, Dauffie left Monaco and headed eastbound along the coastal route toward Menton. After a few miles, he pulled into a parking lot next to a modest seafood restaurant that overlooked Cap Martin. The Russians parked on the street and waited until the two other men had disappeared inside the restaurant, then rendezvoused in the parking lot.

"So far, so good."

Klemberk nodded. "Why don't you go inside and keep an eye on them. I'll work on their car."

THE FOUR MEN who'd laid ambush to the French army's search party weren't members of the Blood Against Oppression. In fact, except for their leader, twenty-one-year-old Felix DesChamps, the four snipers were all teenagers, local farmboys who'd tired of work in the fields and longed for a chance to rebel against the dull future they felt had been laid out for them without their input or approval. Inspired by the attention the BAO had received for their reckless daring in their seemingly relentless raids on the French Riviera, the youths had plotted this assault, using weapons and ammunition secured for them by their ringleader.

And now, like it or not, they were committed to carrying matters out to their grisly conclusion. To a man, each of the gunmen believed that if they inflicted sufficient casualties on the seven army officers they'd pinned down, they would achieve enough notoriety to ensure that, despite their age, the BAO would welcome them into their ranks with open arms.

Three men already lay dead in the clearing below, and another two had been wounded during the youths' initial fusillade, which had drilled into the search party as it ventured through a narrow gorge flanked by tall, sheer walls of basalt.

Whether by design or sheer luck, the youths had picked an ideal snipers' nest, and although the men below had been returning fire, they were at a decided disadvantage having to shoot uphill at targets well concealed behind clusters of boulders crowning the top of the basalt formations. None of the snipers had been wounded as yet, and they'd brought along enough ammunition to keep up their offensive and also to contend with any other ground forces that might arrive.

What the youths hadn't counted on, however, was a counterattack by air, and they were woefully unprepared when the Reed-279 helicopter suddenly materialized above them like an avenging angel, stirring up clouds of dust with its fierce rotor wash. Before any of the snipers had a chance to react, a hail of M-16 gunfire was raining down on them. Two of the youths were slain outright, and DesChamps was put out of commission by a volley of rounds that ravaged his upper right arm, almost severing it from his shoulder.

The fourth gunman managed to scramble over the side of the cliff and secure a tenuous footing on a narrow ledge a few feet down. He crouched low and inched along the outcropping, still clutching his high-powered rifle. He could hear the chopper clearly, and when he heard it drifting toward him, he planted his feet firmly on the ledge and leaned his hips against the rock facing to balance himself. On a count of three, he was going to rise from his crouch and empty his rifle into the chopper.

One...

The youth tightened his grip on the rifle, planting the stock firmly against his shoulder.

Two...

He tensed his leg muscles and tilted the rifle upward, resting his finger on the trigger. He could see the front end of the chopper as it drifted toward him.

Three...

The youth sprang upright, but before he could draw a bead on the chopper, a hand reached out and grabbed the rifle barrel. Bolan, who had leaped from the chopper and raced along the edge of the cliff, jerked the rifle to one side. It went off, firing wide of the Reed-279, which banked sharply and backed away.

"Give it up, pal," Bolan said in passable French, shifting his grip to grab hold of the youth's wrist.

"No!" the sniper cried out, struggling to free himself. In doing so, he lost his balance and one foot slipped off the ledge. He started to fall, pulling Bolan with him.

The Executioner instinctively dropped flat on the ground, spreading his legs and his free arm to anchor himself as he continued to hold on to the youth, who was now dangling over the side of the cliff, both his legs swinging in a wild panic.

"Stop it!" Bolan cried out to him. "Just let me pull you up."

The youth, however, either didn't hear Bolan or didn't understand him, because he continued to writhe to and fro. Bolan could feel himself losing his grip on the sniper, but there was nothing else he could do. Several seconds later, the youth slipped free and let out a loud, anguished cry as he plummeted down the steep precipice. His cry was abruptly silenced when he slammed into the floor of the gorge, landing less than two feet away from one of the army officers he'd slain only a few moments earlier.

Bolan peered down over the cliff's edge, seeing the survivors in the search party staring back up at him.

"All clear!" he called down to them.

Grimaldi set down the chopper, and Kissinger climbed down onto the rocks, ducking to avoid the whirring blade overhead. When he got a close look at one of the fallen gunmen, he shook his head sadly.

"They're just kids."

"Tell that to the search party," Bolan said. He moved back from the cliff's edge, seeking out the lone surviving sniper. DesChamps was curled up on the ground next to his fallen rifle, grimacing in pain as he clutched his wounded arm. Blood streamed through his fingers. He stared up at Bolan. Any trace of the naive arrogance that had led him on this course of self-destruction was gone, replaced by a look of abject and total fear.

"I'm not going to hurt you," Bolan said as he picked up the man's rifle. "But you've got one hell of a lot of explaining to do...."

CHAPTER TWENTY-FIVE

"She's still holding her own," Ed Dauffie said as he hung up the pay phone in the restaurant lobby.

"Good," Brognola told him. "Audrey, too?"

Dauffie nodded, following Brognola toward the exit. "Thanks again for dinner, Hal," he said on their way out. "I really bent your ear."

"No problem. Glad to help."

Once outside, Dauffie paused on the steps, looking out over the Mediterranean. It was dusk, and the calm waters mirrored the sunset's fiery golds and jagged streaks of purple. A few sailboats floated tranquilly around the cape. In the foreground, couples dining on the patio enjoyed the view as well, carrying on their myriad conversations between bites of swordfish and calamari.

"It's hard to imagine," Dauffie reflected. "All this butchery and mayhem going on all around them, and yet people still go about their business as if all's right with the world."

"Sometimes that's really the only solution," Brognola said. "You go through the motions and ride the hard times out."

"Yeah, I guess so." Dauffie started down the steps toward the parking lot.

"I don't know, it's just still so hard to accept. You raise children and do everything you can to protect them, but once they're free to make their own decisions, it's suddenly out of your hands. You have to let them make their own choices, take their own chances. You tell yourself that no matter what you'll be there for them, but it's a crock. Your lives go separate ways and the next thing you realize, you look in their eyes and there's someone you don't even know."

Brognola nodded. "I've been there, too, Ed. It can be rough."

"There I go again," Dauffie chastised himself. "Okay, end of subject. Maybe we should talk baseball or something."

"Fine by me."

Dauffie unlocked the door for Brognola, then circled around and got in the other side. He started the engine and backed out into the street, then headed back toward Monaco. They discussed the first few weeks of the baseball season, losing themselves in heated discussion about how players' overall statistics had declined in recent years proportionate to their increased salaries.

They hadn't gone far, however, when Dauffie's car suddenly began to act up, misfiring and losing power.

"Gas?" Brognola wondered.

"No, I just filled the tank a couple days ago."
Dauffie switched on his emergency blinkers and
veered toward the shoulder. "Must be something
under the hood."

Brognola was concerned. "It seemed to be running fine on the way out."

"Yeah, but you know how these rental beasts can
be," Dauffie said. "A hundred different drivers,
slipshod maintenance..."

"Maybe so," Brognola said unconvincingly. On
his guard, he checked the surrounding flow of traffic. There were a handful of other cars on the road,
some of them blasting their horns as they sped by.

"What are you saying, Hal? You think somebody
tampered with the engine while we were eating?"

"Could be."

As Dauffie pulled onto the shoulder and brought
the car to a stop, Brognola unbuttoned his jacket,
giving him quicker access to his handgun. The car's
engine bucked a few times more, then died.

"Well," Dauffie said, "there's one way to find
out."

Reaching under the dashboard, he pulled the remote hood release. At the same time the hood latch
sprang open, there was a second, softer sound, a
hissing under the steering column. Dauffie reached
under the column, but by the time his fingers fell on
a small aerosol can rigged up to the hood release, it
was too late. The can had already sprayed its fast-

acting, odorless vapor into the car. Dauffie slumped over the wheel, and even as Brognola was grabbing for the handle to open his door, the gas overcame him and he fell unconscious.

Moments later, another vehicle pulled off the road and stopped behind the rental car. Anatoly Klemberk remained behind the wheel while Evan Willan got out and circled around to the front of the first car. He raised the hood, tampered briefly with the engine, then got in the front seat, shoving Dauffie to one side. When he turned the key in the ignition, the engine started up, showing no traces of the malady that had forced Dauffie to pull off the road. Shifting into first gear, Willan pulled out into the flow of traffic. Klemberk followed from behind. Within a few miles, they were on the autoroute, headed for Menton, where a hydroplane was waiting to fly them to the northern provinces.

EMMA SKODYNOV PULLED the Alfa-Romeo into an old cemetery on the outskirts of Vitteaux. An equally old dirt road wound up through hillsides dotted with weather-beaten grave markers, some of them more than two centuries old. In the ebbing twilight, the grounds took on a haunting quality. Stirred by a faint breeze, tall, brooding oaks swayed their gnarly limbs like fearsome sentinels trying to scare off intruders. In one of the upper branches, a horned owl perched and whooped mournfully as it awaited the coming of night and a chance to feed nocturnally on whatever small creatures might venture through the untamed grass.

"A cheerful place, isn't it?" Babdi chuckled as he took in the dreary surroundings.

"Romantic, too." Emma smiled thinly. "Pity we didn't pack a picnic lunch."

"Now, now, you promised to be a good sport."

"Yes," Emma admitted, "and you promised to tell me at some point why it was you've dragged me out here."

"You'll find out soon enough."

"Just so you know," she told him, "I draw the line at necrophilia."

Babdi laughed heartily. "That's a relief. Don't worry, this graveyard hasn't been used in decades. The worms have already had their fun with everyone buried here."

Emma smiled again, doing her best to mask her uneasiness. It concerned her that Babdi had insisted they drive here, miles from the nearest town, while refusing to disclose his motives. It occurred to her that perhaps he had been stringing her along much as she'd been doing to him. If that was the case, she could be very well driving herself to her own execution. It didn't seem likely, but she was prepared for any contingency nonetheless. The Bogsley miniautomatic was within easy reach inside her jacket, and the Combat Magnum was still concealed under her seat. And, as she'd proved to Tristam Donlier's chauffeur, she was adept enough behind the wheel to use the car itself as a weapon if the need arose.

"It's over there, to the right," Babdi instructed, pointing to a family plot surrounded by a crumbling brick wall.

"Your ancestors?" Emma wondered aloud as she turned down the narrow road and parked downhill from the plot.

"My ancestors are dust in the wind back in Turkey," Babdi told her. "Come, let me show you something."

Emma warily followed Babdi out of the car and up the steep decaying staircase leading to the plot. The gate had long since rusted off its hinges, and inside the walls years of fallen, decaying leaves formed a fecund carpet across the ground.

"Watch your step," Babdi told Emma as he passed through the gate. "There are some markers hidden under the leaves."

In the center of the plot was a large marble mausoleum, covered with moss and eroded around the edges from exposure to the elements. Its walls were still intact, however, as was the cast-iron door, which was held in place by a heavyweight padlock that was clearly a recent addition.

Babdi produced a key from his pocket and slipped it into the lock.

"You have something stored here?" Emma guessed. "Is that it?"

Babdi smiled enigmatically as he removed the lock and swung the door inward. The hinges groaned loudly, sending a chill up Emma's spine.

"After you," the Turk told her, gesturing inside the mausoleum.

Emma casually slipped her hand inside her jacket as she ventured into the darkened chamber. She clasped her fingers around the Bogsley and switched off the safety.

The Turk left the door half-open, letting in just enough light to allow him to track down a large flashlight set in the corner. The batteries were weak, but still managed to cast a beam of light on the mausoleum's cobwebbed interior. There were three elevated sarcophagi in the center of the chamber, each with its heavy lid secured by a padlock similar to the one on the main door.

"Here, hold this," Babdi told Emma, handing her the flashlight. "And aim it at that casket over there."

Emma held the light in her left hand, keeping her right clenched around her gun. Babdi used the same key as before to unlock the lid, then groaned slightly as he raised it up on its hinges. Mission accomplished, he grinned back at Emma.

"Have a look," he told her.

She cautiously stepped forward and peered into the sarcophagus. With an unexpected gasp, she exclaimed, "I don't believe it!"

CHAPTER TWENTY-SIX

Instead of a body, Emma saw that the cavity of the sarcophagus was filled with oblong wooden crates, each stacked upright and extending down to the floor. From the size of the crates and the markings on the sides, she knew what they contained even before Babdi pried off one of the tops to show her.

"Rifles," she whispered.

"Kalashnikovs," Babdi told her, laying a hand on one of the exposed guns' distinctive barrels. "Two dozen of them, never used."

"These are the ones I helped secure for you when we were in Germany," Emma said after a closer inspection. "I assumed you'd taken them with you down to Mougins."

"There was no point. We already had more than two guns for everyone in the group. I figured, why bog ourselves down with the surplus when I could just store it here, for when we had more troops."

"This is wonderful!" Emma said with genuine delight, although not for the reasons Babdi suspected. Emma knew that this shipment of rifles was easily traceable to a Russian munitions plant in Saint

Petersburg, and as such they would be perfect weapons for use in Operation Rekindle.

"And that's not all," Babdi boasted, tapping the sarcophagus behind him. "This one is stocked with ammunition, and the third is packed with grenades and explosives."

"Enough to rearm the BAO from scratch," Emma deduced.

"Exactly. They might have thought we were neutralized after the arsenals they seized in Mougins and Hanover, but no. All we need to do is gather our men and recruit a few replacements, then we can rise from the ashes. And we can do it in a matter of days, while the iron's still hot."

"Amazing," Emma repeated.

"A nice little surprise, yes?" Babdi asked her.

The woman smiled coyly at the Turk. "I should have known you would have planned ahead."

"You're forgiven," Babdi said. "*This* time, that is. But you must learn never to doubt what I—"

The terrorist's voice trailed off and he stared past Emma at the half-opened door.

"What is it?" Emma asked.

"Shh," Babdi hissed, withdrawing his automatic from the pocket of his coat.

Emma listened intently, then she heard it, too—there was someone outside the mausoleum. Withdrawing her Bogsley 3-shot from her jacket, she quietly followed Babdi to the doorway, then back outside. The sound continued, but they both realized that it wasn't coming from as close as they'd thought when they were inside the structure. They traced it downhill to where the Alfa-Romeo was parked.

"It sounds like it's coming from inside the car," Emma remarked quietly as she peered down over the brick wall. "But I don't see anyone."

Indeed, from where they were standing, the car looked much the same as they had left it moments before. Then, to their utter amazement, the vehicle's engine suddenly turned over.

"It can't be!" Emma cried out, spooked by the sight.

Babdi had little fear of the supernatural, however, and he broke into a run down the decrepit concrete staircase, all the while keeping his eyes on the idling sports car. Suddenly a figure popped into view behind the steering wheel, and Babdi realized that the car had been hot-wired.

As the vehicle began to pull away from him, Babdi slowed to a firing stance and carefully raised his gun, drawing the sights on the back of the head of the car thief. When he pulled his trigger, the Alfa's back windshield shattered. Moments later, the driver pitched sideways, dropping his hands off the steering wheel. He hadn't picked up much speed yet, and the car rolled slowly off the road before crashing against a raised marble headstone.

Emma followed close behind as Babdi approached the vehicle, gun still at the ready. The Turk opened the side door and the slain driver fell chest-first onto the ground. Babdi pried his toe under the man's shoulder and flipped him onto his back. Judging by his disheveled garb and unshaved face, Babdi assumed the would-be thief was a harmless vagrant who'd blundered onto the wrong temptation at the wrong time.

"I'll stash him in the mausoleum for now," Babdi told Emma. Glancing at the blood-soaked front seat and shattered back windshield, he quickly added, "We need to get our hands on a truck, then we can pick up the other men and come back here for the weapons. By tomorrow we can be ready to strike back and let the world know that Ali-Jahn Babdi is still a force to be reckoned with!"

GRIMALDI BROUGHT the Reed-279 down onto a helipad inside the military base Yakov Katzenelenbogen had called from. Phoenix Force, however, had already headed back into the field. Kissinger had remained back at the scene of the ambush, leaving room in the helicopter for Felix DesChamps, the snipers' wounded ringleader. The Frenchman was feverish and in a state of delirium, babbling incoherently. Grimaldi had already radioed ahead about the man's condition, and a medical crew was waiting near the pad with a gurney, ready to wheel the man to the base hospital for treatment.

Bolan bounded out of the chopper and helped an orderly move DesChamps onto the gurney. The way the youth was flailing and thrashing his unwounded arm, it was no easy feat.

"Strap him down," the head medic told the orderly.

Grimaldi helped hold the sniper still as the orderly secured sets of cloth straps across the wounded man's legs and torso. The medic, meanwhile, inspected DesChamps's ravaged shoulder.

"I had to use a tourniquet to stop the bleeding," Bolan explained, pointing out the blood-soaked strip of fabric bound tightly above the man's right bicep.

"Well, he's apt to lose the arm," the medic said, "but you probably saved his life."

The medic opened a kit bag and removed a syringe filled with fluid. As he prepared to give Felix an injection, Bolan asked, "Is that morphine?"

"Yes. It will help to calm him down."

"Can you hold off?" Bolan asked. "Or at least give him a dose that won't knock him out?"

"Why?"

"He's been rambling the whole way back, and I think he keeps saying something about wanting to impress a recruiter. I didn't know the dialect, so I can't get him to explain himself."

"He really needs to be treated," the medic replied. "How urgent is this?"

"I think you know the answer to that. If he has any kind of link to the Blood Against Oppression, it's vital we get whatever information he has."

The medic glanced down at the prisoner, then sighed and squeezed half the morphine dose into the dirt before shooting the rest into DesChamps's thigh. "I'll be your interpreter," he told Bolan, "but let's make this fast."

The morphine took effect almost immediately, dulling the sensation of pain racking the sniper's body. DesChamps relaxed slightly on the gurney. The medic calmly told him that he was going to ask some questions and that he needed the man's cooperation so they could get him treated. The sniper nodded his head and mumbled something. The medic turned to Bolan.

"He said he'll talk."

"Ask him if he was acting on orders from the BAO when he ambushed that search party."

After the medic asked the question, DesChamps shook his head, then said something.

"No," the medic replied, "but he was trying to make an impression on a recruiter for the Blood."

"What recruiter?"

The medic relayed the question, and DesChamps gave him a lengthy answer.

"He says there was a man working on a farm near Domrémy who approached him a few weeks ago. He didn't come out and say he belonged to the BAO, but he gave that impression. He said that he knew of some people dedicated to change who were looking for men who weren't afraid to fight for a better world."

Without prompting, DesChamps elaborated a little further, then the medic continued. "He and his friends said they were interested in joining, but this man told them he thought they were too young, not strong enough to do what was needed."

Bolan guessed the rest. "So they pulled off this ambush just to show how capable they were."

The medic rephrased the Executioner's words, putting them into a question. Again the sniper nodded and elaborated.

"He says that when they heard this morning about the BAO's attacks in the Riviera, he rounded up the other youths and staged the attack to show solidarity, and to shame the recruiter into admitting they were worthy enough to join the Blood."

Grimaldi glanced up from the prisoner and shot a glance at Bolan. "Sounds like street gangs back home."

"Yeah, only the stakes are a little higher."

"Do you guys have all you need?" the medic asked. "I really need to get him into surgery."

"As soon as he gives us the location of that farm and a description of the recruiter."

As Brognola surfaced from the void, he felt a sensation of weightlessness. He was disoriented, and when he tried to open his eyes he realized he was blindfolded. Fast on the heels of that discovery he became aware that he was was lying on his side on a hard, vibrating surface, bound at the wrists and ankles as well. His full weight was on his already-inflamed thigh, aggravating the injury further, and his skull throbbed from some residual after-effect of the drug that had knocked him out back in Monaco.

Monaco.

Slowly Brognola recalled his last conscious moments, particularly with regard to his suspicions about the engine problems with Dauffie's car and the hissing of aerosol from under the car's steering column.

So that was it. He'd been knocked out. So had Dauffie, as he remembered. And whoever was responsible had taken considerable care to ensure that he and Dauffie could be taken alive.

His immediate assumption was that he'd been taken hostage, probably by the BAO and most likely in retaliation for the defeats that had been handed to the terrorists in Cannes the previous night and that morning at the airport in Nice. If such was the case, he also knew it was a reasonably safe assumption that once he'd served whatever strategic use the BAO had him for, he was going to be a dead man.

It took the big Fed only a few minutes to think all these matters through, and now, aware of the odds against him, he was ready to see what he could do to buck the odds against his survival.

Lying still and relying on his senses, Brognola slowly took stock of his situation. Between the vibration around him and the whine of high-powered engines on either side of him, he felt certain he was inside an airplane probably no larger than a Cessna. He was aware of someone breathing shallowly next to him and assumed it was Ed Dauffie, no doubt bound as he was.

In the background he could hear two men quietly speaking to each other. Brognola assumed one of the men was the pilot. It was difficult to make out the gist of the conversation, not only because the men were speaking in a foreign language, but also because the drone of the plane's engines created a wall of sound that the men's voices could not fully penetrate.

Taking care not to move or otherwise tip off that he was conscious, Brognola tried to tune out the sound of the engines and focus solely on the voices. It was a difficult endeavor, but after a few minutes he was able to discern the rhythm and cadence of the speech to realize what language they were speaking in.

Russian.

Brognola was taken aback. He would have bet money that his captors were from the Middle East. And there had been a part of him that had speculated that he had fallen into the clutches of none other than the leader of the Blood Against Oppression, Ali-Jahn Babdi.

But Russians?

It wasn't a totally unexpected wrinkle; Brognola recalled being told by Denis Scautt that some of the handwritten notes on the map of France found at the BAO hideout in Mougins were in Russian. But the assumption had been that one of Babdi's cohorts was merely bilingual and had written in Russian to prevent underlings from becoming privy to more information than was necessary for them to know. If, on the other hand, those notes had been written by a Russian adviser, the implications were ominous. Brognola knew it was ludicrous to think that his abduction wasn't directly tied to the events of the past twenty-four hours, and the realization that Russians were involved changed everything. Suddenly the forces of the West were no longer fending off the brutality of an isolated demagogue and his fanatic followers. Instead, Ali-Jahn Babdi now had to be looked upon as a stalking-horse for a far more formidable foe, a foe that some had foolishly presumed had come to change its outlook on the West and the way that it dealt with the countries of the Free World.

The cold war, Brognola thought, for whatever the reason was about to be reactivated, and there seemed little he could do to prevent it.

CHAPTER TWENTY-SEVEN

Tristam Donlier's main farm was easily the largest in the area, employing between four dozen and a hundred workers, depending on the season. When Bolan showed up at the front gate with Kissinger and Denis Scautt, who'd just flown up from the Riviera, they quickly learned from the farm's manager that there were currently seventy-three laborers on the payroll. They were apparently behind on their production quotas, and even if there was barely any light left in the evening sky, the manager wasn't about to have his operations disrupted by any sort of mass interrogation.

"Absolutely not," the man snarled in French, wagging a disapproving finger. He was in his late sixties, a crotchety World War II veteran whose tobacco-filled cheeks were scarred from a knife fight in a Nazi prisoner-of-war camp. "Take a look around here. We raise pigs and cattle, grain and poultry. Not terrorists."

Bolan glanced past the gates and could appreciate the man's point. The farm looked like a well-run, rural enterprise that had more in common with the preatomic world than modern-day headlines. The idea that it might serve as a breeding ground for terrorists seemed ludicrous, but then Bolan knew that appearances could be deceiving. Many had been the time he'd wandered into even more benign and innocuous settings, only to unearth the clandestine operations of anarchists and other murderous lowlifes.

"Perhaps you misunderstand the situation," Scautt told the manager, his patience clearly strained to its limits. "This is a national, not to mention, international emergency. One way or another, we're coming through this gate and we're going to question your men."

"On whose orders?" the old man demanded.

"You've already seen our credentials." Scautt sighed. He gestured behind him, drawing the manager's attention to a khaki-colored personnel truck carrying sixteen uniformed soldiers from the military base in nearby Fienne. "If you want, we can force our way in and make you look like an unpatriotic fool in the eyes of your workers. Is that really what you want?"

The manager eyed his uninvited guests with unbridled animosity. He was flanked by two shotgun-wielding employees, but they were clearly outgunned. In addition to the military backup, Bolan and Kissinger made no effort to conceal the fact that they were armed as well.

Cursing under his breath, the manager turned his head and spit tobacco juice on the ground. "Some choice you give me." He scowled at Scautt as he signaled for his guards to open the gates. "Fine, do what you have to. But you're wild geese as far as I'm concerned."

"Thank you," Scautt replied with mock graciousness. He turned and waved the convoy through the gate. As soon as it rumbled past, Bolan, Scautt and Kissinger turned from the manager and followed the truck on foot. The old man glared at them, clearly anxious to get in one last word.

"International emergency indeed!" he finally scoffed, raising his voice as he once again wagged his arthritic finger at Scautt. "I'll be speaking to your superiors! Yes, that's right! I fought in the war, I'll have you know! I earned my stripes!"

"What does that have to do with anything?" Kissinger wondered.

"My guess is he's putting on a little show for his workers, letting them know he still has his backbone," Scautt said.

They continued walking and the manager continued to rant at their backs.

"I might be mistaken," Kissinger told Scautt, "but I don't think he cares much for you."

"Then that would make him a kindred spirit with you two gentlemen."

"Hey, wait a minute," Kissinger said. "Who said anything about—"

Scautt cut him off. "I hear the talk."

"This isn't the time to get into this," Bolan told him.

"I just want to clear the air," Scautt said. "I know I'll never win a popularity contest, but I have my job to do, and I have to do it the best way I know how."

"Fine. Then let's just do it."

Scautt's features hardened momentarily, then he nodded and excused himself, heading off on his own to supervise the troops, who were just now filing out of the parked truck.

"He's a hard case," Kissinger murmured.

"Yeah, but I trust him. Let's just give him a wide berth until this is over."

There was a drone in the sky overhead, and the men glanced up to see the lights of a helicopter skimming above the tree line at the far edge of the farm.

"Speaking of a wide berth," Kissinger said, "that has to be Jack."

As the chopper drew closer, both men recognized the now familiar outline of the Reed-279. Grimaldi was providing aerial surveillance in the event that the recruiter was flushed out and tried to make a run for it before the troops located him.

Bolan unfolded a sheet of paper from his pocket and stared at a photocopied composite of the man

DesChamps had described on his way to the operating table. The likeness had been created with the latest version of the Identi-kit process, which used overlays of various generic physical attributes that were then embellished by a professional sketch artist to incorporate more individualized traits. Scautt and Kissinger also had copies of the composite, as did the soldiers, who were beginning to fan out in teams of two, brandishing NATO-issue Belgian FN rifles.

Although the circumstances warranted it, it turned out that the large manpower deployed in the search was unnecessary, because within five minutes several workers had identified the recruiter as David Laix, a onetime resident of the area who had since left the farm. And yes, the workers confirmed, Laix was prone to political rhetoric, although no one else on the farm was willing to go so far as to claim the man was affiliated with the Blood Against Oppression or any other organized group.

When asked if any other men Laix associated with had left with him, the workers had provided three more names—Bari Sihn, Colaz Douke and Zeita Hu-Perzar, all immigrants who'd been hired only a few weeks before they had been transferred, along with Laix, to another of Donlier's farms more than a hundred miles southwest of Domrémy.

As to why the men had been transferred, Bolan, Scautt and Kissinger were referred back to the farm's manager, who by now had retreated to the livery stable to fortify himself with several long draws from a flask of whiskey. When confronted again, the manager eyed his interrogators mirthfully.

"How should I know why they were transferred? I'm just a lowly soul who follows other people's orders."

"Then someone else ordered them to be transferred?" Scautt inquired.

"Aye, you're a sharp one, *sir.*" The manager snapped off a mock salute. "I bow to your keen intellect."

"Listen to me, you pathetic sot!" Scautt raged as he strode across the stable toward the manager. The old man fumbled for a pitchfork, but Scautt easily batted it aside. "I want a simple answer to a simple question!"

"Roast in hell!"

"You don't want to talk?" Scautt yelled. "Then don't! I'll even help keep you quiet!"

Scautt glanced back at Bolan and Kissinger, offering them an inexplicable wink, then turned back to the manager, pinning him against the wall and beginning to strangle him. The old man's eyes bulged with sudden terror and he clawed at his assailant's wrists, trying to pull his hands from his throat.

Bolan and Kissinger rushed forward.

"Hey, take it easy!" Kissinger shouted at Scautt. "There's no point in killing him!"

"Sure there is! It'd make me feel good!"

"That's enough!" Bolan grabbed Scautt and pulled him away from the old man. "Leave him alone."

The manager slumped to the floor, gasping for breath. The fight had been choked out of him, and he stared at the other men pleadingly. "Donlier!" he said. "He's the one who wanted them transferred!"

"You're sure?" Scautt asked harshly.

"On my life!"

"Where's Donlier now?" Bolan asked. "Is he here?"

The manager shook his head. "No. He's in Paris."

Kissinger held out a hand and helped the old man to his feet, then handed him his flask. The manager clutched it in his trembling fingers and raised it to his lips, closing his eyes as he drank.

"We won't bother you any further," Scautt told the man, softening his tone.

The manager eyed Scautt sullenly but said nothing, staying put as the other three men turned and left.

"What do you know about Donlier?" Bolan asked.

"Aside from the fact that he owns the farm?" Scautt said. "Not much, I'm afraid, but I ordered a background check the minute we found out about this location. My people might have something by now."

"Good." Bolan motioned toward the helicopter, which Grimaldi had just set down in a nearby field. "There's a radio in the chopper. You can call and find out."

It was dark now, with a scattered winking of stars in the night sky. As they headed toward the field, Bolan glanced to his right and saw the soldiers piling back into the convoy truck. "Is there a base near that other farm?" he asked Scautt.

"No. Should we send these men down?"

"Definitely," Bolan said, "and if we can squeeze them into some kind of air transport so they can get there quicker, let's do it."

"I'll look into it."

The chopper was idling in the field as they approached, and Grimaldi jumped down to the ground, heading out to intercept them. He had a troubled expression on his face.

"What's the matter?" Bolan asked.

"It's Hal," Grimaldi reported. "He's missing, along with Ed Dauffie!"

ALTHOUGH BABDI STILL HAD access to the grave digger's truck parked back at Wintze Inn, he had reservations about the vehicle's durability, particularly if he was to load it down with additional men and the weapons cache from the cemetery.

As he and Emma Skodynov drove through the outskirts of Les Laume in the Alfa-Romeo, Babdi set his sights on a grocery market that was just about to close for the night. There was a delivery truck parked out back, with its driver helping two stock boys unload pallets of boxed goods.

"That would suit our needs perfectly," the Turk said.

"But is it really worth drawing attention to ourselves stealing it?"

"I'm not going to haul my gun out and start blasting away, if that's your concern," he chided her as they drove past the parking lot. "We can steal it with cunning just as well as we can with force."

Emma was finding it increasingly difficult to hold back from telling Babdi how ridiculous his obsessive quest for a truck was under the circumstances. Even if she was truly the Turk's ally and not just trying to lure him into a trap, logic dictated that they show themselves as little as possible and make straight for the secure isolation of the hunting lodge. But Emma knew that stubbornness was Babdi's Achilles' heel, and to question his judgment too harshly would only make him more unyielding.

"Very well," she said with resignation. "What's the plan?"

"First, turn right at the next corner and stop the car once you're clear of the streetlights."

Emma obliged, pulling over once she'd made the turn. She left the engine running. Babdi climbed out, leaving the door open as he crouched low and stared back at his companion.

"It's very simple," he told her. "What I want you to do is circle around to the front of the market, then make a commotion, something that will draw the attention of the men in the parking lot. You should have no trouble with that." Emma smiled tightly but said nothing. Babdi went on. "Keep them occupied long enough for me to get to the truck and drive it away, then I'll meet you down the road near the turnoff to Donlier's farm. Understand?"

Emma nodded. "Yes, only give me a few minutes. The timing will have to be just right for this to work."

"Whatever it takes," Babdi told her. "I saw a trash Dumpster I can wait behind. Now, go."

The Turk quietly shut the door and slipped into the darkness. Emma drove off, seething with frustration at Babdi's foolhardy scheme. A part of her was tempted to just leave the Turk behind and proceed to the lodge alone, but she knew that the Gray Hand would frown upon carrying out the executions of the other BAO members without including their leader. It would diminish the results of Operation Rekindle, and she would undoubtedly be held responsible for any shortcomings—not a fate she wished to tempt.

By the time Emma had circled the block, she had a clear idea of the diversionary ploy she was going to attempt. First, however, she wanted to make a quick phone call. There was a public booth down the block from the market, and Emma idled the Alfa-Romeo at the curb as she hurriedly called the number of the senior agent she'd spoken with earlier. She didn't plan on the call taking too long. There was, after all, only one thing she needed to know.

"Do we have Dauffie?"

"Yes," the agent told her. "And more."

"More?"

"Klemberk also abducted someone from the U.S. Justice Department."

Emma was ecstatic. "That's fantastic."

"I gave them the location," the agent reported. "They're flying up by seaplane and should be there shortly."

"We're on our way."

"You're not there yet?" The senior agent sounded concerned.

"It's a long story," Emma said. "But I promise we'll be at the lodge within the hour."

Emma hung up the phone and got back in the car, driving to an alley two buildings away from the market and backing in. She shut off the engine, then feverishly ran her fingers through her hair, mussing it into a state of disarray. She unzipped her jacket, exposing her already-torn blouse, then rubbed the back of her hand across her mouth, smearing lipstick across her face.

She slipped the ignition key under the front seat, next to the Magnum, then got out of the car, leaving the door unlocked. Taking a deep breath, she closed her eyes, trying to summon tears. When they wouldn't come, she slapped her face several times, then dug her fingernails into the soft flesh of her earlobe until the pain intensified to the point where she found it easy to weep.

With a sudden scream of mortal anguish, Emma lunged out of the alley and staggered toward the market. By the time she reached the front doors, two customers and a cashier were charging out to investigate her cries. Through her tears Emma noted happily that they were all men. This was going to be easy.

"He hurt me!" Emma sobbed. "He was going to kill me!"

"Who?" the cashier asked, unable to take his eyes off the woman's exposed chest. "Who did this to you?"

Emma pointed across the street, toward an alley that led back behind a bakery that was closed for the night. "He took my purse, too! He's an animal!"

"Take her inside," one of the customers told the cashier. "We'll go after him."

As the two other men rushed off across the street, the cashier took Emma by the shoulders and carefully guided her inside the market. There was no one else in the store. Emma sobbed even louder and pretended to lose her balance briefly, toppling a stacked display of canned peas. The cans tumbled loudly down around her and she flinched as if startled, letting out another scream.

"It's okay," the cashier said. "It's okay."

"I'm sorry." Staring over the man's shoulder, she saw the trucker and the two stock boys entering from the rear of the store, drawn by her screams. The cashier explained what had happened and dispatched the stock boys to join in the chase for the supposed attacker while he reached for a phone to call the police.

"No! Not the police! Please!!"

"But, madam," the cashier protested, "they should be informed of this, so they can help."

"But he...he raped me!" Emma cried. "The police, the papers...please, I don't want to have to deal with all of that!"

As the cashier continued to plead with Emma to let him call in the authorities, the trucker suddenly cocked his head to one side and glanced toward the rear of the store. A look of anger and disbelief crossed his face.

"My truck!" he bellowed, starting back toward the exit. "Someone's stealing my truck!"

"It must be the man that attacked me!" Emma said, turning to the cashier. "Go help catch him! Please! I'll be all right here."

"Are you sure?"

"Yes," Emma insisted. "Please, I want him caught!"

The cashier paused long enough to remove a label gun from underneath the cash register, then stormed down the aisle fast on the trucker's heels.

Emma maintained her facade a few moments longer, but as soon as both men were out the back door, she turned and fled through the front. With long strides, she ran to the alley where she'd left the Alfa-Romeo. Slipping quickly behind the wheel, she keyed the ignition and put the vehicle into gear. Tires screeched, and she barreled out of the alley and sped away from the market. Glancing in her rearview mirror, she caught a quick glimpse of two of the men she'd sent chasing after her imagined assailant.

"Thank you, my knights in shining armor," she murmured as she sped out of town and made her way to the turnoff where she was sure she'd catch up with Babdi and his truck. From there they'd go to the lodge at Donlier's farm, and Operation Rekindle, after months of planning, would finally be ready to unfold.

CHAPTER TWENTY-EIGHT

"Are you sure we have enough clearance?" Anatoly Klemberk asked worriedly as he eyed the approaching treetops.

"Relax, comrade," Evan Willan told him as he worked the controls of the seaplane. "Are you forgetting that I was a stunt pilot before I joined the KGB? They wanted me because I was good at this sort of thing."

"Yes," Klemberk said, "but you've flown less and less since you were assigned to Operation Rekindle."

Willan laughed. "There's a parachute behind your seat. Perhaps you'd feel better jumping."

"I think not."

As the plane continued its descent, Klemberk tore his gaze away from the window. Flying had never agreed with the Russian, and the smaller the plane, the greater his anxiety. He would have preferred closing his eyes, but was reluctant to make himself the butt of more taunts from his younger colleague. Instead, he stared down at his lap and busied himself with reloading his .357 Magnum pistol. His hands were shaking, however, and he fumbled the ammunition onto the floor.

"You have nothing to worry about," Willan said. "Flying a plane is like riding a bike, Anatoly. Or like making love. One doesn't forget how it's done."

Klemberk exhaled slowly, bringing himself under control. He had to concede that Willan was right about one thing; there was no way Klemberk would forget what it was like making love, especialy with Emma Skodynov. He longed to see her tonight, to witness the expression on her face once she saw that he had managed to apprehend not one, but two viable fall guys for the conclusion of the first phase of Operation Rekindle. She would be forced to see him for what he truly was, a crackshot field agent who could perform heroics as readily as he finessed his way through the world of paper shags. When they made love again, as he was sure they would, she would bring an even greater passion to their union.

Such fantasies proved to be a potent diversion, because the next thing Klemberk knew, Willan had cleared the treetops and was angling down for a landing on the still waters of Tristam Donlier's private lake. Klemberk drew in a quick breath and tensed in his seat as Willan cut back on the throttle and the plane's hollow floats slapped against the lake's surface. The touchdown was rougher than most ground landings, but not by much, and Klemberk gradually relaxed as they motored slowly across the lake toward a wooden dock reaching out from a dirt path leading up to the hunting lodge.

"Where's the welcoming committee?" Willan wondered.

"I'm not sure," Klemberk replied, eyeing the docks and the shoreline. He saw no signs of activity. nor were lights on inside the lodge. "Perhaps we're early."

"But we had farther to travel than any of the others," Willan said. "Even Gott should have gotten here from Geneva by now."

"I'm sure there's nothing to worry about," Klemberk said, rallying his nerve now that the plane was safely down. "Pull up next to the dock and I'll have a look around."

A special feature of the seaplane was the hydraulic lift system built into the struts supporting the plane's floats. When activated, it was possible to raise the main body of the aircraft to as much as six feet higher than the floats. And because the plane's wings were roof-mounted, Willan was able to maneuver alongside the dock as if he were easing a car into a parallel parking spot. When he opened his door, Klemberk had to take only one wide step to find himself standing on the dock. Willan passed out a length of thick rope, and Klemberk used it to moor the plane to the dock's lodgepole uprights.

"Wait here while I check the lodge," Klemberk told his subordinate. "I'll be right back."

Willan nodded, leaving the plane's doors open to allow for some cross-ventilation. He pulled a pack of cigarettes from his leather flight jacket and hummed to himself as he lighted one. Staring through a cloud of smoke trailing up from the cigarette's tip, Willan watched his comrade stalk up the dock, gun in hand.

"Ah, you're a brave one all right, Anatoly, as long as you have two feet on the ground."

By the time Willan finished his cigarette, Klemberk had gone up the path to the lodge and entered through the front door. Willan flicked his butt out into the lake, then extended his arms and yawned. He decided to climb out of the plane and stretch, but as he was getting out of his seat he suddenly stopped, thinking he'd heard a sound in the cargo area behind his seat.

Willan's hand went for his gun, a Colt Cobra .38 Special. He flicked on an overhead light, then glanced into the back of the plane. Both Ed Dauffie and Hal Brognola were still laid out on the floor, bound and gagged. Neither was moving, but Willan could hear something making a faint grating sound, not unlike a rat scratching its way across a wooden surface.

Puzzled, Willan squeezed around his seat and stepped over Dauffie, trying to pinpoint the source of the noise. Without warning, Dauffie suddenly sprang into motion. Even though his legs were bound at the ankles and he couldn't see through his blindfold, he was still able to kick his legs upward with considerable force, directing his shins into Willan's groin. Taken by surprise, the Russian doubled over in sudden agony.

Simultaneously Brognola joined the fray, shifting his weight quickly so that his shoulder rammed blindly into Willan's knee, bowling him over. The Russian's head struck the wall before he could break his fall, and he tumbled to the floor, stunned. Both Dauffie and Brognola lashed out at him as best they could, getting in a savage series of kicks to the body and shoulder blows to the head. Despite their binds they were a formidable duo, and they managed to overpower Willan and knock him unconscious before he could make use of his .38.

Once the Russian had ceased to struggle, Dauffie and Brognola concentrated on freeing themselves as best they could. Able to move about without fear of being heard, the big Fed was able to position himself in such a way that he snagged his blindfold on an exposed bolt behind the pilot's seat. By carefully wriggling his head back and forth, he was finally able to work the strip of cloth off of his eyes. Moments later he liberated his gag in much the same manner.

"We'll get out of here yet, Ed," he said to Dauffie, who was still blindfolded and gagged but had focused on the knot binding his wrists, loosening it with the help of an open latch on one of the cargo hold's doors. As the knot gave way, he worked his hands back and forth, trying to free them.

"Keep it up, Ed. You're doing great!"

It was slow going, however, and by the time Dauffie had finally freed his hands and begun to untie his blindfold, he and Brognola heard footsteps on the docks, headed their way.

"Damn!" Brognola cursed, eyeing the .38 Special lying on the floor a few feet away from him. With his hands still tied, there was little he could hope to do with it, but he called out to Dauffie, "Don't bother with your gag! There's a gun just to your left, next to the guy. Grab it, quick!"

As he tore the blindfold off, Dauffie looked around him, trying to spot the gun. His eyes were slow to adjust to the dim light, however, and before he could reach out and grab the weapon, someone climbed into the plane and pointed a gun of his own at the two captives.

"Stay where you are!" David Laix warned.

ONCE AGAIN the Reed-279 was aloft, carrying Bolan, Grimaldi and Kissinger across the French interior.

Thanks to Scautt's people, they now knew that Tristam Donlier was linked to the Lawtin-313 missile launcher that had been implemented by the BAO during the unsuccessful assault in Cannes. What remained to be seen was whether the computer baron was directly involved in the theft of the weapon or had been used somehow by other forces. An interrogation team from the French Ministry of Intelligence was in the process of questioning Donlier, and Scautt had promised to pass along any new information.

As for Brognola and Dauffie, they were still missing in action, with the only clue to their disappearance being the discovery of Dauffie's rental car in a shoreline parking lot two miles from Menton. A pack of matches from a seafood restaurant farther up the coast had been found in the car, and the establishment's maître d' had confirmed that both men had been at the restaurant a few hours before.

"And Babdi's still hiding in the woodwork somewhere," Kissinger stated as he stared down at the farmland below.

"Not for much longer," Bolan said. "I've got a feeling we're going to hit paydirt in Les Laume."

"I'd be all for that," Grimaldi told him. "I don't know about you guys, but the way we've been hopping all over the place I'm starting to feel like a checker piece."

The transceiver suddenly squawked to life. It was Scautt.

"My men have just finished with Donlier," he reported. "Their feeling is he's in the clear, but was unwittingly duped by one of his clients, a woman working for the Russian Ministry of Commerce."

"Bingo," Kissinger whispered.

Scautt went on to relate Emma Skodynov's business relationship with Donlier, concluding, "And not only was she the one behind his transferring those people from his farm in Domrémy to Les Laume, but she borrowed his company plane to fly there just this morning. Personal business, she'd told him."

"Right," Grimaldi said. "Global terrorism's about as personal as it gets."

"I'm not sure that you'll find her at the farm, though," Scautt went on, "because we just received word that a woman matching her descripton was involved in the theft of a delivery truck just outside of Les Laume. She was driving one of Donlier's cars, but abandoned it near the linkup with the main highway running between Paris and Dijon."

"Then who was driving the truck?" Bolan asked.

"We don't have a description, but we've talked with the staff at Donlier's house in Les Laume, and his chauffeur's missing. There was apparently some gossip about him having had a fling with Emma during one of her earlier visits, so he has to be a suspect."

"And the four workers from Domrémy," Bolan said. "Any word on them?"

"No. The staff doesn't deal with the laborers," Scautt said. "However, according to my notes here, Donlier said something about one of them being a caretaker at a hunting preserve he owns. It's right next to the farm, so it might bear looking into.''

"That leaves us with three choices," Kissinger said. "The farm, the hunting grounds, or the highway."

Bolan went with his gut. "The hunting grounds."

A BACK ENTRANCE to the hunting preserve allowed Babdi and Emma to approach their rendezvous without being seen from the grounds of Donlier's farm. After driving three-quarters of a mile down a narrow dirt road, Babdi idled the stolen truck before the rear gate. Emma climbed out of the cab and swung open the gate, which had been left unlocked according to her instructions. She stepped back and waved Babdi through.

As the Turk drove onto the grounds, Emma heard a twig snap behind her. She was turning to take a look when she felt the barrel of a gun stab her in the ribs. Before she could let out a cry, a hand was clamped over her mouth and she was pulled backward until her abductor was close enough to whisper threateningly into her ear.

"Not a word," Zeita Hu-Perzar warned.

Emma remained silent and offered no resistance. As she saw Colaz Douke appear out of the nearby brush and steal toward the truck, she realized that a mutiny was in progress.

Be calm, she told herself. They were after Babdi.

Inside the truck, the Turk slowed to a stop once he was inside. He glanced in the rearview mirror, expecting to see Emma closing the gate. When there was no sign of her, he shifted the truck into neutral, figuring to get out and see what was keeping her. He was halfway out of the cab when someone grabbed his ankle with both hands and twisted it sharply. Letting out a surprised shout, Babdi tumbled forward to the ground, spraining his wrist as he tried to break his fall. As he tried to get up, Douke strode over and swept his booted foot upward, kicking the Turk squarely in the jaw. The terrorist groaned, spitting blood and broken bits of teeth as he toppled over onto his side, dazed. Douke loomed over him, a .22-caliber pistol in his fist, a malicious grin stretched across his lean face.

"Good to see you, Ali-Jahn."

CHAPTER TWENTY-NINE

"I keep telling you, there's been some kind of misunderstanding," Anatoly Klemberk told David Laix. "We're your allies! We came here to *help* you!"

"I don't think so," Laix replied, unmoved by Klemberk's pleading.

They were inside the main room of the lodge. Klemberk was spread-eagled atop a picnic table, tied securely with nylon cord. Evan Willan was similarly bound on another table a few feet away. By contrast, Ed Dauffie and Hal Brognola lay on the cold stone floor, their gags and blindfolds removed but otherwise tied up as they had been in the seaplane. In the background, Bari Sihn leaned back against a huge brick fireplace, guarding the prisoners with a Detonics .45 pistol.

"Didn't you speak with Emma Skodynov?" Klemberk asked his captors. "She was supposed to explain all of this to you."

"I spoke with her," Laix told the Russian. "She mentioned nothing about you, nothing about us agreeing to be pawns for Russian Intelligence."

"You're not pawns!" Klemberk insisted. "I'm telling you, you're allies! Equals!"

Laix chuckled as he wandered close to Dauffie and Brognola. "And you two," he said, picking up the men's identification papers from a nearby chair. "You are both Americans. I suppose you are our allies, too."

Neither Brognola or Dauffie spoke.

"No, I didn't think so," Laix said, tossing the IDs back on the chair.

There was a stack of firewood next to the hearth, and next to that a rack filled with fireplace tools. Laix nonchalantly picked up a small ax and dragged his thumb across the edge of the blade as he ventured back toward the picnic tables.

"But the Russians, they say they are our friends. Our *close* friends. But it occurs to me…why stop at that?" He eyed Klemberk and Willan. "Why don't we become even closer. Blood brothers!"

Suddenly Laix tightened his grip on the ax, raised it over his head, then prompty brought it crashing down. Willan strained against his binds and let out a curdling scream of agony as the weapon hacked through his left thumb and bit into the tabletop. A torrent of blood spouted from the stump.

When Willan continued to cry out, Laix raised the ax again and warned him, "Maybe you'd like me to carve out your tongue next, yes?"

The threat quickly sank home and Willan fell silent, clenching his jaw to keep his cries buried in his throat. The pain in his hand was overwhelming, and when a cold sweat enveloped him and he felt himself becoming light-headed, he went with the sensation, seeking the welcome refuge of unconsciousness.

"Let me advance a theory," Laix said, moving away from Willan and addressing his remarks to Klemberk and the two Americans. "I think Russian Intelligence had a plan that our beloved Emma was helping them with. I think the plan was to bring the Americans here, then kill them along with us, and make it look as if we were somehow collaborating. Is that right, Mr. RI?"

Klemberk followed the Americans' cue and remained silent. To himself, though, he conceded that Laix wasn't far off the mark. Yes, Operation Rekindle called for the execution of the members of the Blood Against Oppression as well as the Americans, but the killings were to be orchestrated in such a way that the world would be given the impression that, contrary to personal disavowals made by none other than the President, the United States was indeed dispatching assassins to deal with terrorist groups. It was supposed to end up looking like Brognola and Dauffie were killed by a BAO member who'd somehow managed to survive his execution long enough to seek revenge.

The Gray Hand was even willing to go so far as to implicate Russian Intelligence as being the real force behind the Blood Against Oppression, their rationale being that if members of the Hand could subsequently kill a few select agents from either side, tensions between the U.S. and Russia would escalate to the point that the cold war would resume and even escalate. Granted, it was a convoluted ploy, but after months of slowly maneuvering the various players into the right positions, it had looked as if all the planning was about to pay off.

Now, however, all bets were off.

Not only was the plan unraveling before his eyes, but Klemberk was also terrified that at any moment David Laix would put the ax to use again, this time on him. The prospect of slow death by dismemberment weighed heavily on him, and he found himself longing for the dull routine of his shag work in Paris. It was a futile exercise, however. Klemberk knew deep in his heart that he'd seen the last of Paris, the last of any sort of life beyond these four walls that seemed to be closing in on him.

"THERE'S THE TRUCK!" Grimaldi said, glancing down at the vehicle threading its way through the forest toward the hunting lodge. A spiral of smoke was curling up from the cabin's chimney, and moored downhill next to the docks was the seaplane. Grimaldi turned to Bolan, seated beside him in the front of the chopper. "Nice call. Looks like you win a Kewpie doll."

"I'll pick one out later." Bolan grabbed the transceiver microphone and tried to make contact with Denis Scautt to check on the status of backup troops. Scautt had good news and bad news.

"We've got nine men in a Sikorsky headed your way," the French agent reported, "but they've gotten sidetracked momentarily. Seems they intercepted distress signals from a single-engine that crash-landed about fifteen kilometers from you. They dropped back to assist."

"Why?" Bolan wondered. "Couldn't they just have radioed someone on the ground?"

"Perhaps, but they figured it was pertinent to the mission."

"How's that?" Grimaldi probed.

"Well, the one survivor putting out the distress call turned out to be a CIA agent who was abducted in Geneva by the RI. He says they were taking him to Les Laume."

"Did he have any idea what was going down there?" Bolan asked.

"Negative—although he did overhear mention of two other men being brought there as well."

Grimaldi traded glances with Bolan.

"Get those troops back in the air and up here, pronto," Bolan said. "There's a cabin by a lake in the middle of the hunting preserve, and from the looks of it, that's our target.''

"They're already on the way,'' Scautt reported. "I'd say at most they're twenty minutes behind you, though.''

Bolan signed off.

"I think Hal's up here,'' Kissinger speculated from the back of the chopper, "along with Ed Dauffie.''

"That makes it unanimous.'' Grimaldi banked to his right and headed the Reed toward the back entrance to the preserve. He didn't want to get any closer to the cabin for fear of alerting those on the ground. He figured they'd have a quarter-mile jog through the woods to get to the lake.

"What do you think?'' he asked Bolan. "Should we stay back and wait for reinforcements?''

Bolan shook his head, reaching to his side for an M-16.

"We might be too late as it is,'' he said gravely. "And if they've killed Hal and Dauffie, I don't want to leave the payback to strangers.''

CHAPTER THIRTY

The hunting lodge was looking more and more like a chamber out of the Spanish Inquisition.

Ali-Jahn Babdi and Emma Skodynov had been lashed to the two remaining picnic tables inside the main chamber. Both of them had been gagged as well. A red pool drenched the floor beneath the table where Evan Willan was in the process of bleeding to death. Klemberk had been spared any mutilation, at least for the time being. Brognola and Dauffie remained on the floor, helpless to intervene in whatever course the mutinous crew of the Blood Against Oppression was planning to take next.

"I have an idea," David Laix said, turning to his three fellow conspirators. "Let's turn the tables, so to speak."

To demonstrate, he went to the picnic table Willan was tied to and, with some effort, tilted it upright. Willan's thumb rolled to the floor and the agent sagged limply as gravity tried to pull him downward. Bari Sihn, Colaz Douke and Zeita Hu-Perzar pitched in to likewise upend the tables onto which Klemberk, Emma and Babdi were tied.

"Now," Laix suggested, "turn our fearless leader's table the other way so that he can have a good look at his beloved Emma."

As Babdi's table was shifted, the Turk jerked back and forth wildly, futilely attempting to break free. He cursed his tormentors, but his words were lost inside his gag. Laix retreated to the hearth, removing a poker that had been placed into the fire so that its tip was now glowing.

"You have something to say, Ali-Jahn?" he asked Babdi as he stood before the Turk. "I could probably understand you better if I took off that gag, don't you think?"

Babdi struggled anew as Laix slowly raised the poker and moved it toward his face.

"Keep your head still!" Laix demanded.

When Babdi only shook his head with greater fury, Zeita and Colaz stepped forward, grabbing him from either side and pinning his head to the tabletop. Laix grinned and closed in with the poker, gently pressing the white-hot tip against the fabric of the gag. Smoke billowed as the cloth ignited, then fell away, allowing the poker to sear its way into the flesh of Babdi's face. The terrorist screamed in agony.

Zeita and Colaz recoiled from Babdi, repelled by the stench of his burned flesh. Laix withdrew the poker and reached for a bucket of water set on the floor. He splashed its contents into Babdi's face, drowning out his cries.

"We'll kill you soon enough," Laix promised, "but first we thought you might like to hear what it was like for us all those nights we slept alone while you and your Russian slut coupled like dogs in heat in rooms next to us."

Laix turned to Emma, reaching out and touching the still-hot tip of the poker against the strand of rope stretched across her chest. The rope burned clear, and Laix pulled the poker away before it could make direct contact with the woman.

"Not to worry," Laix told her. "I wouldn't dream of scarring that velvet flesh of yours...especially not before I've had a chance to sample it."

Even with the one length of rope burned free, Emma was still too securely bound to free herself from the table. She glared with hatred as Laix unzipped her jacket, revealing her torn blouse and partially exposed breasts.

"Very nice," he said.

"Leave her alone!" Klemberk shouted from across the room.

Laix ignored him. Setting the poker aside, he ran his fingers slowly up Emma's leg and then closed them around the hemline of her skirt. With a sudden tug, he tore the skirt away from her. She tried to kick out at him, but the ropes tied around her knees and ankles restricted her.

"I'll be gentle, I assure you," Laix told her as he began to unbutton his shirt. "After all, my friends here will want their turn, too, and I don't want them to be disappointed.''

Twenty feet away, Brognola closed his eyes, burning with silent rage at his helplessness. Nearby, Ed Dauffie likewise turned his head, unwilling to witness the sorry spectacle before him.

Laix had taken off his shirt and was unhitching his belt when the main window of the lodge suddenly disintegrated with an explosive crash. Rapid bursts from an M-16 ripped into the cabin, cutting down Laix and Zeita Hu-Perzar before they had the faintest idea of what was happening.

As Colaz Douke instinctively retreated toward a rear exit, the back door burst open and Kissinger charged in, Stealthshooter raised before him. When Douke tried to get off a shot with his .22, Cowboy brought him down with a quick volley.

Bolan appeared in the window he'd shattered, leveling his M-16 at Bari Sihn. The terrorist dropped his own gun and threw his hands up in surrender. To his right, the front door swung open and Grimaldi stormed in, ready to blast away with his Government Model .45. He quickly realized it wouldn't be necessary.

Almost as quickly as it had begun, the siege was over.

The Executioner climbed in through the window, taking care to avoid jagged shards of glass still clinging to the frame. Taking in the tableau of bound captives and tortured flesh before him, he felt an upwelling of fury. He'd seen carnage this bad and worse, but it would never cease to amaze him the depths to which his fellow man could wallow.

"Hey, Hal," Grimaldi called out as he came over to untie Brognola and help him to his feet. Kissinger did the same for Ed Dauffie. "We had a feeling we'd find you here. Are you all right?"

"I'll be a lot better once I'm back in the U.S.," he said. "And in the future, I think I'll leave the field-work to you guys."

"I tell ya, it's gonna be nice traveling in something a little cozier than that flying peapod," Grimaldi said as he settled into his first-class seat aboard the Concorde.

"Amen to that," Kissinger said, tilting his seat back and stretching. "And this is one flight I'm not going to have any problems sleeping on."

Across the aisle, Bolan was seated next to Brognola. They were at DeGaulle International Airport in Paris, preparing for a return trip to the States. Through his window, Bolan could see a groundswell of security forces flocking around Air Force One, which had just brought the President to France to pay a visit to his daughter, whose condition had stabilized. Vera Maris was in guarded condition, and Ed Dauffie was already at her bedside, trying to be there for her in a way he hadn't been for years.

"So what do you think?" Bolan asked Brognola, who was in the process of peeling the cellophane off a high-priced cigar. "Does all this mean that the cold war is back on?"

"No way. But when you think that one of the reasons for an attempt to have it rekindled is because some old-guard former KGB honchos want to keep control of their black market, it's a little disturbing."

"Then you think Klemberk was telling the truth?"

"I doubt that *he* even knows if he's telling the truth," Brognola speculated. "From the sounds of it, he and that Skodynov woman were straddling so many different fences they'd lost track of their allegiances."

"They pledge allegiance to themselves," Bolan said. "I think that's the bottom line."

"Yes, and the same goes for Ali-Jahn Babdi. Seems only fitting that he was brought down by his own followers, don't you think?"

Bolan nodded slightly. "As long as he stays brought down. I have to tell you, it wouldn't have broken my heart if he had been caught in the line of fire."

"They'll all go before a tribunal, and justice will be served. Trust me.

"In any event, that whole ball's out of our court now." Brognola propped the cigar in his mouth. "I'm going to put on the headphones, find some classical music and try to wash all this out of my system."

"Not a bad idea," Bolan said.

A steward appeared in the aisle and stared apologetically at Brognola. "I'm sorry, sir," he said, "but there's no smoking in this section."

"So who's smoking?" Brognola replied, removing the unlighted cigar and waggling it between his fingers as he arched his eyebrows, doing what Bolan could only guess was supposed to be an impersonation of Groucho Marx.

The steward smiled wanly and moved on to tend to other passengers. Brognola chuckled to himself and reached for the headphones. Bolan closed his eyes and leaned back in his seat.

It was definitely time to go home.

Take
4 explosive books
plus a
mystery bonus

ATTENTION ALL ACTION ADVENTURE FANS!

In 1994, the Gold Eagle team will unveil a new action-packed publishing program, giving readers even more of what they want! Starting in February, get in on even *more* SuperBolan, Stony Man and DEATHLANDS titles!

The Lineup:

- MACK BOLAN—THE EXECUTIONER will continue with one explosive book per month.

- In addition, Gold Eagle will bring you alternating months of longer-length SuperBolan and Stony Man titles—always a surefire hit!

- Rounding out every month's action is a *second* longer-length title—experience the top-notch excitement that such series as DEATHLANDS, EARTHBLOOD and JAKE STRAIT all deliver!

Post-holocaust, paramilitary, future fiction— Gold Eagle delivers it all! And now with two longer-length titles each and every month, there's even more action-packed adventure for readers to enjoy!

CATCH THE FIRE OF GOLD EAGLE ACTION IN 1994!

GOLD EAGLE

A struggle for survival in
a savage new world.

JAMES AXLER

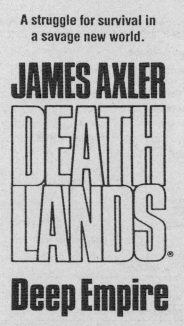

DEATH LANDS

Deep Empire

The crystal waters of the Florida Keys have turned into a death
zone. Ryan Cawdor, along with his band of warrior survivalists,
has found a slice of heaven in this ocean hell—or has he?

Welcome to the Deathlands, and the future nobody planned for.

Don't miss out on the action in these titles featuring
THE EXECUTIONER, ABLE TEAM and PHOENIX FORCE!

The Freedom Trilogy

The Executioner #61174	BATTLE PLAN	$3.50 ☐
The Executioner #61175	BATTLE GROUND	$3.50 ☐
Super Bolan #61432	BATTLE FORCE	$4.99 ☐

The Executioner®

| #61178 | BLACK HAND | $3.50 ☐ |
| #61179 | WAR HAMMER | $3.50 ☐ |

SuperBolan

| #61430 | DEADFALL | $4.99 ☐ |
| #61431 | ONSLAUGHT | $4.99 ☐ |

Stony Man™

#61889	STONY MAN V	$4.99 ☐
#61890	STONY MAN VI	$4.99 ☐
#61891	STONY MAN VII	$4.99 ☐

TOTAL AMOUNT		$
POSTAGE & HANDLING		$
($1.00 for one book, 50¢ for each additional)		
APPLICABLE TAXES*		$ _____
TOTAL PAYABLE		$ _____
(check or money order—please do not send cash)		

To order, complete this form and send it, along with a check or money order for the total above,
payable to Gold Eagle Books, to: *In the U.S.:* 3010 Walden Avenue, P.O. Box 9077, Buffalo,
NY 14269-9077; *In Canada:* P.O. Box 636, Fort Erie, Ontario, L2A 5X3.

Name: _____

Address: _____ City: _____

State/Prov.: _____ Zip/Postal Code: _____

*New York residents remit applicable sales taxes.
 Canadian residents remit applicable GST and provincial taxes.   GEBACK

GOLD EAGLE